SHE WALKED INTO
HIS WELCOMING ARMS—

and there they kissed, deeply, in full and grave surrender. These arms, this body, these lips were Jenny's home. She had never had a home. She melted into his shaken strength . . . for he was shaken by his own thirst, her answer, and their ecstasy.

It was the memory of why she was there, of what she must do to this man, that tore her free. . . .

Lady in the Tower

by

Katharine Newlin Burt

A SIGNET BOOK

NEW AMERICAN LIBRARY

TIMES MIRROR

SIGNET TRADEMARK REG. U.S. PAT. OFF. AND FOREIGN COUNTRIES
REGISTERED TRADEMARK—MARCA REGISTRADA
HECHO EN CHICAGO, U.S.A.

SIGNET, SIGNET CLASSICS, MENTOR, PLUME AND MERIDIAN BOOKS
are published by The New American Library, Inc.,
1301 Avenue of the Americas, New York, New York 10019

FIRST PRINTING, FEBRUARY, 1975

1 2 3 4 5 6 7 8 9

PRINTED IN THE UNITED STATES OF AMERICA

To
MARGARET *and* NATHANIEL BURT
enthusiastic listeners

Chapter One

Nick Landis had not meant to fall in love. It was an extravagance that he despised. He had diagnosed it as a psychopathic condition to which men and women surrendered of no necessity. His profession was his love and he had already, in his own mind, selected Alice Morell, who had everything he would demand at home and abroad for the wife of his career.

Nevertheless, he had surrendered, and before Jenny Thorne's graduation from the Nurses' Training School he had admitted contagion and set about its only bearable cure. He would marry Jenny Thorne, a trained nurse—than whom he considered no physician could have a less appropriate wife! Jenny Thorne, a nobody, coming from nowhere, poor, her home two rooms in Mrs. Clarke's tourist house, her mother and only apparent relative some sort of a nervous invalid, whom nobody ever saw.

That Mrs. Thorne was neither insane nor incurably ill he had meticulously assured himself, forcing her more than once to stay her habitual flights for adroit and searching examination. A beautiful, strange creature as unlike Jenny as possible which, Nick Landis considered, was all to the good.

When they were married, he would persuade Jenny to send her mother "somewhere." He had the usual vague masculine assurance of getting his own way.

He had to reckon, of course, with the girl's devotion. Her face, even at the mention of that mother, burned white, like an angelic sword. But a husband has power to exorcise such possessions and Jenny, in love with him, as he dared to hope she might be, would become an altogether different girl. The new feeling would absorb the old. This was a creature of strong and concentrated passion. If she loved him strongly . . .

Nick Landis, preparing for courtship before his mirror, looked himself in the blue eyes, and said, "Don't even think *if*, my boy. That way failure lies," and went marching down the stairs of his own mother's house with an air more military than medical, as was justifiable because he would be mil-

7

itary in a few weeks. But not Mrs. Nicholas Landis! No army nursing for Jenny Landis. She should remain here in the comfortable old house with his own comfortable, authentic sort of mother, until such time as the war would be over—wars do end sooner or later—and his real life of surgical practice and pleasant hominess would begin. It was a good prospect. His face, handsome at any time, was very pleasant to look at with the glow of its anticipation. Too bad about Alice Morell. But she had a half dozen beaux and he had not so far—thank the Lord and his own caution!—in any way committed myself.

Jenny was waiting for him at the appointed place, the steps of the Public Library on Holly Street. Her training had grounded her in punctuality. "Poor girl!" thought Landis, running up to meet her running down; "that trait will increase her suffering as a doctor's wife. The meals she will have to keep hot for me! The engagements I won't be able to keep!" This one, however, would be kept.

"How does it feel to be out of harness, Jenny?"

He liked the way she looked in her grey flannel suit, straight and short-skirted, with a glittering something at its shoulder. She wore no hat and her head was bright with brushing. Her light, long legs were bare, brown as polished horse chestnuts. He was glad to see her out of uniform.

"Wonderful! I had breakfast in bed. Think of it! After three years!" There was an undercurrent of sadness in her laughing voice which gave everything she said color and depth.

"You do look rested," he said. His own voice was deep and serious.

"I don't think I was so very tired. But the suspense got me down. I was morbid for fear I'd fail or get snatched away before I won my cap."

Sitting beside him now, the wind stripping her temples of its sun-gilt hair, she gave him and the whole world beyond him a look which he surprised himself by calling "haunted."

"I didn't believe," she murmured, "I *couldn't* believe I'd be allowed to put it through."

"Why not?"

But this witness could not be startled into inadvertent evidence.

She turned her strange, narrow face away from him. The profile ran out a trifle from brow to chin, her eyebrows and eyelids lifting towards the temples where the dark gilded hair grew forward. When she looked quickly at him and away, he saw that she had the face of a faun, naturally wild and panicky, but controlled for the most part by a will stronger than her emotions, stronger than her youth.

This day, on which Nick Landis meant to put the seal on his document of surrender, had intensified his powers of observation. The girl beside him, who was to remain beside him, he hoped, for all his life, was not the girl she had been yesterday. It was not only being out of uniform. He was seeing deeper into her consciousness. He was feeling towards something in her that was disturbing, poignant. He could not yet name it, but, before sundown, surely he would. And its naming would influence, not his intention which was immutable, but his happiness in its fulfillment.

Now, at last, she was answering his "Why not?" as though, at the end of a debate, she had come to a decision of her own.

"Because I've never been allowed to finish anything before. Mother's health ... she's never found a climate that really suits her. Change is the only thing that does her any good at all. After we move ... First it was New England, then California, New Mexico, Old Mexico ... no use enumerating them. It's just a lesson in geography! But, after we move, for a while she's well and cheerful. Then she runs down like an unwound clock. You're no psychiatrist and I've had only a short experience in that sort of work, but I do know that her condition is due to nerves, to some sort of behavior-pattern. If I had the reason ..."

"I should think, by now, you'd have that," he said, impatient of mystery and of inadequate behavior.

"You would think so." She sat, drooping, penitent. "Mother's strange," she said.

They drove in silence until he shook off his own. "Let's forget it. Let's leave our worries back in Bonnetsville. Before we're through with them, though—just this: when you can learn to share your worries with me, Jenny, I think you'll find them a lot easier to bear."

He was amazed by her response. Her brilliance melted. A warm, startled, shaken face, a hand on his against the wheel pressing it, tears on her eyelashes. He was half afraid of her but, at the same time, he had never before felt for anyone such yearning tenderness.

The sun of that April day was past its setting and faced already a brightening moon above the mansard roof of Mrs.

Clarke's old house, when Jenny Thorne mounted the stairs to its third story. She moved slowly, looking about her at everything. Yes, it was the same dingy dwelling, the brown wall paper had not changed its spots nor the dark halls their Ethiopian complexion, but there was a light upon them that had nothing to do with setting sun nor rising moon. She stood reflecting its unearthliness, one foot on the step above, hand on the rail, head tilted back, eyes closed.

Jenny Thorne had not dared to hope for a heart so reassured. All her life, until this moment, had been darkened by a nameless fear. She did not know what she feared but it was the feeling of the man in the haunted house, at dusk, alone, peering about the corners in expectant dread. She had not looked for this sudden splendor of love. Life had made her serious and "poor in spirit"; poor, that is, in her expectation of personal happiness. Unlike most mothers, hers had never chattered about present lovers or the husband that was to be. In halting phrases Jenny had been encouraged only to stand on her own feet, to dedicate herself to unrewarded service, to take no root, to ask for no securities.

And now, this ambitious man, splendid with health and youth, had taken up her life into his strong hands. From now on she would never, God willing, be alone. Her mother had a champion. Not the least part of Jenny's ecstasy was the prospect of sharing it with this pathetic creature, whom, in reversed mother-daughter role, she had cherished.

The thought of that mother opened her eyes and restored her to upward motion. How wonderful to be bringing good news!

At the door of her room, she said a short prayer, then, smiling, opened it. Inside she stood back, closing the door behind her. She had become, in that short step, a different girl.

She heard her mother in the bedroom beyond but here in the living room was the more than sufficient evidence of Jenny's familiar dread. The big old trunks had been brought up, the boxes were half-packed, bags open, all the small accretions of ornaments and draperies and pictures had been taken down and wrapped and put away. The drab, familiar necessity of "moving on" had overtaken this poor home. Jenny had been allowed to finish her nurse's course but not more than one day's margin thereafter. Whatever Mrs. Thorne had seen of Nick Landis' obvious devotion, whatever she had imagined this might mean to her daughter—the consideration had had no extra weight. She was going away. She was leaving Bonnetsville, North Carolina, as she had left St. Ingris, Winston, Monterey and Tasco and all the other shabby uncertain stations of their insensate pilgrimage. And certainly she expected to take her daughter with her.

The blood of shock, of fear, and, for the first time, of anger rushed from Jenny's heart to her face. She ran across the room and broke into her mother's sanctuary.

Pale Clara Thorne straightened from packing a small case on her bed, saw her daughter's face and sat down as though she had no strength to stand before it.

She was taller than Jenny and even more slender. Her beauty was far more explicit so that she could no more pass unnoticed than a torch in a dark street. The white streaks in her hair were decorations; the blasting of pain, the long rigidity of self-control, the wincing lines of her timidity, were only a sort of intaglio upon a jewel. Sitting there, white and scared, upon her narrow bed, her hands writhing together in her lap, her eyes lifted, she was and she would be forever, the first and the last sentence of a romantic tale.

"Mother!"

"Darling! I know. Don't look like that. Please be reasonable ... be patient. I've been waiting for you to get your diploma. I didn't want to tell you until you'd passed your examination ... but the doctor said ..." Her lashes shadowed her thin, beautifully modeled cheeks, her voice faltered.

Jenny said, "What doctor?" and went over to one of the windows to hide her face.

Clara Thorne's low, hesitating voice lied, "Dr. Chartis, of course. How *can* you, Jenny? It's nothing new."

"No, mother. It's nothing new. But this time, for me, it's different."

A long silence, broken by that unendurable, scared voice, "Different?"

Jenny said, "What doctor?" and went over to one of the hands over the two that struggled there. "Stop it, mother. Things are going to be different from now on. This time we are not going to run away." It was the first time that she had so worded their departures and she knew that she had at last faced a truth.

Clara's lips shaped "run away" without interrogation. Jenny hurried on. "No silly old Dr. Chartis is going to do that to us. And you, yourself, darling, are not going to let him. This time, dearest darling," here Jenny flung her arms strongly about her mother, drew her close, "poor, dearest darling, I am going to take control."

There was no word of contradiction but the feel of the gentle body was adamant.

"Mother, I am going to marry Nick Landis." She waited, laughed shakily and asked, "Doesn't that make any difference at all?"

Clara gave one of the long sighs that had so often waked her little girl at night to distressful sympathy, drew herself away and rose. She walked over to the big cheap bureau and stopped before it, setting her hands down on the top, leaning on them, and looking at her own reflected face. This was so unlike her ordinary behavior that Jenny forgot everything in surprised suspense. She, too, stared at the tall dark figure with its white frill and its lovely racked countenance. It seemed to her that the streaks in her mother's hair burned white with an especial intensity of color. Her eyes, looking into themselves, were bright, not happily, as though pain had rejuvenated them.

"Yes, it makes a difference. It forces me to tell you, Jenny. I knew some day it would happen. I've tried to prepare myself and you . . . a little." Here she looked past her own reflection to Jenny's still seated on the bed. Jenny instinctively looked too and saw her own vividness. The faun face of panic. To herself she said, "Don't give in to it," repeating a charm she had used before, "Love casteth out fear." "Love casteth out fear." There was love for her now everywhere! there couldn't be fear.

Her mother was saying, "Stay where you are, dear. I can't bear to look at the real you. I can see only too much here in the glass. I am going to tell you a name . . . maybe you've heard it before. I think you have. I've even helped you to hear it." She forced herself to look at the reflection of her child and spoke the syllables softly, spurning them from her pale lips.

"Enid Ambrose."

Jenny whispered after a pause, "Wasn't she an actress, mother?"

"No, think again."

Jenny's mind groped back toward some experience dim and distasteful. She repeated the name under her breath, "Enid Ambrose."

Then it came back to her, rising up, hideous, like an enormous octopus monster from deep sea water. There had been a time when that name was a household word. Such names have a long life. They persist on human tongues and in human memories. Jenny had heard the story. Her mother had told it to her once ... by her bed in the dark, whisperingly. Long ago. And she had heard the name from other children, "Let's play Enid Ambrose" ... and the history.

Jenny's tongue ran across her lips but she asked in a loud careless voice, "What of it? What's the name mean to you, mother?"

Mrs. Thorne leaned down heavily on her hands but kept up her dark and gentle eyes.

"It is my own," she said.

"Mother darling, I think you must be very ill."

"Stay where you are. I am not ill at all. I've never been ill. There was never anybody stronger and healthier than I am. I've never had a day's sickness in my life. I am Enid Ambrose and you are my daughter, Sheila."

Jenny heard herself like another person, laughing. "Well, I must say I prefer Jenny Thorne." Then she saw that her own hands were struggling on her lap and she controlled them angrily.

"You were accused of ... killing someone? You? That's just ... impossible."

"It happened. Do you want to hear?"

"Of course. But I'm not frightened. You don't frighten me a bit. In fact, I never felt better about you. If anyone was fool enough to suspect you of doing anything so wild, so out of character, that someone ought to be shut up for lunacy. And if he isn't I'll see to it." She spoke through her teeth, holding herself down because she had been told to stay where she was.

"Hush, darling. Wait until you hear."

"Please come and sit down then. It can't be a short story ..." She repeated dazedly, "Enid and Sheila ..." and heard herself laughing again.

"No. I'm going to stand here, no matter for how long. It will make it easier." Still leaning on the two long slender hands, still looking at the reflection of first one and then the other face, she began to speak, forcing the words from an unwilling throat.

"It all happened years ago, when I was very young. At Barent, in the house they called Castania."

Chapter Two

The town of Barent climbs crookedly up the high and sudden bank of the Hudson River. It is an ugly town; cobbled, treeless, grey, a pale snake in the beautiful, bright hill-country. Along Ferry Street after it leaves the yellow railway station, every other house is a saloon, changing from speakeasy and back according to legal exigency, so that it is never safe for a decent girl to frequent it after dark. The square or pentagon to which it leads, however, is respectable. It is known as The Corners. Five streets go out from it; the Main, a decent, shop-lined extension of Ferry Street. Along it, closely, grind the trolleys day and night, well supplied with passengers by a factory on the stream above the town. A few doors beyond The Corners on Main Street stands The Dutch House, largest of Barent's hotels and the most hideous.

In its chocolate-coated lobby on a dark day of April, 1942, a visitor wrote her name in the greasy register, engaging a modest single room "indefinitely."

The elderly clerk showed a dim interest.

"Miss Jenny Thorne, Savannah, Georgia. From the South, eh?"

"Yes. But I wasn't born there. I'm a Californian. Is there someone to carry up my bags? And can you tell me where Dr. Roger Dean lives? Or, better, where he has his office, please?"

Dr. Dean's office, it appeared, was in his house, just around the corner on Elm Street. And at his professional door a few hours later, Jenny Thorne entered, leaving her umbrella to leak in his vestibule and shaking moisture from her rain cape before she took it in.

The office, small and crowded with ambulatory cases, smelled of disinfectant and of damp clothes and was visited, every time the outer door opened and closed, by Dr. Dean's attendant, a prim, middle-aged woman who took, with an air of reproof and reluctance, the note Jenny Thorne handed to her.

In five minutes she returned to say, "Miss Thorne, Doctor

14

says will you call on him at eight this evening, using the other door? He'll probably be at home then and will be able to talk to you."

Jenny went out again into the rain. It had slackened; the pavements showed here and there a gleam of pale sun. By the time she got back to The Dutch House, the sky was clear. Jenny left her rain togs with Mr. Slade, who had learned already to smile at her, and went out for a walk. She stepped fast, looking about her, quick and keen. In spite of their long and intimate relationship, Clara Thorne had never but once mentioned to her child the name of this town but it had for her now a dream-like familiarity. She watched the faces on the street. "There goes an old man who may remember Enid Ambrose. There's a child who surely doesn't yet know her history. There's a woman who may just now have come from talking to Felicia."

Felicia . . . to Jenny's literal and vivid memory, the name returned on her mother's tongue which had produced for it a sudden thrust-like chord of adoration.

"Then came Felicia. Oh, Jenny," and she had looked up with all her lovely eyes, "never forget Felicia. I say her name in my prayers every night. She was Philip Grise's wife at Castania."

"Mrs. Philip Grise." Already Jenny knew, from a search in the Barent telephone book, that Mrs. Philip Grise still lived in the house of Enid's tragedy. The clear afternoon tempted Jenny to walk out in that direction, hoping that from some sheltered spot she might be able to look down upon Castania and study it. But her unwillingness to ask questions and her ignorance of local geography led her astray and the town coming "by way of neat and pleasantly shaded houses" quickly to the open fields, she found herself following a rough path along the river. Here the railroad cut across a bay and there was a narrow rock-strewn beach. No path seemed to lead along the shore beyond it so Jenny's walk had come to an inevitable end.

She stood and looked at the little precipice above her. It was so steep that only the green fingers of a cedar clump showed against the sky but, up there somewhere—for the Grise house had been "only two miles out of town along the river"—must have stood the garden summerhouse where her mother had had tea so often with Philip Grise, his small son playing somewhere not too far away. "He didn't like children. He didn't want another child in the house. That's why I had to leave you with my cousin. Felicia had even to keep his own child out of his way"—and there Enid Ambrose had paused, wrinkling her brows with that vague air of bewilderment. "I've never understood all that," she had said—a phrase that ran indeed like a plaintive bird note through her confession.

At the end of that confession, Jenny had had but one desire: to escape from Bonnetsville. She had not cried, she had asked few questions but she had begun to pack furiously. Enid Ambrose's daughter, knowing that someone in Bonnetsville had recognized her mother, wanted only to be gone. Her face was indeed panic, a marble faun's, as it bent over the trunks. She had written a letter to Nick Landis leaving it for delivery by Mrs. Clarke.

Dear Nick: My mother's name is Enid Ambrose. If your mother can't tell you about her, you can read her story in any newspaper of 1920-21. You will find her picture there too. She was tried for the murder of Philip Grise in New York State and, for lack of sufficient evidence, received a suspended sentence. It was a very celebrated case. Apparently everyone believed her guilty and she has never been able to stay anywhere without sooner or later being recognized by somebody. She has a very noticeable face. Now you will understand why I am leaving at once and saying goodbye to you like this. I don't even need to tell you never to see me again. Not only just to forget me but to dig me out of your mind and heart. This is no time for softness . . . not for you and certainly not for me.

I need hardly say I believe her innocent. I know her innocent. What word is there to add?

Sheila Ambrose (alias Jenny Thorne).

For some reason Mrs. Thorne had chosen Savannah, Georgia, for their next retreat and they travelled south through that sad country, shortly after break of the next day, two pale and silent women. It rained and the drops, hunting one another down the pane, etched a sad pattern in Jenny's memory. For nearly the whole of that journey she kept her hand, warm and strong, about her mother's under the shelter of her skirt against the dry plush seat.

But, little by little, as the day wore on, a change had come into Jenny's face until by night it was no longer panic or faun like. It had that whiteness of an angelic sword.

Now, a few weeks later, Jenny sat on a boulder and stared out across the Hudson River. Its noble faring was beautiful, consoling. On its far bank low blue hills ran away and up towards the distant Catskill range. Courage was manifest to her in the soaring horizon, steadfastness and faith in the great movement of the water. "I will love this river," she said, "this river will be my friend." And she rose, comforted, and looked up once more bravely at the cliff.

She then saw that a man was looking down at her. He had come part way along the side of the small precipice by some rocky path she had not been able to detect and he was leaning at its edge against a high rock which hid his body, showing only his shoulders and a dark pale face. What struck her instantly, and sent her moving back quickly by the way she had come, was the expression on that face.

It was not until she had turned into one of the home-bordered village streets that she was able to recapture her composure and to analyze her shock. "Perhaps," she thought, "there is a sanitarium up there. And he is one of the patients. Certainly there's nothing about me to scare a sane man out of his wits. He looked"—and for the first time the slang phrase took on the original freshness of its imagery—"he looked scared to death. He might almost have been dead." She stopped on the dirt path, her heart stopped too and a quick chill went over her skin. Philip Grise . . . and oh, kind Heaven! the manner of his death!

She flung away the morbid terror.

Did she perhaps resemble Enid Ambrose? No. Not in the very least, not in any line or feature. Of this she had thoroughly assured herself. Besides the man was very young, not more than twenty-five and probably younger. He could remember nothing of that tragedy. Was he in uniform? She couldn't recall but his shoulders seemed to have been dark, not khaki-clad, and there were no visible insignia. His head had been uncovered but the wind, moving across it, had not stirred a single hair of its sleek darkness. The face seemed to be spare, eyes set, narrow, between the bones of cheek and brow. Maybe he had just been normally startled at seeing her there. Maybe he just had one of those "exaggerative faces." Or perhaps there was some assignation and an unexpected figure gave him a shock. Perhaps he had been dreading to see someone . . . So, phrase by phrase, she reassured herself and by the time she had come back to The Dutch House, she was able to be angry with her discomposure.

In her ugly little room she sat down at a table by its one window, which looked down upon Main Street with the grinding trolleys, took out of its locked brief case her stenographic report of her mother's story and the diary she had bought. In it she wrote, using the hieroglyphic she had been taught as a child in one of the efficient California schools, the record of "My First Day at Barent." At its close, or nearly at its close, for the day was not yet over, she set down a black mark against her own behavior.

In Savannah, two weeks before, she had registered in the heightened language of youth and girlhood her own new resolve: "I have undertaken what may be my life work and to its accomplishment I have dedicated myself. It may lead to an increase of misery. It may lead to triumph. I will go to Barent. I will plant myself there. I will root myself there. And, before I leave the place, I will reconstruct the scene and circumstances of my mother's experience with such patient skill, with such exhaustive research and new keen observation that the truth will be inevitably exposed. My mother will never again be hunted from one hiding place to another. She will be proud and free and I, her daughter, if God give Nick Landis patience and courage and real love, I too may get back my own happiness. It is a desperate undertaking. I must myself have simply enormous patience and great courage. I must never give up. I must absolutely conquer my doubts and fears.

"Mother's life has been an embodied fear. My own first reaction to her story was panic. But from this day of April seventh, forward, until my work is done, we must both be done with fear. Enid Ambrose is innocent. Innocent people are not afraid. They do not run away. If mother had stayed near Barent, if mother had looked the world straight in its suspicious eyes, if she had worked with persistence, as I now intend to work, indifferent to public opinion, to discouragement, surely she would long ago have come upon the truth. The passage of twenty years makes the job pretty desperate but there *is* truth. It can't cease to be. It lives. It endures. It must be resurrected. I am the agent of its resurrection.

"I have told mother and, as the first hard test, I've stood out against her resistance. She kept crying to me, 'It will be no use. It will only hurt us more. It may even hurt Felicia.'

" 'For me,' I told her, 'Felicia doesn't count. Even if she did take you in when you were so poor, even if she did stand by you, even if she has supported us both by her extraordinary parting gift she does not count. Only one human being counts and she is ... Enid Ambrose. That name is going to be clean and open to free use again. It is going to be a happy and triumphant name.' Mother cried and begged, fought me to exhaustion; refused to give me any aid in my undertaking. Her lips are sealed by my purpose as they were sealed during the trial by fear of bringing unhappiness to Felicia Grise. When I left her, half an hour ago, she lay on her bed, her face turned to the wall. There is no fight in her. She was never a fighter. But I, who am now shamefully Jenny Thorne but who will some day proudly be Sheila Ambrose, am a fighter. I am going to New York City. I am going to find out what the chances are for a trained nurse at Barent. I am going to get a letter of introduction to its leading physician. These days, when trained nurses are so scarce, none of this should be too difficult. I am leaving Savannah tomorrow. I am going to Barent with my diploma, my uniforms, my own $150.00 of cash—for I cannot begin my investigation of Felicia Grise's household on her own past charity!—and my heart is fixed as the sword in the stone.

"I am twenty-two years old and I am what the world calls only a girl but I am as dangerous to one person, whose name I do not know, as steel."

That was what she had written only two weeks before, and yet today she had been scared breathless, scared into flight, simply by the face of a startled man looking unexpectedly down upon her.

She set down the story of her day and the confession of her failure and she renewed her vow. By her bed, before she slept, she prayed again for—and to—the Love that casteth out fear.

This was after she had returned from her first interview with Dr. Roger Dean.

Up to the moment when he came into his little sitting room, Dr. Dean had been to Jenny Thorne merely one of the agents of her adventure. She had decided that the leading physician of Barent would necessarily be a familiar of the leading family of Barent. Philip Grise's widow had been an invalid for years. She would have the habit and the need of medical supervision. Dr. Roger Dean would be, she hoped, Felicia's oldest and most intimate professional acquaintance, if not her oldest and most intimate friend.

But when the tall man, switching on a light near the door to brighten the dim, book-lined room, came towards her,

Roger Dean became in his own right a very living part of her experience.

"I don't have to tell you that I'm glad to meet any trained nurse at this juncture, Miss Thorne," said he, "especially one with your credentials. How does it happen that you've chosen Barent?"

It is always exciting to meet an attractive fellow creature of the opposite sex. This man was very attractive. He held himself with a grace half-military, half-diplomatic, was strong and sunburnt, slender. His high head was whitely helmeted. He had the beautiful hands of his profession. Jenny found herself, like any schoolgirl, hoping he was a bachelor and had not time to blush for herself before he had taken her hand and was looking through her with the brightest of dark eyes.

She told the story she had prepared: she had wanted to work in a small town not very far from New York City, with a fine, small hospital and under a distinguished physician. These requirements Barent had met. The Board had given her a starred list and, after a lot of consideration and some advice, she had made her choice, arranged her credentials and, "I hope you'll be able to make use of me, Dr. Dean. I do indeed."

He laughed at her, a low short sound concentrating much amusement and crinkling his eyelids pleasantly. "I can make use of you. I've studied your papers. I've an appendectomy tomorrow at eleven A.M. A patient, male, fifty years old. No complications so far. Simple case enough . . . for a starter. Meet me here at 8:30 with your bag packed and I'll run you out to the hospital. I can give you instructions on the way. Where are you staying? Not at The Dutch House? That's pretty awful, isn't it? Well, for the next week you'll be at the hospital, then I may send you out on a private case. I can keep you busy, Miss Thorne. I suppose you know that you're an answer to my prayers."

Jenny was glad, just then, to be an answer to anyone's prayers, rather especially the prayers of Dr. Roger Dean. She was able almost to feel glad or, perhaps more accurately, relieved, at the prospect of working with this man. Could she call herself lucky? Could she dare? She . . . Sheila Ambrose? Yes, in this instance she could and she would. And, though the dim glow faded, and, for all her strong will to courage, she wept herself to sleep again upon the hard and lonely pillow, still it remained a small, small glow, like Stevenson's dark lantern under a coat, symbolizing the unconquerable romanticism of youth.

The hospital was on the north side of town, just off the north-south highway. It stood, Jenny thought, about halfway between Barent and the old Grise mansion. She had no need to question. Castania, as it had been called for the two great chestnut trees that had once flanked its entrance but had since succumbed to the blight, *was* a mansion and a landmark. The town had little enough drama in its history and could not afford to allow any newcomer to overlook its unsolved mystery.

One of the first things, moreover, that Nurse Thorne saw, when she went on rubber soles along the hall of the hospital to her patient's private room, was a brass plate on one of the closed doors.

"To the memory of Philip Marshall Grise this room is dedicated by his loving wife Felicia."

Every time she passed it she could not help looking and her heart missed a beat. She was glad that Mr. Hughes was not occupying that room.

After his recovery, she was sent to a house case. Pneumonia. A Mrs. Carter. This fragile lady had clung to the big old estate back from the river until neither her shrunken income nor her shrunken self could properly maintain it. "She should go to the hospital," grumbled Dr. Dean, "but I can't pry her loose. It will be a troublesome case for you, I'm afraid." Under his bright, impersonal gaze Jenny felt that she was being probed, tested for some more exacting ordeal. "She has only the one woman to help her. It's lonely and it's going to be a night and day matter until we get her past the crisis. I won't, of course, insist ..."

"I'll take it," smiled Jenny Thorne.

And Dr. Dean, still looking at her probingly, gave her his smile.

Jenny liked the doctor and she was determined to take root in Barent. Besides she had the conscience of her calling. Her grief and her longing for Nick, the horrible lingering hope that made her cry in the dark, lonely nighttime—for he *could* trace her, he *could* find her, he *could* follow and help and be the St. George of her dreams—drove her to action like a spur. She waited upon her chance for further knowledge that might aid her quest. But it was not exactly chance but another person's purpose that rewarded her.

Mrs. Carter was getting well and had been taken out onto the high old verandah. There she sat in one of the creaking wicker chairs, pathetically glad of the warm June sun and of the wisteria vine's phenomenally rich bloom.

"It seems just to take care of itself," said she, lifting her eyes of so faint a blue that they matched the delicate flower clusters, "that vine." She laughed airily. "I had a colored man once who called it the Mysterious Vine."

Jenny sat on the steps and looked across the down-treading roofs of Barent to her friend the river. It was very blue to-day and she could see from this high vantage point away and away to the Catskill ranges against their bluer sky. The thunder of the passing trains was not here audible . . . only their faint cry of passage, mournful and adventurous.

"Felicia used to love that story," murmured Alethea Carter, "about the Mysterious Vine."

It was the first time Felicia's name had been mentioned. The hands of the young nurse paused in their knitting. "Who is Felicia?"

"It's Mrs. Grise. Mrs. Philip Grise. I had such a sad little note from her. It makes me feel guilty, Miss Thorne, to have you here taking care of a useless somebody when my darling Felicia is so troubled!"

That panic heart was running wild again. Jenny drew slow breaths. "You mean that . . . that Mrs. Grise needs a trained nurse?" She tried not to sound incredulous, for why, after all, should Miss Jenny Thorne find in the statement anything incredible?

"She needs just everything. That house of hers with its pretty old name and its ugly old history—Castania—now, I ask you! Why, it's a white elephant such times as these. She can't get servants. She has only the cross old cook and the deaf old woman that pushes her round and waits on her. And she has something that calls itself a handy man and drives her car to market and the post office. But with this recent complication . . ."

She gave a loud and happy exclamation for just then up drove the doctor in his Ford and he "must stay and have tea" and he must congratulate her on being out of doors and he must tell her all the news.

Roger Dean lingered with Alethea Carter under the Mysterious Vine for these mild diversions, while Jenny, after helping with the tea service, went tactfully into the hall. From there she heard herself warmly recommended. "That child is just a wonder, Roger. It's not only that she's so sweet and so delicious to look at, but she's so clever. Honestly, Roger, she has a genius for bucking you up. You ought to put her on every depressed case you can find. She gives a person courage."

Jenny, flushing with uneasy pleasure, moved farther away, "which," she told herself, facing an undistinguishable portrait of someone in a white stock against the dark wall of the parlor, "is just what I must learn not to do. I must stay as much as possible within earshot of conversations. I must learn to be an expert eavesdropper. It's only by such stale little crumbs accidentally let fall that I'll ever be able to begin to reconstruct and to reshape that old history." And, ignoring the heat of shame in her face, she forced herself to go back and sit down in the stiff chair by the console in the hall.

The front door stood open. She could see Dr. Dean's arm ending in the teacup. Mrs. Carter was saying in a voice plaintive and beguiling, "Couldn't you possibly, Roger? Just for a few weeks. It might be everything to both of them just now. She's *so* discouraged."

But what could possibly be done and for whose encouragement Jenny failed to discover. And it was not until she was on her way back, in Dr. Dean's car, to her room in The Dutch House, that enlightenment was bestowed.

They turned from the highway in through a gate.

Dr. Dean looked at her and away. His eyes were even brighter than usual and more impersonal.

"Miss thorne," he said, "this, if you don't know it already, is the road into Castania."

Chapter Three

The road to Castania ran straight and level between its bordering larch trees, a sad, beautiful entrance lane that gave no hint of the harsh house above the river. The trees from which it had its name were dead and there the house they had sheltered stood bare, a rack of gables, angles, cupolas and balconies, expressing the fantastic taste of some Victorian architect.

It was a jumble of a house such as Jenny had never dreamed of, part of blue-grey wood and part of green-grey stone but all scalloped and eyeleted like the ruffle of an old-fashioned muslin petticoat ... too high for its width, too tall for its foundations, it toppled there above the river so that a wind, she felt, might push it down. And a wind it had forever, sucked up and down through a cleft in the river bank as though through a funnel.

After leaving the larch colonnade, the drive turned about a prettily wooded meadow then plunged steeply. This last piece of road had been built in the horse and buggy days ... Dr. Dean said bitterly, "Every time I take my Ford down here I feel I'm never going to get her up again ..." and coiled its end about in front of the high verandah. A gloomy old verandah hung with vines, holding its windows and a row of wicker porch chairs and a big front door flanked by panels of colored glass.

"You wait here, Miss Thorne, in the car," said Dr. Dean, and in he went being admitted promptly by one of those old servants described by Mrs. Carter.

Jenny was left with her rapid pulses, her feeling of nightmare and victorious adventure. For there she was, daughter of Enid Ambrose and her avenger, in the very shadow of Castania. Twenty years before, a girl no older than herself had come along that sad and level driveway, had plunged down the steep hill towards the river, near now and audible in its wide rushing. Twenty years ago she had come, innocent, timid, grateful, to serve Felicia.

The name, for all its tripping syllables, thundered in her

24

mind. The owner of that name was in peril. Generosity and championship must now avail her nothing. Nothing could make her proof against the acid of this search. Innocent she had been proven twenty years ago, her alibi had been unbreakable, her character above suspicion, her loyalty to her poor younger protégée of a moral splendor that could not be decried. But to Sheila Ambrose, she could never be above suspicion. There must be nobody in this house, nor in this house's memory, above or below investigation. "If God lets me in here," Jenny told herself, "I will be as blindfold against prejudice as His own justice, Amen." Already she was hardening herself against a spell.

Then, before ever seeing her, she heard Felicia's voice.

"But, Roger," it said wistfully, "what makes you think she'll come?" and, immediately thereafter, Dr. Dean opened the door and came quickly down the steps.

As he stood beside Jenny, she thought how beautiful a human face can be when it is dedicated to service, when it is absorbed in the wish to help other people. He spoke gravely. "I want you, Miss Thorne, to come in and talk to Mrs. Grise." He must have seen Jenny's face go white for he put his hand quickly over hers. "Don't be afraid of her. She's a lovely person," he said and Jenny nodded and climbed down. She felt numb. It was like walking out of real life into a remembered dream.

She crossed the verandah, went in between the blue-paned windows, remembering the superstition that "hants can't cross blue" and in the great square hall, she waited; for Felicia was not in sight.

She was surprised at the interior pleasantness of this ugly Castania. The hall went straight from front door to back and this, being open, showed sunlight and greenness. There were flowering bushes and a breezy entrance of flower perfume. The stairs turned nobly down under wide, sunny windows and, from the hall, furnished mainly by a great carved chest below a portrait, doors opened right and left to other rooms. They could open, that is, for all of them now were closed so that Jenny wondered how she had been able to hear Felicia's voice so clearly, high and sweet and curiously young.

Jenny moved instinctively to stand beneath the portrait as though it had become her host. It was the likeness of a young man, high-colored, with curly auburn hair. His head was lifted eagerly, like a hound's. An open shirt collar and a sash about his narrow waist gave him the look of an artist. If this were Philip Grise, the apparition on the side of the cliff had been no ghost.

At a very slight sound, she turned to see Felicia.

Moving on the rubber-tired wheels of her invalid chair, Mrs. Grise had come noiselessly in from the back porch through that open door. The light was behind her and Jenny held her breath. She was so radiant.

"Will you come into my room here at the left, Miss Thorne? I do want to talk confidentially with you, if the doctor will allow it. He thinks," she went on as Jenny followed her, she not trying to look back but talking ahead as she propelled herself, the doctor holding open the door for them both, "Dr. Dean thinks ... and I can't quite believe him ... that you might be willing to come here for a few weeks and ... help me out a little.

"Now that we're alone," she added, in a changed, more earnest key when the door was closed, "I can tell you what I'm up against."

It was hard for Jenny to do anything but stare, the room like its mistress was so exquisite. Like the inside of a sea shell—peach and blue and palest green. The few ornaments were opalescent in color, fragile, precious. It was a woman's sitting room and had all the useful and amusing appurtenances: the writing desk, the sewing stand, the window boxes of flowers. She saw that Felicia, alone, played solitaire and, with someone else, chess and backgammon. There were a mandolin, a music stand, a bowl marked "Puss" on the hearth before an open fireplace and the user of the bowl lay like a little drift of snow across the peach-silk-covered lounge. The rug, very deep piled and large, was like an old, dim flower garden. Her footsteps across it made no sound.

She was directed to the sun-filled window seat. Felicia wheeled herself opposite and took out, from the pocket of her chair arm, a piece of knitting in soft light-colored wool. She worked without looking, her fingers swift and pale. The sapphire on her left hand matched her eyes.

She said, "I'm supposed to need help. I don't. I have two wonderful old women who could take care of a palace. You won't see a speck of dust anywhere in Castania and I'm sure that's true of very few houses these days. And a houseman who is no more lazy and useless now than he ever was. I've the gardener and the gardener's family, which means my washing and my weeding both get done. I've never felt the need of a trained nurse. You see," she laughed and flashed up a young, almost a mischievous look, "when you've been an invalid for so long, you're practically well. I never think of myself as 'sick'; just, let's say, 'odd' or perhaps 'distinguished' as though everyone would prefer to go about in a wheeled chair if they could arrange it." She laughed again. Here is a woman, Jenny thought, without bitterness. It has made of her a lovely, eternal child. "But now," Felicia went on, "I'm playing martyr and all my friends are bleating about me and I've got you here—so far—on false pretenses. But it won't do me any good to go on with my faking. Because," all laughter went out of her face, left it no color but the sapphire of her eyes, "my dear girl, I need your help for someone else and that someone mustn't guess for an instant that you are here—if you *are* here!—on his account."

"Who is he, Mrs. Grise?"

She looked past Jenny towards the river and Jenny wondered if she too thought of it as her friend.

"It is my son, Adam."

Her forehead, smooth as a girl's beneath its curly mist of fine and very thick grey-blond hair, frowned deeply, suddenly, mounting two perpendicular sharp lines. "He has been honorably discharged. He was an aviator, in China. He had a terrible experience. He is out of hospital. He's supposed to be well enough for a quiet, regular civilian life. But, my dear girl, he isn't. Definitely. Nobody but me knows how profoundly and frighteningly he is *not*."

Jenny waited, trying to veil the intense interest she felt in every gesture, look and word.

"Dr. Dean says that you have had some psychiatric training and Alethea Carter says you are a marvel in building up morale. Now my poor boy needs just exactly that. I mean the reconstruction of his normal attitude towards life. I thought . . . I hoped . . . that if you could come here"—again her eyes were on the river—"as my nurse—I've been faking pain in my back and headaches and such vague ailments—you might be able to get round Adam to the point where you could give him the push he needs. I feel that it would just take a push. In the right direction. You wouldn't guess it, mind you! to look at him or to hear him talk. But watch him, watch him closely." She tightened her hands on the needles and held them still. Her whole body went stiff. She let out her caught breath and her voice and eyes were piteous. "Won't you help me? Won't you help me to save *him?* He's all I have left."

It was not easy for the child of Enid Ambrose to bear the emphasis on that pronoun. Jenny's impulse was to cry out, "No. No. You mustn't ask me to come in." But she held fast, held iron-cold.

And she acted out her reluctance, her gradual yielding. Felicia was begging. Felicia was thanking "Miss Thorne" almost with tears. Had she once been as grateful to Enid Ambrose for coming into her home? That had been to help her with Adam too . . . and the same Adam.

"You will try your very best to keep the truth from him and from everyone else, won't you, Miss Thorne? Even from Dr. Dean. You won't let anyone imagine for an instant that you are here on anyone's account but mine?" She was moving towards the door but stopped her wheels, turning to look at Jenny. There was a change upon her.

"Oh, there's one thing," she paused, finished hurriedly, "I've only the one room for you. We're very luxurious in the matter of space at Castania, and it's a mansion only in name and because there are no real mansions hereabouts. We've spread ourselves out very thin. I have the apartment down here including my husband's old rooms. Anna sleeps in his bedroom. Upstairs old Mrs. Grise, my husband's mother, occupies two rooms and a bath while Adam has taken over the whole other side of the second story. That, except for the servants' quarters, leaves only one really decent bedroom, the one in the tower." She added, while Jenny tried again to manage her quick heart and breath, "We have a tower, you may have noticed. Most girls like the idea of living in a tower, the old princess-complex. When I first came here, I wanted to live in it myself. But it's a maiden's bower. I wonder—it's a little lonely and detached but I won't even pretend to need any other night attendant but Anna—I wonder if you'd mind . . . ?"

Chapter Four

PAGES FROM JENNY'S DIARY

This is a strange night, my first night in the tower room. Physically a beautiful night, starry and still, and sung to by the river. Mentally for me a night of such excitement as to be a torment to my nerves.

Mother has been writing to me constantly, using my old typewriter (for the script of Enid Ambrose must not be seen in Barent), addressing her envelopes to the General Delivery Post Office where I collect them. In every letter she urges me to give up my mad purpose and come back to her. "Weren't we happy together, darling? Wasn't it better for us both than this? You've known Nick Landis such a little time and me such a long time. He can't mean so much to you . . . not now when you know that marriage with him is impossible. Aren't you afraid that what you are doing now may make it harder for us both?" I had told her never to mention the old names or the old history but her constant pleading treads so closely to it that it scares me. I always destroy her letters as soon as they are read. I'm not going to tell her, if I can help it, that I have moved to Castania.

Tonight—for I arrived after dinner and was taken at once to my room, climbing after Anna up the wide stairs and the narrow winding one, through a house as quiet as a shuttered nursery—I am thinking of my mother with such intensity that she might as well be here within touch of my hand.

The room has been beautifully cleaned and charmingly prepared for me, the bed is turned down, the linen everywhere is fresh and smells of lavender. The curtains are drawn across the windows. The tiny bathroom, a mere closet with one small window, shines and is perfectly appointed. Anna, in the muffled voice of deafness, said, "I hope you'll be comfortable here, miss. And won't feel lonely-like. There's no one in the room below, but if you look out and down a bit to the right, you'll see the window of Lizzie's room and you can wake her easy. She's not got my trouble, I can tell you. She's quick to wake as a cat. I'll bid you good night now, miss. Lizzie says she'll fetch you up your breakfast tomorrow morning as long as you don't know your way about but, after tomorrow, you can come down to the breakfast room, if you please. About eight o'clock, if it suits you."

At the top of my voice I assured her that "whatever suits Mrs. Grise suits me" and won her meek smile and her mute nodding.

I had carried up my own suit case and, after I had looked about me and down from my airy "casement," I unpacked all my belongings. I wanted first to re-read a certain portion of my mother's story, although I knew it all by heart. And then I wanted to write down, while it is fresh in my mind, all my own first impressions. In this shorthand diary I mean to record every detail and every word. I can't tell what may turn out to be of importance.

Sitting on my bed close to the lamp that stands beside the pillow, I turned to my mother's story spoken to me first in Mrs. Clarke's room at Bonnetsville, with our trunks standing open and the glory of my first love in my heart . . .

(My mother speaking:

"I left you, Jenny, my little baby, with an aunt of mine as poor as I was and glad to get what I would send her from my ample salary, and, in the spring, May 2, 1922, I went to Castania.

"It was a fascinating house.

"Felicia gave me a charming room in a sort of tower that looked down on the river. How glad I was to be there then . . . and how I hate now to think of that room!

"Philip Grise . . . I think, Jenny, that a modern psychologist would call him an 'escapist.' He was perverse in a charming, spoiled-boy way. There's no doubt that he adored Felicia. And was afraid of her. I mean, afraid of her loveliness. I don't make it clear because Philip always puzzled and bewildered me. I think there was too much of the son in his relationship with his wife. He liked to keep things from her . . . to have secrets. He liked to have fun she didn't know about. I think he even liked being a little afraid of her finding out. That's the way he was about me, at first. It began with his playing with little Adam when the child and I were together. For he soon got over any unwillingness to be 'with children.' [That pleased Felicia. She used to say, 'You've been able to make a father of him, Enid, and that's the most wonderful repayment.' You see, I was always worrying about how I could show my gratitude to her.] He spent a great deal of time with us ... more and more. Felicia never knew how much. He was a very idle and extravagant young man. He pretended to be writing a history of New York State. He had his study and his library. Books were always coming by post for his 'research.' But he spent most of his time mooning. There was never a better word for Philip's favorite occupation. He was a 'moon calf' if ever there was one. And had the charm of all dreamers ... gentle and coaxing and ... I guess you'd call it ... ineffectual. He was lovely to look at, tall, and auburn-haired and whimsical. Oh, I know it's 'dated' now but that was the time when every romantic hero had to be 'whimsical.' He had a delicious, sly, unexpected sense of humor, a laugh as captivating as any sound you ever heard. Any woman in the world would want to mother him. He was born to be a spoiled darling. Felicia indulged him to the limit. But I don't think she understood him. Or any of us— for that matter! The money was hers, you see, though the house was his. And of course he worshipped the ground that she, poor child! could never tread upon. You mustn't forget, Jenny, how young we all were. Philip was twenty-four, a year younger than Felicia; and I was only twenty-two. Your age, Jenny!

"Felicia never went upstairs at all. She had her own rooms on the ground floor. I felt as if those rooms were the real tower, a place of ivory enchantment. Philip slept there too. But his study was in the tower room just below my own. You see, little Adam had his nurse. They occupied rooms on the second floor opposite his grandmother's. And I had nothing to do with the child's sleeping or eating or dressing. I was strictly his governess. So it wasn't necessary for me to spend my nights near him, though I often tucked him in and sang to him. He was so sweet!

"There was a circular staircase in the tower. When I went up and down I passed the door of Philip's study and he got into the habit of leaving it open and of lounging on the threshold; later, of calling me in, asking me to help him with this or that.

"It was such a beautiful room, Jenny; morning, noon, and night.

"I don't think Felicia was capable of suspicion. She'd been surrounded all her life with worshippers and Philip was so especially her slave. He was—or seemed to be—completely hers.

I can't understand. I don't think I ever understood men ...
Philip Grise least of all. But, in the end, oh yes, in the end
there was something I did understand. He loved me. And I
loved him. I loved him, Jenny!")

As I finish this, my own report of her speech from memory, the house lies silent and I hear the river. It is the same
house, the same river, but in the mirror above my dressing
table is the reflection of another girl. There was once love in
this place, love in this tower ... a strong, secret passion,
wrong and wild. And that other girl, so beautiful and gentle,
so alone, sitting here must have felt shame, no doubt, and
sorrow but also, I am sure, a certain burning happiness.

It was that wrong happiness so long ago that has destroyed
my own;—for my love though it is good and promised a sane
and clean fulfillment is all sorrow.

Nick has not written to me.

Will he ever write?

In the morning Lizzie brought in to Miss Thorne her
breakfast tray.

Jenny heard her climbing the stairs a little before eight
o'clock and sat up in bed to be ready for her. Those two old
women had known her mother. They had been there at
Castania at the time of Philip's death. Jenny was afraid of
them. She had always been afraid of old women, who seemed
to her to have powers not given to other people. And of
these two old women she was especially afraid. They were to
be, she hoped, the mainspring of her resurrection of those
past events. She felt that she must make friends of them both
and win their confidence. Anna was a humble and friendly
soul but Lizzie, like most cooks, had the artistic temperament. Her old eyes were dark and quick, her stout body
moved lightly and with precision. She was not given to smiles
and nodding like Anna. She had dignity and temper. Jenny
saw at once that, as a trained nurse—anathema to servants in
any household—she must walk warily.

She greeted Lizzie and thanked her, therefore, not too ob-
sequiously, with no over-emphasis, rather as if she was used
to breakfast-trays, and told her gravely that it was nice of
her to make things easy for her first morning in Castania.

"It was Miss Felicia's orders," said Lizzie and added with a
sharp, forbidding look, "That's Mrs. Grise."

"Miss Felicia ..." It was too soon to ask questions but that title could mean only one thing: that Lizzie had come to Castania with Felicia at the time of her marriage, that she had been part of Felicia's girlhood life.

"Mrs. Grise," said Jenny with gravity, "is very kind."

"She's too kind ... to everyone ... is what I say," Lizzie announced but went about pulling back the curtains, plumping the pillows, and arranging little things in the room.

Just before leaving, "Tomorrow," Lizzie said, "you'll be coming downstairs at eight o'clock, I suppose, miss?"

"Yes, Lizzie." Jenny hoped she had not been too meek. She wanted Lizzie to feel that she was submissive to tyranny only up to a certain point. The old woman gave her a sharp look before she went out that set Jenny's heart to beating. Was there something here that reminded Lizzie of that other girl who once lived in the tower room above Philip's study?

On her way down the spiral staircase Jenny dared to try that door. It was not locked. It opened silently. She stood in an arc of radiant sunlight, pouring in through three big, uncurtained windows.

Philip's room was kept in order, swept and dusted. His bookcases, still full, were all about the walls and under the three windows of the bay. The room reminded her of a pilothouse on a ship. The desk was neat and completely appointed. She wondered, with a sick unease, if anyone now used the desk and read the books. She had meant to explore this room repeatedly and she had been hoping that it would be unlocked but neglected. This morning she stayed only an instant, not daring to be caught investigating. She wondered if she could get Felicia's permission to use that desk for her own letters. Much too soon for any such request and what slight hope she had was immediately defeated.

Felicia, who received the nurse in that downstairs sitting room, said almost at once after the greeting, "Adam uses that room beneath yours, Miss Thorne. That's one reason, I must confess, why I put you there. It will make it natural and easy for you to get acquainted, to see something of each other."

She spoke so tranquilly, smiling her mischievous smile, that Jenny had much ado to keep from staring. For there had been a time—a time that must be black within her memory—when two other people, a man and a woman, had found it easy to get better acquainted in those rooms. Could it be possible, thought Jenny, that Felicia's memory had been affected by her illness? that her almost unnatural child-like loveliness had been painted upon her forty-five year-old face by some sort of amnesia? Jenny decided to test this rather frightening theory . . . but not this first day. She must never forget to disguise her curiosity. She must not ask one unnecessary or untimely question.

Felicia was saying, "Now we must plan something for you to do for me, Miss Thorne. I loathe massage and electric treatments but that's no reason why we shouldn't pretend to indulge in them. I have all the needed apparatus. Suppose we arrange for ourselves a strict regime. You report here at nine o'clock every morning and stay in my bedroom—strictly private!—for two hours. I am then supposed to be exhausted by your ministrations and I am left to sleep. And you will need a free hour or more before your midday meal. Adam," went on Felicia, "is as restless as a monkey and never does anything with regularity. But I'll leave you to discover his vagaries and get yourself in touch with him. He uses that room below you sometimes but not consistently. He rides all over the country. He walks for hours. He sees his grandmother and me at dinner. I have breakfast and lunch in here alone. You'll have lunch with Mrs. Grise. I want you to dine with us all at seven-thirty. And, please, not in uniform."

"Outside of my uniforms, I haven't much of a wardrobe, Mrs. Grise."

"One informal evening gown?"

"Yes."

"Then begin with that and pick yourself out something nice from one of the ads . . . from a good New York shop. The papers are full of them. It's for my benefit so it should be part of my provision. You're size twelve, aren't you? Anything will look well on your figure." She wheeled closer to Jenny, put one of her beautiful and fragile hands on the girl's arm. It was her left hand and the sapphire winked. "Get a red dress, won't you? I adore red. It's such a happy color."

Jenny, glad when she was free of the cool kind pressure, asked, "Does your son come to lunch with his grandmother?"

"Never. He doesn't lunch at all. You don't mind lunching with old Mrs. Grise?"

"Mind? Of course not. I'm here only to do just what you want."

A flash of pleasure crossed Felicia's face. "That's nice," she said in a tone of such profound satisfaction that Jenny almost laughed. It was as though Mrs. Grise tasted something delicious on her tongue.

"Then in the afternoons, until five o'clock," she went on, "when I go out on the lawn or onto the verandah, you might read aloud to me . . . and how I loathe being read aloud to! . . . or bring your work. I suppose you have 'work' . . . and chat with me. Possibly Adam will join us. At least, he'll have to pass us on the verandah going in and out. I do want you to observe him very closely, Miss Thorne."

Jenny promised that she would; close observation, she said feeling treacherous, being part of her profession.

". . . and report your impressions to me. I want," said Felicia and paused for a long time, gazing out at the river, "I want to understand Adam. I must understand Adam." Her face was pale.

The proposed regime was begun at once but all day there was no sight or sound of Adam. He must have left the house early and did not return until just in time to change for dinner. Old Mrs. Grise appeared at lunch, a hollow bent reed of a woman with a dark peering face. She was silent and very much interested in her food. She looked, being so small and hooked, like a mute interrogation point.

At seven o'clock towards the close of this long, strange day, Jenny was alone in the fine drawing room, wearing her one informal gown . . . a simple straight frock of blue crepe, when Adam came in, stopped, then walked straight towards her.

He stopped short of a handshake and said, without smiling, "Good evening, Miss Thorne," then turned and walked over to the lamplit table from which he took up an evening paper. He stood there, reading it, and gave her not another word or look. "A moody, arrogant, handsome boy," wrote Jenny later, "if ever there was one!"

She recognized him, but not immediately, as the man who had been so startled by her presence on the beach. It was, no doubt, a private beach and she had no business to be there. Certainly, she thought, this fellow would be a stickler for his prerogatives. Her interpretation of his look must, of course, have been a mistake, some trick of light or shade, for Adam Grise would not "scare" easily. He walked almost with a swagger, holding himself straight and proud. His face, as she had then observed, was spare with narrow eyes set between the bones of cheek and brow. They were grey, of a light peculiar grey, which made the pupils and the lashes seem intensely black. His bone structure was heavy, hands large and strong, but his thinness gave him a slender look.

After a considerable time, he said without looking up, "Dinner's not until eight o'clock."

Jenny murmured, "Oh ... I understood 7:30" and realized that Felicia had laid a small trap. Her son, no doubt, always came down to read the evening paper, the two women joining him only just before dinner was announced. Jenny had been tricked into a tête-à-tête. Clumsy of Felicia, she thought, her hazel eyes darkening with discomfort, and defeating of that purpose.

She said, "Then I'll have time to get some air. After all, it's a June evening," and went out quickly onto the verandah. Her slippered feet tap-tapped and her head was held high.

On the verandah she walked up and down, digesting her impressions. She could not help contrasting this thunderous fellow, this second victim of Felicia's indulgence, with her Nick. Those clear intelligent blue eyes of Nick's smiled again, and again she could hear him say so gravely and so gently, "When you learn to share your worries with me, Jenny, I think you'll find them a lot easier to bear." Tears rushed to her eyes as they had rushed before.

Why, after all, temptation suggested, not share her worries with Nick? Why not write to him? Just as a friend. Tell him her mother's history, describe this desperate undertaking, have his sympathy and his advice? He was very clever, had had more experience in life. This thought surged through the lonely-hearted girl like a tide of rapture. For fifteen minutes she forgot all her surroundings. Castania faded into a thin mist. She hardly heard the river's patient voice. She was not alone. She was with her lover. She was happy, hopeful, young ...

A musical dinner gong sounded; the more formal announcing, Jenny supposed, couldn't be kept up by Lizzie and the handy man. It was this John, young, red-cheeked, awkward, with a big Irish mouth, who waited on them after they had all met in the hall and had marshalled themselves behind Felicia's chair which Adam pushed into its place at the head of the table.

It was, in a certain sense, Jenny's strangest moment. That brief return to her old life and her old self, induced by the indulgent recall of Nick's devotion, had made her present adventure fantastically unreal. She was cold with a sudden terror. What was she doing in this house and with these people? Castania—a musical dream-name—had had its victim. Must she offer herself now, after twenty years?

The four candles in their silver holders blurred before her sight.

"You're looking pale, Miss Thorne," said old Mrs. Grise in a sudden deep voice she used, "or maybe it's just the color of your dress. That shade of blue's trying to a blond complexion."

"I always think of myself as a brunette," Jenny began and stopped as she saw the flash of amused contempt in Adam's eyes. She could feel with mortification that she had lost her pallor. It was, in fact, distinctly bad form for her to focus attention on her personal attributes.

Felicia, however, with her sensitivity to the happiness of other people, put her at her ease. "A blond skin with dark hair and hazel eyes . . . you can take your choice of categories, can't you, Miss Thorne? They say 'Gentlemen prefer blondes' but they very often fall for brunettes, don't they?" Then, hurriedly, for there had come a dark flush into old Mrs. Grise's hollow and hooked face, "It's not for me to boast but doesn't Lizzie make a delicious onion soup? It's Adam's favorite, so we have it very often."

The wretched boy laid down his spoon and drew his eyebrows together. His mother's consideration, her playful attempts to please and to placate him, ruffled his temper. After that, Felicia and Jenny had the conversation entirely to themselves.

Jenny's liking for Felicia grew. "She cares so much for other people," the diary recorded, "that it is impossible not to care for her. And yet—and here is the only important discovery of my second day at Castania—how is it that these two people, who share her home with her, don't seem to care?"

In setting down this impression, she found herself at once explaining it: "Old Mrs. Grise and young Adam are both spoiled people. Felicia has spoiled them as she spoiled her husband, and, perhaps, I am beginning to suspect, my young dependent mother. Shut up with her in this queer, lonely house, on her bounty as I imagine both Adam and the old woman at present are, Felicia's very magnanimity is on their nerves. No doubt Adam would be better off if he could go away."

Chapter Five

The first thing Felicia said when Jenny came into her room at nine o'clock the next morning was, "Now tell me quickly what you think of my son?"

She was on her lounge, covered from thin bare shoulders to feet with a light, peach-colored blanket. Jenny could see the outline of her beautiful slim legs, apparently undeformed by the long helplessness. Beside her Anna had set up the infra-red lamp, the electric vibrator and a table holding towels, massage cream and alcohol. She said smiling, "I'll rub a lot of this stuff into my face and neck and hands. It can't hurt my poor old complexion . . ." which was really like the inside of a shell . . . "and it may even help it. Sit down, please, and turn on the lamp for a few minutes. Now, go ahead!"

"Mrs. Grise," Jenny answered slowly, "it's very difficult to make any report because I don't know at all, you see, what Captain Grise was like before."

"Oh yes. Well, let me tell you. He was the sweetest, gayest, lovingest boy you can imagine. He sang and whistled and was in and out of my room fifty times a day. Above all . . ." she turned her delicate face aside but I could see the rush of tears to her eyes, "he adored me. Never in all his life did I have a rude speech or even a cross look from him." She put a hand across that moisture, smiled wistfully. "You see! There's one very obvious symptom."

"You mean that now he's . . ."

"Irritable. Unpleasant. Rude. Not to his grandmother. Not to the servants. But to me."

"That often happens, Mrs. Grise, in nervous disorganizations. The patients are apt to do just that, turn against the very people they adore."

"Oh, that's so helpful, Miss Thorne. Just that would make it worth while to have you here."

"Tell me another thing—Captain Grise—does he show symptoms of what used to be called shell-shock?"

She laughed. "I don't think that's possible. I just can't imagine Adam being hysterical or scared. He was a great

38

mountain climber, you know, and a skier. He seems to be greedy of danger ... of taking chances. I suppose that's why the aviation service attracted him."

"But now? After the crash?"

"It wasn't a crash. He had a fall back of the lines, after he had come down. He suffered a head injury and was unconscious for days. His men helped to get him back. But no, I don't think he ever lost his nerve. And all the physical effects are over now. He's entirely normal. He would be, that is, if—well, if he just *were*. Doctors say he must be careful to avoid strain, excitement, responsible work but . . ."

"Then really it's only his bad temper and his rudeness to you that worries you so, Mrs. Grise?"

The surprise was audible and Felicia looked confused. Nervously she fingered the silk-bound edge of her "throw."

"It's hardly fair to me, Mrs. Grise, not to tell me if there's anything else. That is, if you really want me to be of any use."

After a long pause, Felicia forced her eyes to meet Jenny's. She spoke in a key so low that it was necessary to lean closer to hear and, at once, listening to her, Jenny laid aside any idea of loss of memory.

"I suppose," she said, "it's almost impossible to escape it even now—I suppose you've been told the . . . the history of Castania?"

Gravely, steadily and at once, Jenny answered, "Yes, Mrs. Grise. I have been told," and for the first time was able to be proud of her courage.

As though that firm answer had steadied her, Felicia went on with more composure. "You'd think they'd forget it, wouldn't you? After twenty years. We here at Castania had almost forgotten it, I think, even Philip's mother whose bitter memory is so long. But we never spoke of it and hardly ever thought of it. We'd put it away, as, thank God, human minds are able to put away ugly things. Oh," here Felicia smote the sides of her lounge with her slim hands, "if I hadn't been like this, it would never have happened. Never in this world. Let's not go over it. It's too painful, even now."

"No. We mustn't. It's only, about your son . . ."

"Yes. Yes. I know. I was so careful always to keep the story from Adam. As much, that is, as it could be kept. Adam never seemed to brood on it or even to be made unduly unhappy over it. I was able to control Philip's mother who was the one to keep the ember alive. But children are very casual, especially a healthy boy like Adam. Now, since his in-- jury . . ." Felicia paused interminably. Jenny heard the white cat purring and the light swift running of the silver clock. She heard a train far away, rushing nearer. Before it passed, blurring the sound of speech, Felicia spoke again. "Since he came back, he's thought of nothing else."

Jenny felt a dryness in her mouth and heard herself swallow carefully. She waited for the train to pass. The windows rattled a little and the whistle gave one of those long, sad, homeless cries.

"You mean," she began, "that Captain Grise . . ."

"I mean he's made up his mind to bring that old story to its conclusion. He's called the ghost to life, called it back to this poor old house and to our time-drugged minds. For time is a drug to horror, you know. A merciful drug. Oh, I don't think it's his own idea. It's Philip's mother. She never forgave me for saving Enid. It was, after all, my attitude that did save her. And now . . . I don't know how or why except that his poor young tortured mind is open just now to morbid influences . . . but she has recently infected Adam. It was his return and his condition that gave her encouragement. They talk about it . . . they go over the whole horrible thing. She gloats on his participation. She swore once . . . I remember that I came out and found her standing before Philip's portrait and with her fist up, swearing to bring that girl to justice. She believed her to be guilty. She has never in her heart given up that will to punishment. And now, Adam's sympathy, his falling in with her obsession . . ."

Felicia, drawn up high and quivering, put out both hands and closed them on Jenny's arm. "If they found evidence that would reopen the case, I couldn't bear it. I don't even know that Enid is alive. I don't know where she is. I gave her some money and told her not to write to me—not to keep in touch with me—for her own sake. Just to disappear. She may be dead. But . . . now . . . to hunt her down, to drag her back!

"You must do something. You *must*. To divert Adam. To change his horrible intention. This will be the end. This will be," her smile was twisted in a pitiful sort of self-mockery, "the death of . . . Felicia Grise!"

Jenny gave her some water, put her back on her pillows, insisted upon quiet, soothed her with irrelevant and gentle murmurings.

"See how we've frightened Beauty! He's stopped purring and come over. He wants to get up . . ." the usual nurse-formulas, and presently she opened her beautiful star-sapphire eyes and thanked "Miss Thorne."

"You do help."

"Won't you leave it to me, Mrs. Grise? I'll do my very best. Wouldn't it be possible, perhaps, to send your son away?"

"No. No. I've tried."

"And you've asked the advice of Dr. Dean?"

"I won't do that. Remember your promise, Miss Thorne. I especially don't want to let Dr. Dean in on this particular case. It wouldn't be playing fair. You see, Roger Dean has never liked Adam."

She was exciting herself again. Jenny said, "It's time for your rest now, Mrs. Grise. I'm going to get Anna."

Felicia nodded meekly, relaxed and closed her eyes.

That afternoon Jenny explored the grounds of Castania. She even drew a map to show how the garden and the stables lay. The tall house, itself, stood at right angles to the river bank, the tower commanding the shore as though against marauders. Felicia's sitting room opened through her river wall upon a terrace. It was easy for her to roll herself down an inclined plane to the turf. And here or on the verandah she "took the air" in true invalid fashion. At five o'clock, as regularly as the sun set, she wheeled out to the edge of the river bank, pulled up the hood of her chair and went into her quiet hour of uninterrupted contemplation—seclusion no one in Castania would dare, it seemed, to interrupt. Jenny wondered why she never went for a run in the car. Mrs. Grise explained this at lunch. "Felicia can't bear to be lifted up or down. She says it hurts her back. Only Anna is allowed to move her."

Beyond the terrace, down one shallow step, lay a piece of level ground at the edge of the cliff. It was on this level that the flower garden had been planted, a beautiful situation, sheltered from above, and high and full of concentrated loveliness. A narrow alley went through it from end to end and at the farther point, where the cliff was steep above the beach and the bright river, stood the little summerhouse so fatal to Enid Ambrose's happiness.

Jenny found only the place where it had been: one of the old posts cut down and overgrown with vines and part of the foundation, making a brief parapet. It had been flanked with big stones set deep into the grass and here she sat at the end of her exploration. It was a lovely late afternoon—her first of freedom—the sun burning in the western hills. The river glowed. Its voice was a constant murmur. The thrushes were melting their crystal laughter into tears. Jenny thought of the lovers, guilty and enchanted, sitting there under that spell. She thought of the little boy, innocent as a bird, digging perhaps in the nearby path with his little spade . . . The sound of a real spade striking stones warned her that the gardener was at hand. He straightened from behind some currant bushes, shaded his eyes against sunset and discovered the slim figure all in white. He smiled—a tall dark cadaver of a fellow obviously unfit for military service or for any work that would keep him out of the air.

"You're settin' in a sort of historic spot, aren't you, miss?" said he.

The uniform had been an identification.

Jenny answered, rising from the rock, "I didn't know . . . is this where . . . ?"

"It's just about the ex-act spot where *he* was settin' when the thing happened. They tore down the arbor and just sort of flagged the edge but there's not many that would sit there since. Likely," gathering up his tools now that he was aware of sunset, "you've broke the spell, miss, and the place has lost its curse—like."

Jenny was moved. It was a kinder and a happier thought than any Castania had yet produced for her.

She asked, "You were here then?" Her voice with its sadness and its laughter was no discordance for the thrush.

"No, miss. Not I. Nor the man before me. It was a chap named Hogan . . . Josh Hogan . . . that was gardener then. He figured at the trial—if you've happened to read about it ever, miss, which isn't likely." (Jenny didn't tell him how closely and how often she had pored over every copy of the papers she found in the New York Library.) "That Hogan had a right smart lot to say at the trial. They tell me down to Barent that Doc still visits him. Doc Dean, he's loyal to his friends."

Jenny was glad to hear this. It confirmed her own impression. Unconsciously she depended more and more upon the loyalty of Roger Dean.

"Where does Hogan live now?"

"Up the river a ways, miss, on his own little old farm. He's got a mortgage paid off and does all right, his grandson helpin' him." He stopped, stood aside and raised a battered

straw object which did him service for a hat. "Good evenin',
Captain," said he.

Adam, in riding clothes, was striding along the gravel
walk. He came as far as the edge of the alley and stopped, a
good four feet short of Jenny's perch. She saw that his face
was as white as chalk and that his forehead was wet. He
must have ridden himself half to death.

"Come back from there," he commanded; "you're too
close to the edge."

She smiled and came towards him, walking beside him as
they both moved housewards.

"I'm not afraid of heights," she said and remembered suddenly the face she had seen from below on the river beach.

"Why," she asked impulsively, "why were you so startled
when you saw me on the beach below the cliff two weeks or
so ago? I wasn't in any danger of falling then."

He stopped short and stared at her. "Was that you? I
wasn't startled . . . or, at least, not to the point of being
scared." He smiled a sardonic, twisted smile. "You're not a
very alarming presence, Miss Thorne."

"That's what puzzled me," she said. "You looked as though
you'd seen a ghost."

His face went scarlet and his eyes glittered with rage. He
struck at his boots with his crop.

Jenny felt like apologizing but refrained. She would not be
subdued to this thunderous spoiled boy's tyranny. She had a
right to protest his look of terror at sight of her, harmless, on
his beach.

He said in a low, not quite steady voice, "Perhaps I did,"
and then swore, not at Jenny but certainly, in military par-
lance, beside her.

His anger amused the girl in a hard bitter fashion. The
Master of Castania, she thought, unused to opposition. He
has never in this place been laughed at or questioned or corrected in his life . . . unless, perhaps, long ago, by that gentle
girl-governess who haunts the garden and my mind.

It seemed to Jenny now, as they came down that alley, just
wide enough for two and more comfortably wide for lovers,
that Philip and Enid walked with them and even *in* them,
stepchildren of that passion as they were.

Adam said, glancing up at the house roof above the locust
trees, "How do you like living in a tower?"

As it was her role to question him, his question put her
about for an instant. Then she gushed, "Oh, I adore it!"

He gave her one of the amused, contemptuous looks. "I guessed you were like that. You read 'Adventure' and 'True Romances' and 'True Confessions,' don't you?"

"I'm not at all romantic, Captain Grise."

"Cut out the captain! I'm not in uniform."

"You expect to get back into the service?"

"Of course. As soon as I'm through here."

"You mean . . . as soon as you're well enough?"

"What in h—" he stopped short, went on jerkily—"makes you think I'm sick, Miss Thorne?"

She would not be confused. "I took it for granted, since you've been honorably discharged from a military hospital and are doing nothing else in the way of war-service."

"So you've found out all about me, eh?" Jenny blushed, furious at his assumption . . . as though she had come to the house primed with information and full of predatory intentions. "That doesn't mean I'm an invalid," he went on, "does it? Do I look like one? Act like one?"

"You have the mean temper of one," she said, smiling her faunlike smile at the flash of anger in his face.

"Trained nurses," he gibed, "are something like these medieval jester boys . . . in two-colored clothes and bells, privileged characters at court who could be just as fresh as they liked without fear of punishment." His right hand had tightened on his riding crop. Jenny laughed, though she was still angry.

"I don't advise you to attempt beating me up, Captain Grise. A trained nurse has a whole medical body back of her."

"Not to mention Dr. Dean and"—his face and voice changed past recognition; he had indeed one of those "exaggerative" faces!—"and my poor mother."

Jenny's anger evaporated. For the first time she had an impression of genuine sweetness and of pain.

"I think that, of all invalids, your mother is the least pitiable."

"Yes. I know. She has the courage of . . . of a saint, I guess. The rest of us aren't saints, though, are we, Miss Thorne? We can't quite attain to her . . . standards."

Now he was sardonic again and hateful and incomprehensible. Why did he gibe, she thought, and at whom? Himself . . . Felicia . . . or Jenny Thorne? She said nothing more . . . they had reached the shallow steps that led up to Mrs. Grise's terrace and there, in her wheeled chair, she sat, bathed in the clear glow. Her face was tilted back, her eyes half-closed. She looked like lovely death and Jenny heard her son draw in the air sharply.

That small sound roused Felicia, her fingers tightened on the wheels of her chair as though she meant to charge forward or back. Then she smiled. "Bad children! You startled me. Adam, you ride too far and too fast. Garvey says the horse comes in lathered and you . . . you look like a ghost."

Old Mrs. Grise spoke deeply from the verandah-end where back of the vines she must have been standing to watch them. "You talk too much about ghosts for my taste, Felicia," said she and Adam shocked them all. He threw back his head and laughed out, long and loud, until Felicia protested. "Stop it, Adam! Please push me into my room. It's getting damp out here."

In her diary Jenny made a note of her deductions:

1—All these people are intensely conscious of the past tragedy. Adam's return and his interest have stirred all of them. The fact of the suspended sentence has kept it alive in their imaginations . . . like an unfinished serial story or a melody that has been interrupted before its final chord. Like me, now, none of them will rest until the word Finis has been written.

2—Philip's son, like Philip's mother, resents Felicia's past magnanimity towards Enid Ambrose and her present reluctance to look for further evidence.

3—Felicia wants me here chiefly to report on their activities in this matter . . . if there are any such activities outside of her own imagination.

4—The root of Adam's mental trouble lies in the past, although it is the disorganization of his war experience that has brought it to the surface. To active life. I would like to consult with Dr. Dean but am forbidden. I don't dare cross Felicia in this or break my promise to her. I wonder if it would be possible for me, somehow, to get up the river to talk to Josh Hogan, the ex-gardener.

I will write to Nick as a physician, as a friend. I must have his advice.

So, I have written a letter, which, on second thoughts, I shall not dare to send.

Chapter Six

Jenny came up the winding stairs to her tower room a little before noon and, from the door of Philip's study, Adam emerged. (She remembered her mother's low and troubled voice, "There was a circular staircase in the tower. When I went up and down I passed the door of Philip's study and he got into the habit of leaving it open, of lounging at the threshold; later, of calling me in to help him with this or that ...") Adam, straight as a soldier, made no ceremony. He said, "Come in here, will you, Miss Thorne."

She came, the crystal height and stillness of the room at once encompassing her.

"You see those books?"

"Certainly." They went from floor to ceiling on every wall except where the big windows interfered.

"I want to catalogue them. Have you any free time? Can you help me?"

"In what way, please, Mr. Grise?"

"I'm no professional cataloguer. I'm just making a list in longhand and then I mean to get it typed. I'm a two-finger typist myself. How about you?"

He smiled at Jenny half-shyly.

"I can type," she said. For some reason this turning on of his charm made her feel stern. He looked away from that hardness out through the great sunlit windows—what a place it was, she thought, for radiance—and his face, without its shy and coaxing smile, was haggard, rough.

"Do you understand filing systems?"

"No."

"Well, you can, if you will or if you have time, take one wall and set down the titles and the authors, can't you?"

"Yes, I can do that. I've considerable spare time." It was a gift from the gods, his offer, from Jenny's own special little god of luck. She had indeed been invited to cross this threshold as evil spirits, they say, must be invited before they can enter any Christian place.

"Beginning now?"

"Why, yes ... if you like."

"I like. Here," he went to the big central desk that faced the pilot-windows, "here's your notebook and pencil; here's mine. There's your starting point. Here's mine. We begin each at one side of the windows and work around the walls till we meet. There's a ladder for the top shelves. The books under the windows are my own ... when I was a kid. My father had me put them there as a reward. If I remember rightly, I was about five years old."

Jenny began at once and so did he, backs to each other, the width of the tower room apart.

"By the way," he murmured in an absent-minded, casual voice, "shake out any loose papers in those volumes. My father was writing a book. There might be notes. I want them."

In a tone as nearly casual as his own, she assented but how her heart was jerking! The note secreted by her mother in one of Philip's books—the note that was never found. That did not appear in the evidence that "would have meant so much," that might "if Philip did not destroy it, be still somewhere in that room!"

Enid had said, "I am glad it was destroyed or lost. I hope now it will never be found. If it were, Felicia's peace would be destroyed forever."

The young man, working quickly, impatiently shook out each volume with violent thoroughness, ruffling the leaves and, Jenny thought, with an increase of strong emotion, "If he should be looking for that note ... if he should find it ... first?" It was terrifying to have an antagonist, a fellow investigator, whose purpose was so different from her own. Nevertheless she thought, "God must have sent me to protect poor mother from this young devil's smouldering life-long vengeance."

Why do you want to hurt her now, she longed to cry out to Adam. "Why, in this horrible red world of pain, do you want to resurrect any old still agony? What good will it do anyone ... now?"

Her sense of justice immediately replied, "That's what your mother told you. That's what you are trying to do yourself, Sheila Ambrose."

Then, why not welcome Adam's co-operation even if the motive should be at brutal odds ... the more so, perhaps, for that very difference? An innocent person does not run away. An innocent person has never anything to fear. Love casteth out fear ...

A mad impulse rose almost to the brink of speech, shaking her lips and, in sympathy, her hands. She could take Adam into her confidence, she could join his search, share his discoveries, annex his intimate knowledge. She could ... she could win him to her side, against the black influence of old Mrs. Grise.

"Go slow. Go slow, you little fool," she told her madness. "You may pull down the house of Castania about your ears. You may ruin everyone: Enid and Adam, Felicia, the old woman and yourself. The chance for your own happiness is very slight indeed. Tread softly. Take care," and, closing her eyes so that the brilliance of the room was misted, she prayed, "God help me to take care" and heard again the clear voice saying, "It will be the death of Felicia Grise."

There was no reason why Jenny should have been startled, that evening, to find Roger Dean a dinner guest at Castania. Nothing could have been more natural. He was, as she had foreseen and hoped, an old family friend. But from the threshold of the living room at half-past seven she was so astonished to see him that she stopped short and gave a little cry.

He laughed.

"Is that dismay at having a doctor to dinner, Miss Thorne?"

Jenny went up to him then and held out her hand. He took it and smiled down into her eyes.

"It's a welcome, Dr. Dean. I don't know when I've been so glad to see anyone."

He looked distinguished in his evening clothes—even in wartime Castania was ceremonious. Everyone "changed" to some extent for dinner and this was an especial occasion. Fortunately, Jenny was wearing her new "mail-order" dress for the first time. She saw the doctor running his eye over it.

"Mrs. Grise ordered this dress for me," she said defensively, "and ordered me to wear it. She doesn't like uniforms after work hours. I must say, though, that I don't feel ethical."

"You don't look ethical. You look beautiful. Well, it makes it possible for us to forget our professional etiquette; which is all to the good, isn't it? Red is my favorite color, the color of courage. *Your* color, Miss Thorne."

He released Jenny's hand and turned from her at the entrance of the others. Adam was in his ugliest mood which meant Felicia at her gayest for she spread her animation like a rainbow wing for his protection. Adam and Roger Dean were obviously foes of long standing. It was a tempestuous dinner, fierce arguments, checked on the brink of a quarrel, in which old Mrs. Grise sided with Adam and Jenny unfalteringly with Dr. Dean. The doctor's eyes were bright and dangerous, softening sometimes to amusement as they met Jenny's but, for the most part, he was tense and keen. It wasn't exactly a happy meal but, for the stranger, it was exciting, a relief after the monotony of the clouded family reunions. And Felicia kept herself serene and beautiful. A tender admiration from all these people haloed her. She kept throwing anxious and eager looks at Roger Dean pleading for peace, for sympathy.

After small coffee, Jenny found it tactful to absent herself and when the others went out onto the verandah for coolness, she stayed indoors with a paper under the lamp. She was interrupted only once, by John bringing in ice water and bidding her good night. "I'm leaving in a few minutes," he said—he lodged with the gardener's family—"so, if there's anything . . ." There was nothing. Almost immediately Jenny heard his departing step stablewards along a gravel walk.

The war news quickly deafened her to the talk she should have tried to overhear and she did not really come to full awareness again until Adam said his surly "good night" to the others outside, came in and went quickly up the stairs. A car engine started presently and drew away. Very soon afterwards old Mrs. Grise asked Jenny to come and help her with a zipper which always gave her trouble in "this stupid old dress."

Jenny had not been in the old woman's rooms before and she was as startled by their ugliness as she had been by the beauty of Felicia's. Here all the big dark Victorian furniture in the world was huddled together. There was hardly space in the high large rooms to move; and amongst all the wardrobes and mirrors and tables and consoles and the big, marble-topped bureaus, this little old hooked woman scuttered like a mouse.

She stood before one of the immense mirrors when Jenny bent to examine her underarm seam difficulty and could hardly help laughing at the absurd contrast in those reflections, a scarlet mermaid trying to unzip a black deep-sea snail.

"The doctor," said Mrs. Grise, "is getting very political, isn't he? How do you reconcile that?" It was a question she asked meaninglessly so often that it had become an irritation to Jenny's nerves. She said, with as little show of crossness as possible, " 'Reconcile?' I don't know what you mean."

"Why, to his professional detachment. He doesn't really give a hoot for public matters; or private ones either except for the symptoms of his patients. That's where he fools so many silly females. He's so handsome and romantic looking with those bright eyes and all the while he's thinking about the functions of their wretched bodies. Of course, sometimes, when something new and beautiful appears like Miss Jenny Thorne, eh?"

Jenny made a sound of protest. "Oh," said Mrs. Grise, "it was sufficiently obvious. He hardly took his eyes off you. Look out for Felicia!"

Jenny refused to ask her what she meant so she was forced to go on without encouragement. "Mrs. Philip, you know, is quite the Saint of Castania ... the saint in the stained glass window or the cathedral niche. Well," her chuckle was as glabrous as that of an enchanted snail, "what else but a saint can she be? A wheel chair isn't exactly a siren's couch, is it, Miss Jenny? But, like every saint, she has to have her worshippers. There were plenty of them in the old days before Adam grew up and mounted guard. A good thing too. There might have been gossip. Even an invalid isn't sacred from town tongues."

"Very dirty and malicious ones," said Jenny, "if they attack Mrs. Philip Grise."

"Dirty and malicious they were and are," the old woman surprisingly agreed, getting out of her dress and into a purple robe. "And it would have been fine medicine for them if she had held her own tongue at the time of our disaster."

"Why, Mrs. Grise?" Jenny wished that she did not so loathe her role of detective, of spy.

"Then they'd have known, all of them, once and forever, that that Ambrose woman was a professional blackmailer, a desperate little ..."

The words struck and coiled about Jenny's heart. She forced herself to stand still. At last, slowly, she spoke. "How you must have hated her!" Then as her hostess fairly spat out her indignation, she added, against her own saner will, "And why?"

Amazement changed the old woman's rage. "Why *not*, Miss Thorne? What a question! Really!"

Jenny stammered, "It's only ... I mean ... all of you here

seem to me to have been so much stronger and . . . and safer than she was. I don't know anything about it of course . . ."

The little hooked mind was now at work and Jenny was thoroughly alarmed.

"No, of course you don't. But I wonder if you wouldn't like to know more. Sit down and I'll tell you the story. It will fascinate you really. Young people are always inquisitive. I think I know why you are inclined to take *her* part. She was a girl of your own age then and beautiful, too, though so different from you. And she had the same sense of inferiority. She, too, was employed by Mrs. Philip Grise. Why, you are living in her room, sleeping in her bed! You may well be haunted by her. Sit down. Sit down." She got herself into a corner of the black old lounge and patted Jenny to a seat there.

The daughter of Enid Ambrose forced herself to yield, turning her panic face from the light, putting her hands down close at her sides where the skirt of her dress could hide them. Like Enid's, those hands betrayed emotion. And the old harsh voice went on and on.

Strange it would be, thought Jenny, strange and terrible to hear her mother's story in this hideous version . . . the reflection of her loveliness distorted in the mirror of this crippled mind.

"You see, it had to be Enid Ambrose or Felicia Grise. Those two were the only people with a shred of motive. As a matter of fact, Mrs. Philip Grise had the most obvious one . . . jealousy. But she came out clean as a picked bone. It wasn't only because of her invalidism either, though of course that was guaranteed by Dr. Elliot's certificate." She stopped and seemed to go off into a brooding world of her own, coming out of it to mutter, "Oh, the difficulty of unearthing fresh evidence now . . . it's simply fantastic!"

"Who," asked Jenny and her voice sounded tired and dry, "who would be wicked enough or . . . or mad enough to try to open the case after twenty years?"

Actually she laughed, the queer bent creature wrapped in her dark robe and hooked there in the couch corner. "I suppose *I'm* wicked enough. And Adam's certainly mad enough."

"Why, why . . . why does he want to do this, Mrs. Grise? I can understand your reason. Philip Grise was your son. But this boy . . . if he loves his mother . . ."

"Oh, he loves her. He loves her. It's just that . . ." She was not laughing now. She was so bent that her head all but touched the dark splotched hands knotted on her knee. "In the eyes of the world, no one, not even Felicia, was proven innocent."

Jenny rose. "You mean that he has a suspicion of ... her?"

"No. No. But someone said something in his hearing and he can't bear it. There's a poem of Browning's—nobody reads him these days, I guess, but he's a great favorite of mine and—wait! I have it here. I'll read you something. It says it better than I can."

She found the book, came back to her place and read to Jenny. In the silent house her harsh voice hacked out the rhythms.

> "Would it were I had been false . . . not you.
> I that am nothing, not you that are all!
> I never the worse for a touch or two
> On my speckled hide, not you, the pride
> Of the day, my swan, that a first fleck's fall
> On her wonder of white, must un-swan, un-do.

"There's Felicia, as Adam sees her. And here ... here ...

> "She ruined? How? No Heaven for her?
> Crowns to give, and none for the brow
> That looked like marble and smelt like myrrh?
> Shall the robe be worn and the palm branch borne
> And she go graceless, she graced now
> Beyond all saints . . . ?

"You see, don't you? You see!"

Jenny got to her feet.

"Wait, wait, Miss Thorne. You haven't heard the story . . ."

"I'm afraid I'm too tired tonight."

She mocked, "Your work is terribly hard, isn't it? A war job. Serving your country. And now you have the cataloguing too!"

"I'm sorry. Some other time. Thank you. Good night."

Jenny was shaking. The sound of that harsh laughter clung to her ears.

From the upper hall, when she had come out thankfully from those hideous rooms, she saw Lizzie below about to turn out the lights. The cook heard her, came to the foot of the stairs and, seeing Jenny at the railing, softly spoke.

"Everyone's gone up, Miss Thorne?"

"Yes, Lizzie."

"And the doctor's left?"

"Oh, long ago."

"Good! Then I'll lock up. Good night, Miss Thorne."

Lizzie locked the doors. Out went the lights. Moon whiteness dropped like linen on the floor.

There was nothing for Jenny to do but to climb up alone to her tower room. It, too, was streaked by moonlight and she went to the window. It was warm until she pulled wide the curtains when a delicious wind lifted her hair. Whiteness bathed her. The river voice began to sing.

But she heard a sound, too, of human voices from a shuttered room below her to the right. Lizzie had reached her quarters and was visited by Anna, whose deafness made the conversation audible. Jenny caught the doctor's name and a phrase that brought a flush to her face. "Well, say what you please, he couldn't take his eyes off her in her red dress!"

All at once, immediately beneath, a light streamed. Adam had come into his study. He leaned from the central window. She could see his dark head and his broad thin shoulders, his hands pressed down hard against the sill on either side. "Shut up, you two!" he called out roughly and the clacking servants' tongues fell to a strained difficult muttering.

Jenny drew in, curtained her window and turned on a single light. Then she discovered that she had left her chiffon evening handkerchief downstairs. Remembering where it was, she went down at once to get it. She had not many such accessories and didn't want a reputation for neglect or carelessness. As soon as she came down from the tower into the upper hall, carrying a small nurse's torch, she could hear the deep-sea snoring of old Mrs. Grise; such a noise as couldn't be imagined!

There was no light anywhere but the small one in her own hand and she went on felt soles towards the main stairs.

Just as she reached the landing, something down below in the darkness, where the moon square had been stretched to oblong, swiftly moved. It was a soft step and upon it came the soft, soft sound of a closing door.

Fear is the most physical of all sensations. It is a taste in the mouth and a clogging of the blood. Jenny went back, step by cautious step. For there was no possible explanation for that step or for that closing door. And sounds without reason are terror made into flesh.

Above, Adam still leaned from out of his window, craning farther towards the river. Anna and Lizzie were very audibly bidding each other good night. Jenny wrapped herself in a coat and retraced her steps as far as the study door. It was ajar. She pushed it wide and called out Adam's name.

He turned with a curse, charged forward, stopped; black brows one line above the white face.

"You! What's wrong? What do you want here?"

She told him. "There's someone moving about downstairs. John left hours ago. I heard him myself. Anna and Lizzie are together in Lizzie's room. You know that. You must have heard them. Mrs. Ferguson Grise is in her own bedroom. I heard her snoring loudly as I went past. I'd left a handkerchief downstairs and went down for it. Your mother is quite alone. Everyone is far out of call . . ."

"There's a bell to Lizzie's room and mine and Grandmother's."

"But Lizzie was yelling to Anna. Mrs. Grise is very sound asleep. You are up here. If someone has got in . . ."

"Give me that flash. I'll go down." He stopped a few steps below her on the winding stairs, put a hand against the wall, turned and looked up. "You go to your room, will you? And stay there. Better give up prowling the house like this. It's not part of what you're paid to do. Get me?"

He ran down. The picture of him, turned about, looking up, a dark hand pressed against the plaster wall, stayed with her. The sharpness of his speech, its insolence, did not this time deceive her. For she had seen that face before . . . it had looked down from the side of the river cliff. It was a face wet and half-dead with . . . fear.

Chapter Seven

Though she sat up until early morning, Adam brought her no report of the fruit of his search and she heard nothing more of it until she met him in the study at noon. There and then he gave her a sardonic look.

"Well, sleepwalker! Your ghost was Beauty, Mother's tomcat. Anna didn't quite latch Mother's door. Beauty pushed out into the hall, jumped down from something probably when he heard you. Mother had been calling him and he went back. She was about to ring for Anna when the draught obligingly closed the door for her. She had all her windows open of course. So, there you are. And may it be a lesson to you."

Jenny looked him straight and hard in those strange narrow grey eyes but said nothing. That sound of a step could not have been the padded leap of a cat; no breeze, strong enough to close a door at all, could latch one with such quiet and controlled precision. "No, Adam," she told herself, "either you have been deceived or you know something you won't tell." But she asked no further question, merely noted down a resolution for further investigation of such midnight prowlings.

Beauty really made a get-away that noon. And Felicia was wild. That day she seemed for the first time an invalid, pale, lined, and irritable. She charged about in her wheeled chair calling for her pet and all the rest of the household, outdoors and in, were driven to search. Soon after lunch came Adam striding grimly into her lovely room and dropping upon her lap the errant drift of snow.

Down clapped Felicia's hands upon him; slim and strong, pressing him hard.

"You bad Beauty!" Her musical voice lifted an octave. "No, here you stay while I tell you what I think of you." The cat made no slightest effort to escape but lay, every nerve and muscle tense for a leap, tail lashing and eyes large.

"You're like all of them, ungrateful, treacherous. I've done everything for you, haven't I? Fed you and washed you and brushed you and petted you, kept you warm and well and cool and safe. And I love you ... do you hear? I love you! Yet you'd run away and frighten me half out of my wits. Well, I'm through with you now. You may, for all I care," and she laughed icily, "go to the dogs!" She swept him from her knees.

He landed lightly, shook himself, bounded to his favorite cushion in the window seat and fell to grooming. Jenny glanced at Felicia to share amusement but found the fair grizzled head bent to her hands, tears bursting through her fingers.

Jenny was deeply distressed, knelt by the wheeled chair, put her arm around its occupant. "Mrs. Grise! I'm so sorry. No cat is worth crying for. Please! Please!"

Felicia let her wet hands fall and Jenny put one of her own over them. It was the comfort she had so often given to her mother but now the effect was very different. A shiver went all over Mrs. Grise's body. She flung away the hand, as she had flung away the cat. She reared back and up as though to force movement into her helpless legs and said in a voice entirely different from her usual speech, "Don't touch me please. Your hand ... your hand is ... like somebody's ... it's so like ... *hers*," and with that went into hysterics.

Jenny got Anna to telephone for Dr. Dean while she applied what remedies she could with no success. Felicia was beyond all ordinary control. At first, the half-crazy creature refused to admit Dr. Dean but at last he reached her and Jenny left them. For a long while Jenny heard his sternly soothing voice, her diminishing cries, her quieter weeping and, at last, silence. He had used, she supposed, a hypodermic. He came softly out into the hall.

Before the attack, Adam fortunately had gone out for his ride. Jenny was alone.

"Phew!" said Dr. Dean. "That was a bad one. What set her off?"

Jenny told him. "She imagined that my hands ... my hands ... were like somebody's."

"Let's see them. Humph! They look like any girl's young hands, prettier than most. You're all in, aren't you? Tell you what, Miss Thorne, run up and get into your coolest frock. It's ten degrees hotter outside than it is in this old cave of a house but I'll bet you're sick of starch and white cotton stockings. I've got to take a longish trip to some outlying patients. Nobody needs you here now. The air will do you good. Make it snappy."

She was up like a flash and down again, slipping in beside him as he started his car. Since that night at dinner when she wore her red evening dress, he had ceased to use the nurse-doctor manner when they were alone. It was, for Jenny, a great comfort and relief.

He said, turning a little to look at her, "I thought last night that red was your color. But now I know better ... it's dryad green." A few minutes later he added, as the strong wind of highway speed smote back her hair and bathed her body and she threw back her head to breathe deeply, "What is it you are like anyway? I keep wondering. It's something familiar but odd. Something we've all seen somewhere and yet something charmingly exotic. A beautiful little gargoyle maybe."

Jenny's expression made him laugh.

"Oh, Dr. Dean!"

"No ... no. More archaic. Some sort of a pagan sylvan deity. I have it! A female faun, wild and scared and naughty. Peering and bold ..."

"I don't *like* it!"

"You can't help it, my child. And don't tell me you object to me being personal!"

"No. That's always fun."

"Good. Now it's my turn."

He was so obviously trying to divert and to distract her that she gratefully acquiesced. "It's hard to know what you're like, Dr. Dean. You're so," she groped, "so . . . sort of *bright*."

"Bright! For the luva Mike! What does that mean?"

"I can't describe it. There's a ... veil of ... brilliance ... like someone hiding behind a flame."

"Flame? You make me sound dangerous."

"Fire can be turned to good, to noble uses." Her voice shook.

After a pause, "Thanks, Jenny. I like that," he said. "A successful sublimation. You're quite a psycho-analyst, aren't you?"

She found herself irrelevantly demanding in a strained, low voice, "What did she mean about my hands?"

As always when he spoke about the Castania tragedy, he was dry and practical.

"They probably reminded her of Enid's; the girl had a way of putting her hand over yours. Rather appealing. Felicia doesn't see many girls' hands these days and yours may have that much resemblance. Youth. Combined with the accident of a similar gesture, it overwhelmed her. On top of her fright about the cat ... Here's my first call. You can stay out here in the car under this elm and keep cool. I shan't be long."

Jenny had only one thought while Roger Dean was in that house. *"I must be careful about my hands."*

His second visit was at a large town house and Jenny's waiting was long and hot. Then they turned south again and, after a mile or so, when he said nothing personal, he turned into a lane and pulled up before a farm gate. It helped to fence the top of a steep small hill below which Jenny could see neatly tilled fields and tidy gardens, a little group of buildings by a stream.

"This time I surely won't be long," he promised, "and you've a nice view to look at."

He opened and closed the gate, went out of her sight down the abrupt hill.

Quite as though a name had been shouted into her ear, Jenny heard it, "Josh Hogan." Garvey had said, "He has a farm up the river. Doc visits him. Doc's loyal to his old friends."

Without an instant's hesitation, Jenny was through the gate. She saw a possible screen and an excuse: a six-foot-high bristling hedge of brush overgrown with sweet peas. It stood between her and the house near which she thought Dr. Dean was talking to his host.

She could get down unseen and, if discovered, what more natural than to want some of those sweet, butterfly flowers? She got there and she heard the old man ... from what was visible through the flower tendrils, he was small and piped up to the tall doctor ... "getting along just fine, doc. That physic about fixed me. Say, if it's as good for me as it was for the old woman, I'll not give you no complaints." "That's the stuff, Josh. Don't hesitate to call me, though." That might be the preface for departure, she thought, and poised for flight. Then Josh Hogan added something in a lower key. "Say, doc, there's something I reckon you had ought to know. Captain Grise, he's been here a coupla times lately, askin' questions."

"Grise? Adam Grise? Questions? About what?" Dean's voice was startled enough to startle Jenny.

"About the old story. Yes, doc, he come a horseback cross

country. He was hashin' over the evidence about tools and diggin's above the beach. God knows what-all."

Here the doctor must have put a hand on the speaker and turned him towards the house for the speech stopped and Jenny heard their feet cross a porch and a door closing.

It was a good chance for escape and she took it, was settled in the car and her breath under control, when Dr. Dean returned.

He showed no perturbation but he seemed thoughtful and whistled softly through his teeth. A few miles nearer Castania, Jenny asked in her most casual voice, "Who owns the pretty little farm where you stopped last?"

"An old fellow whose wife I treated in her last illness years ago, when I first came to Barent. He's persistently grateful, darn him! persistently dependent."

Jenny took a risk. The progress of her search was necessarily slow but sometimes she felt she could not bear this slowness. "His name isn't, by any chance, Josh Hogan, is it?"

The doctor's brightness flashed upon her. "Now where did you pick up that name?"

She felt her own flush but told him the truth. "Garvey gave me the name. He said that Hogan had been gardener at Castania when Philip Grise was killed. He said Josh Hogan had a farm up this way and that you still visited him. He said you were loyal to your old patients."

"Very nice of Garvey. How did he happen to loosen up on the subject?"

"I was sitting on the top of the cliff and he told me it was the spot of ... of the tragedy. And I asked him if he'd been the gardener at Castania at that time."

"I see," Dr. Dean sighed. "It hasn't been easy for Hogan, or for any of the others. Being on the scene of such an event isn't so good for anyone's prospects. And Mrs. Grise has felt a certain responsibility towards this man. She rather makes a point of my taking care of him."

"Dr. Dean, how did it affect you? I mean, being on the scene ... and ... everything?"

He looked amused. "In other words, was I under suspicion? No. Luckily for me, I wasn't the family physician in those days. I was very rarely at Castania, except socially now and again when they needed an extra man for dinner. You see, I hadn't been in Barent more than a few months. Old Dr. Elliot, since dead, was Felicia's doctor. So, though they gave me a going over, I came out quick and clean. I'd been called in for Anna a couple of times. You see how humble was my role at The Mansion."

Jenny braced herself for further venturing. This time her breath itself had to be disciplined. "Dr. Dean, tell me, won't you? I can't help being interested. What's your opinion? Whom do you suspect?"

His answer came at once, quite dry and clear. "There was no possible doubt about it. The girl did it."

The girl's daughter managed to force a "Why?" past her closing throat.

"Well, if you want a re-hash: Philip had put them both—himself and the girl—in a tight spot. A very tight spot. He'd been making love to her in his very insouciant fashion for some time. Felicia quite unsuspecting. And he found himself with a tiger cat on his hands. Served him right!" Roger Dean here passed a truck carefully. "But there were other things involved. Felicia, poor little saint, had promised to lend the girl capital, a sizeable sum to start a little business somewhere. Philip got scared by the fervor of Enid's passion and by her demands. She wanted him, it appeared from conversations that were overheard and from notes produced in court, to divorce Felicia and make an honest woman of Enid Ambrose. He threatened her with confessing his folly to his wife and having her thrown out. Enid had a child somewhere, hers by a husband deceased, and Enid's intentions were certainly honorable domesticity. Not so Philip's. He cared for his wife—'in his fashion'—and he also knew quite well where and how his bread was buttered *and* sugared. He was sick to death of this clinging, weeping, lovesick girl. So they had more quarrels than one; overheard as such quarrels usually are . . . and the crazy thing wrote notes threatening him. She even wrote, 'I'd rather kill you than have you hurt Felicia.' You see, she stood to lose quite a lot: her prospects for a fine business and for a fine husband. Her plan evidently was to get the money from Felicia, leave the house and let Philip do the rest . . . force Felicia to start divorce proceedings . . . Enid knew what a proud woman Felicia is. On what grounds I wouldn't know. Nothing worked according to plan. Philip was obstinate, wanting like most males I suppose to have his cake and eat it. In any case, the hysterical, desperate little fool, thinking I imagine that her financial future was more important than the lover whom she began to hate—and one could hate Philip!—made her plans. They were clever too. She got the poison somewhere, by mail perhaps, or she may have

had it in her possession. She was distinctly the suicidal type."
(Jenny thought, "My darling mother! Who has taken her bitter life with a silent courage I am only just beginning to understand!") "Anyway, she always prepared tea and took it
out to that garden house in the afternoons and Philip was in
the habit of visiting her. She invited him 'for the last time'—
that was another note!—and he accepted. She had sawed almost through the rail back of his seat and dug away the
earth under the rock that supported that corner of the silly
structure. You see how it would be? Philip would drink the
poison. It works fast. He would fall and, with or without
some aid from her, he'd crash through the railing and down
upon the stony beach. If he didn't smash his head, she could
run down and smash it for him ... What's wrong? Feel
faint?"

"No ... No. It's just the heat."

"And an ugly story. Put your head down. Better?"

"I'm all right. Really. Go on. It's ... quite a story."

"Quite a story! The teacup would be lost and broken in the
general crash. Who would find the sawed rail or the excava-
tion? No fear of detection. It worked all right. I was with
Mrs. Philip Grise discussing Anna's tonsils, I remember, when
the poor crazy thing came screaming and crying, 'Oh, Felicia!
I think he's ... dead!' And then of course we were all out
there above and below the cliff at once. I discovered that he
was indeed dead. He'd smashed his head all right, and most
convincingly. And all would have gone according to plan if
old Mrs. Grise—not so old then as she is now of course—
hadn't found a piece of the teacup holding a queer white powder that had never been sugar. She'd always hated Enid. Trust
her to know about the tower romance! So she put the china
very carefully in her handkerchief and went to the police.
Analysis showed the powder to be cyanide, a lethal dose—
strong enough to kill a dozen Philips. The little fact of the
sawed rail and the dug away earth then came to light and
Enid was arrested. I suppose you know the rest."

"I should think," Jenny said after a while, speaking as
though her lips were a mechanism she worked carefully on
wires, "I should think she would certainly have been convicted."

"She would have been but for these things: she was very
beautiful, gentle and appealing. They couldn't find a scrap of
evidence as to her having or using the necessary tools or hav-

ing or buying the necessary drug. Motives seemed insufficient.
And then . . . Felicia."

"You mean that Felicia . . . ?"

"Went all out to save the girl. She didn't believe 'dear little
Enid' was guilty. She wouldn't have 'dear little Enid' sent to
prison. She worked and talked and pleaded and guaranteed.
Well, Felicia herself is something to look at and twenty years
ago she was a blond angel to set against Enid's dark loneliness. It was a drama . . . those two in court, the one pleading for the life of the other. Oh, Felicia got her off at the last
by a very skillful bit of evidence, refuting one of the wit-
nesses. And I honestly believe, Jenny Thorne—though I can't
expect you to take my word for anything so preposterous—
that she gave the woman that cash she had promised her . . .
almost as a bonus for Philip's murder! And all the while the
poor child was broken-hearted over her husband's death.
That's how queer a saint Felicia was . . . and is. The money
was enough to keep the wretched Ambrose woman going for
the rest of her worthless life."

"Why do you hate her? I mean, you sound as if you did
. . . personally, even more than seems natural under the awful
circumstances?"

"Do I? Well, it's because of Felicia. You can't see a
woman like Felicia so outwitted and wronged and not feel
some degree of indignation, can you?"

"No, of course you can't."

"So now you have the story and, I hope, for you, the ghost
of Castania is laid."

He looked at the pale straight girl tense beside him. "Poor
little Jenny!" Eyes and voice were tender. She felt weak and
horribly alone. She put out her hand gropingly, not to him
but to some invisible Helper. He took it, lifted it quickly to
his heart, his cheek, his lips, then let it go. And from the gesture she received a strong impression of helpless pain, frus-
tration and defeat.

A few minutes later they were at the house.

She was able to thank him. She was able to get up the in-
numerable steps. A few hours later she was able to write
down the record of the awful day.

"Oh, my poor darling mother. And, oh, Nick, Nick, Nick!"

Chapter Eight

PAGES FROM JENNY'S DIARY

For three days I have set down nothing in my diary and yet I have so very much to write. It is difficult reporting ... and for more reasons than one.

After my surprising trip with Dr. Dean I was unable to sleep. His story shrieked itself in my head. I tried to master my nerves, to analyze his account impersonally. I got out my mother's confession and contrasted it.

My mother, standing before Mrs. Clarke's bureau, leaning on her hands, had said:

"I meant to be loyal to Felicia. I'd have cut out my heart. Oh, Jenny, I did cut out my heart, rather than hurt Felicia. But Philip's feeling became unmanageable and, though I tried first to laugh it off, then to show anger and at last my misery, nothing would stop him. In spite of all I did and said, or even perhaps because of it, he felt that I cared. There was an arbor, Jenny, above the river bank. I often carried out my tea. Philip discovered this; he'd join me. It was the time when he'd be walking or riding and that was a pleasure his poor wife could never share. It was easy for him to stop in at the arbor on his way to or from the house. And, Jenny, I did love having him; my life was lonely and dull as the life of a governess must be. And Philip was the gayest, the funniest, the most charming boy!

"After I knew how much he cared, I tried to stop him from coming to the arbor. I didn't go to his study ... truly I was good. But all the time ... oh yes ... I knew that the only really honorable thing for me to do was to give up my job and go away.

"I kept from the arbor but, one day, Philip sent me a note—you see I was refusing to talk to him. He didn't send it, really, he climbed up on the sill of his study window and somehow managed to throw it into my bedroom window. It was the strangest note. A threat! The last sort of message you'd expect from Philip. It said ... and I remember every word although I tore it up at once. I wish he had been as careful with mine! . . . 'You're playing fast and loose with me, Enid, and I won't stand for that. You'll be sorry if you take this line. If I should go to Felicia you'd have quite a lot to lose, more than you imagine.' The letter went through me like a sword. And I was furious. In my first fury I wrote to him and put the note in a book we used for our silly correspondence—for I went on with our romantic correspondence in spite of all my good resolutions. Indeed I know that note word for word. It was read out at the trial. It was in the newspapers. 'How dare you threaten me, insult me, Philip. After all we've meant to each other . . .' (And he had meant so very much, Jenny!) . . . 'As though you hadn't a hundred times more to fear from Felicia's knowledge than I have. You should even be afraid of me.' (Yes, Jenny, I wrote this as so many people have spoken and written such rash words!) '. . . Rather than have you go to Felicia now, I think I'd kill you with my own hands.' This served to prove it was my wish to force him to divorce Felicia and marry me. They made it appear that, because of some money Felicia was supposed to have promised me, I wanted first to leave carrying the cash and then to have Philip start divorce proceedings or get Felicia to start them. And, believe me, Jenny, though it seems that Felicia did speak to other people about the money she was going to lend me to start a little school, she never once mentioned it to me. Nevertheless that note of mine was shameful and frantic.

"So Philip and I quarreled wildly, loudly, recklessly. At last, when he melted into tenderness—yes to tears! because I'd 'hurt him so'—I let him come to the arbor once again. I wrote a note inviting him 'for the last time.' O, what a fool I was. And on that day and at that hour . . . it happened. He'd gone to the city a few days before; he was not expected back by anyone but me.

"It was a beautiful bright day—he sat in his usual place leaning forward, holding his teacup, looking up—he had a favorite cup with a medallion at the bottom of the bowl of a little grinning clown. He refused to drink from any other cup—that's what a child he was! I'd found only a little sugar in my tea-bowl so I gave it all to him—he had a way of gulping half the tea down, then throwing himself back in his chair with a breath of satisfaction. He sat there, sulky and sweet and beautiful, and I talked to him, angrily and sadly because of something I had discovered in the last few days.

He took the big drink as usual and set down his cup. A train rushed by, drowning out everything. I saw a dreadful change in his face. He flung himself out of his chair, pushing it back—it was one of those heavy rustic ones—and he cried out something; with that the whole side of the place gave way. It was on the edge of the cliff above a stony beach. He fell. There was a rock. When I could get down to him—I went by a dreadful dangerous little path ... he was ... quite dead.

"I ran screaming to the house.

"I hope you will never be able to imagine how I felt. Two terrible days later I was taken into custody, charged with the murder of Philip Grise. They had found poison in the broken teacup. The handle and one big piece were intact. They had found that the arbor rail had been all but sawed through and that earth had been dug away from the corner of the arbor.

In a voice broken with exhaustion my mother said, "If it hadn't been for Felicia, I would have gone out of my mind. If it hadn't been for Felicia, I'd be in prison now ... or dead. Felicia saved me. All through the trial she fought for me. If I could only go to her now, thank her, bless her. But I am an exile from Felicia. That was my real sentence, imposed upon me by her."

Beside this story I set Roger Dean's. There are many discrepancies, not so much in fact as interpretation. I can see how the evidence might bring him to an honest conviction of her guilt. But there were several questions I simply dared not put to him. I had already showed too much curiosity in the matter of Josh Hogan. So I made an engagement with old Mrs. Grise. I said to her at lunch, "If you really care to tell me the rest of that story—I mean, if it's not too painful for you—I'd of course be terribly interested to hear it."

Hear it I did, up in the hideous crowded sitting room in the harsh voice at gloating length. It was much the same version as Roger Dean's, only more venomous towards Enid, less censorious towards Philip. But since it was my second experience, I bore it better. "Tell me please," I cried at the end, as though impulsively, "where was little Adam that afternoon? And what about his nurse?"

Her receding, half-toothless jaw dropped. It was so long since anyone had questioned her that, for an instant, she was angry, about to refuse an answer. But she did speak after a moment in a scowling and reluctant fashion. "The nurse? Mary Ryan? Oh, she was out. It was her day off. But as for Adam ... we never knew. We found him in the midst of us there on the beach, crying and shaking. Dean carried him in. He had seen something ... perhaps he had seen his father fall; though how he had got down except by a crazy danger-ous path about the width of a string, I can't imagine. But he was entirely incoherent and, after he came to from the hypo-dermic Dean gave him, he seemed to have forgotten the whole thing. Never since that day has he been able to remember anything at all about the events of that afternoon ... either before or after Philip's death. Though, God knows, we worked over him and he, himself, has tried."

I have my answers. The nurse was called Mary Ryan. She was out on the afternoon of the crime and seems to have es-tablished her alibi. Her evidence in the newspaper report of the trial seems almost too completely negative. She was ei-ther stupid or primed. Where is she now? Does anybody know? Whom shall I ask and on what pretext? I must be very careful.

And Adam has a secret, buried even from himself.

Here are a few other observations that have come into mind:

Felicia loves the power of her love ... and the worship of her lovers. Of Philip, Enid, Adam, Dean, Lizzie, and Anna. I saw this in her treatment of Beauty. When she is hurt she is capable of flinging someone away—"to the dogs." There is also a secret visitor of some sort. Perhaps Roger Dean re-maining or returning late to her rooms after his apparent de-partures ... though why, as her physician, he should make a mystery of any of his visits, I wouldn't know.

Adam is afraid ... of I don't know what.

As for old Mrs. Grise, I see that there is more to her wish to fasten guilt on someone than the mere vengeance-motive for Philip's death. She hated Enid, yes, but I believe she hates Felicia. Why?

The two old women servants are completely sealed. What-ever they may know or feel is not to be evoked. Have they been bribed? Or scared? Or have they merely forgotten? My efforts to draw them out have fallen completely flat.

Josh Hogan's report of Philip's last speech was discredited in court by Felicia's clever evidence. He is in Felicia's ... and in Dean's confidence. He knows something about tools. Adam is questioning him and that is certainly a matter of concern to Dean ... probably on Felicia's account. Her great dread is that the trial should be opened to further evidence. I remember her saying, "It would be the death of Felicia

Grise!" These things point to her guilt but that would seem to be impossible. She saved Enid, at the risk of being herself accused. Besides ... Felicia? A loving invalid. A saint in a wheeled chair. Gay in her own fashion ... gay and beautiful.

Chapter Nine

Adam and Jenny had been working steadily, hour by bright hour, day by warm day, in that shining library, rarely speaking. Sometimes he was beguiled from duty by a book and leaned back against the case, reading. Jenny could feel, without half looking, his lean big-boned grace and the absent gaze he lifted, sometimes towards the window, sometimes towards herself. It was strange to her to discover how mutual knowledge may progress in a physical nearness without speech. She was beginning to know the queer angry young soldier, this son of Felicia and Philip Grise, better than she could have believed possible. They were left completely undisturbed, no doubt by Felicia's orders. It was what she had wanted, this increase of intimacy, the opportunity for quiet examination. And Jenny had really learned a great deal, some of which she reported to Felicia.

For one thing . . . Adam was afraid of heights. He winced if she went near the window; when she leaned out, he held his breath. She did this sometimes, to look at a bird or to feel the delicious river wind on her hot face. And yet he would go there himself and lean out much farther and look down. It was a steep view, the height of the tower added to the abrupt falling away of the land—just a ribbon of turf to break the descent. But when he did this, Jenny could feel it was by stern constraint. His tenseness was visible and, coming back, he often showed that white and sweated face. He was defying his own phobia, fighting it with a courageous fury she could not but admire though her knowledge told her it was not the wisest course. Poor boy! she found herself thinking, he must have enormous powers of self-control. They could not have guessed when they let him out of hospital how far from normal he still was. That was the reason, she decided, for the face he had presented on the cliff her first afternoon at Barent. He had gone part way down the giddy and perilous cliff trail, as far as the big rock. Jenny had since then looked down it from above and had seen that after it passed the rock it was simply a neck-breaker. But he had forced himself

LADY IN THE TOWER

to that point and was standing there, flogging his fear of the further descent, when he saw Jenny. Her presence on the beach had nothing to do with the look on his face. For some reason this discovery gave her relief.

Once, in the library, a sweet thing happened to her, an indescribably sweet thing. She found it impossible to recapture its sweetness in her report. For she tried to set it down, perishable as the memory was.

He came over to show her something he had come across in one of his books. He stood beside her, placing his big finger on the place. "Look here, Jenny," he said, "don't you like this?" and he read aloud in the warm, natural voice, which was one of his most attractive gifts. His eyes, for once, as clear and happy as a child's, sought for the sympathy of hers. "No," she wrote, "it doesn't sound like anything. It wasn't anything. It was my own imagination that made it sweet, the result of my own loneliness. But to have him near and amused and confiding, like a brother, like a son . . . well, I've had so little of anything as charming and as simple and as . . . masculine as that. It moved me profoundly, touched something in me that nothing ever has before."

He had other ways that stirred her to unexpected sympathy. He would walk up and down, an arm bent across his back, the other hand cuddling his pipe; his step was rhythmic, like a soldier's marching. Sometimes he whistled softly and very beautifully. It sounded so joyous, without care. It made her forget. She thought of the Magic Flute, of the Pied Piper. She felt that she could follow that piping . . . not the piper, never the piper! . . . down into drowning water and not realize her danger or her fate.

He was very skillful with his hands, she noticed, he never stopped or misplaced anything. Perfect coordination, she told herself, in spite of the shock he suffered from. She could see how expert he would be on skis or mountain trails. She remembered Felicia's description which at the time she had thought a mother's wishful phantasy, "He was the sweetest, gayest, lovingest boy . . ." Yes, Adam was like that. He could be . . . he would be if it were not for what her mother and his father had brought about. For she knew now that it was not the war that had wrecked him. The war was just the final agent. It was that past horror, so long buried in his helpless memory.

He startled her. Out of a long, long silence that seemed to

be weaving a tapestry to and fro across the room between their minds, he spoke.

"Are you writing a story about Castania, Jenny? You sit by your window all hours and your silhouette is of a patient and prolific penwoman."

So Adam, she thought, prowls about the tower at night!

She kept her head and answered without too noticeable a delay. "I'm silly enough to keep a diary and . . . and I write long letters, Adam."

"I bet he appreciates them. They mean a lot to the boys, those long letters, almost more than food and ammunition."

She wanted to tell him that she had no soldier or sailor sweetheart but she remembered that the letters to Nick she never sent were really to a soldier sweetheart. By now Nick must be in the army and though she had given him up and he had apparently accepted her decision, he was still the embodiment of her hope for happiness. So Jenny knew that she blushed and she knew that Adam interpreted her blush.

"What do you say about us in your diary, Jenny? 'I don't like Adam Grise.' " For a whirling second she thought he must have read that shorthand record! " 'Mrs. Philip Grise is beautiful and kind. Old Mrs. Grise scares me. And as for Dr. Dean, he is the most adorable, wonderful, handsomest man in the world.' But you keep that out of your letters, don't you?"

"You couldn't be further off, Adam . . . about everything," she said and presently looked at her watch. "I think I'll go out. There's a thunderstorm coming up and I'd like to get my air and exercise before it's on top of us."

"O.K., secretary. You are excused," said he smiling but when she tried to pass him he put out his arm. "Will you swear to me that you are not here to get material for a murder mystery?" Now his face was white and there was no banter in his voice.

"I'm a nurse, not an author," said Jenny, her own face white, "and I *loathe* murder mysteries."

"Pass, friend," said he softly, dropping his arm and she tried to leave without any appearance of flight.

From the garden alley, the storm did not look immediate. Jenny decided to make a long-cherished attempt to go down to the beach by that historic path. She had studied it from the top and, not minding heights and being sure-footed, saw no danger. Down she started, therefore, smoothly, steadily, as far as the big rock. There she could see that the danger for her was not so much from giddiness or scanty foothold as from sliding stones; a sort of rubble which had spilled down at one point across the track.

She set out cautiously, planting one foot on the uncertain ground, brought up the other and, with that, the whole side of the bank gave way below her and, with a loud cry, in a great clatter of little stones, she went plunging to the beach. It was not a bad fall but she was shaken and bruised, dirty and torn. Something had scraped her leg painfully. Before she could so much as sit up and examine this wound, Adam, who must have been at her heels, was beside her. He had come down that path in a few bounds, light and casual as Mercury. His face was white but only with concern. In his fear for Jenny, the boy had forgotten his phobia.

"You're hurt?"

She was wise enough to show no surprise or gratitude.

"My leg . . . not badly. No bones broken. Something scraped off my stocking and my skin here. It doesn't look as if these rounded stones could have done it."

It was a nasty surface wound and it smarted.

"Here's what did it." Adam picked up a bent piece of rusty iron attached to what once had been some sort of wooden shaft. Jenny looked, thinking of iodine. Adam looked with a face of intense, of almost agonized, excitement.

"It's my little old spade. The one that was taken from me . . . by someone. I had garden tools and carpenter's tools. I'd lost my spade and saw. It's what I was looking for that day when I came down the path."

Jenny saw that it was, in fact, the remains of a child's shovel, a sturdy, heavy little tool, buried on this hillside for twenty years!

"Better go on up to the house, as fast as you can," said Adam, "and get that wound of yours clean. I'll get this thing on another trip. It's badly rusted. I wonder," he added, staring at Jenny as though in communion with another self, "I wonder if fingerprints could possibly last . . ."

"Underground for twenty years, Adam? Never."

"I suppose not. But this is the shovel that was used to dig away the ground under the corner of the arbor. There was no trace nor evidence at the trial of any garden tool being taken or used for that purpose. The gardener kept everything locked up."

"Adam," Jenny asked, standing now and in considerable pain but with her dark eyes searching his face, "Adam, tell me if you will . . . do you believe it? Do you believe that . . . it . . . was done by . . . Enid Ambrose?"

He laughed shortly. "Of course not. That girl? Who played games with me as though she'd been another child? And sang songs and told fairy stories? That girl who moaned if you pulled a kitten's whiskers? Who listened to your prayers and tucked you up at night and sang, 'Now the day is over' and 'Softly now the light of day' . . . Here, don't cry, you big baby. Is it as bad as that?"

And he picked her up in his arms and went up that path on a run, the storm suddenly pursuing them, crashing and glittering and streaming so that before they reached the house they were both saturated with rain. And they were both laughing.

Jenny was happy. It was almost frightening to be so glad. Never in the whole dark angry world had there been for her such comfort as in Adam's answer and in the strength of his young arms.

At the worst point in the path, the wind tearing at him, the rain and thunder at his back, he bent his head and kissed her lips. And his mouth felt warm against her heart.

Chapter Ten

Dr. Dean called. It was about four o'clock, the time Felicia and her nurse spent on the verandah, sewing, knitting and reading, in the hope, more and more forlorn, that Adam might be tempted to join them. It was pitiful to watch the dwindling of that hope in his mother's patient face. He would stalk past, sometimes with a short nod and a smile, sometimes as if they had been made of thin air.

Felicia went in with Dr. Dean at once to her sitting room. One of its windows opened on the verandah not far from where Jenny still bent over her handiwork. She could hear their remarks until Dr. Dean abruptly shut down the sash. After that, only the tone of their voices reached her. But the tone was interesting enough. Subtly and gradually it changed, from friendly chit-chat to a low, fast-spoken dialogue in which one interrupted the other constantly until Jenny was amazed to recognize a quarrel.

The doctor's voice lifted to a loud masculine crescendo, broke off. There was silence, then a strange sound. Jenny moved to the far end of the verandah, close to the house corner, beyond which opened Felicia's long French windows. Here the sounds from the room were more distinct. Someone was weeping . . . a series of deep gasps. That was not Felicia. It was the sound of a man's violent and resentful pain, a pain beyond endurance which, after long crushing under, rips through the membrane of pride. Jenny turned away in shame and sympathy and fell to pacing. What was it Felicia had said to her old friend that could so move him? What is the sore spot in his heart? She herself had often felt his pain, it had broken through in his sudden tenderness when she put out her hand for help. This man, she knew, was naturally tender, sensitive, of strong affections.

More and more it seemed to Jenny that the key to her enigma lay in the natures of these people rather than in the small factual clues she might be able to discover: in Adam's fearful investigation, in Felicia's magnanimity, in the malice of old Mrs. Grise, the stolidity of the servants, the complaisance of Josh Hogan, the effacement of Mary Ryan.

Dr. Dean came out.

Jenny was standing then with her back to the door, her hands on the verandah railing, looking towards the river. She did not turn at once because she dreaded to see his face but he came to stand beside her and spoke in the crisp doctor-to-nurse tone he used except when she was out of uniform or off the grounds of Castania.

"Miss Thorne, I want to speak to you privately a moment, if I may."

She led him down the verandah steps along the path John took stableward. There in a circular turfy spot, surrounded by flowering bushes and holding a stone bench and a river view, they stopped. They were well out of hearing from the house.

Jenny dared to look at her companion. He showed no trace of emotion; face clear, eyes and lips steady. But he looked tired.

"It's a personal matter ... personal to you. I always thought your coming to Barent must, in the first place, have had some private motive. Well, a few days ago I had a letter."

She heard herself repeat, "A letter?" and was glad to know that he could not guess how cold she stood there in the hot June sun.

"And I am not going to answer it without advice from you. It is a letter of inquiry from a Lieutenant Nicholas Landis, in the Medical Corps, and now stationed at Camp Benning." He took out the letter. Its writing spoke to Jenny audibly, like a deep, serious voice.

DEAR DR. DEAN:

I am writing to ask you if you have been approached recently by a nurse, graduate of Bonnetsville County Hospital of North Carolina, named Jenny Thorne. I have good reason to believe that she is at Barent, and have a strong personal reason for getting in touch with her ... an urgent reason, urgent for her as well as for myself. She left Bonnetsville in April, went to Savannah, Georgia. From there to New York City. I have been able to trace her to Barent and, as your name was given to her, believe that you must have been in recent touch with her. You have only to look up my credentials to be

assured that my inquiry is based on honorable grounds
and that any information you see fit to let me have will
be used by me for her benefit. She is 22 years old, about
five feet, five inches tall, dark hair with bright, peculiar
lights in it, hazel eyes, that, with the eyebrows, slant up
a trifle towards the temples. It may be that she is using
another name but this description should serve for identification.

Let me assure you again of the importance of my inquiry. I have no wish to do Miss Thorne the slightest injury, either professional or personal. She is entirely up
to the standard of her credentials. I know that you will
regret deeply any lack of co-operation for no matter
what reason.

Waiting your reply with impatience, I am

Sincerely,

NICHOLAS LANDIS

"So," said Roger Dean, "you are running away from this
gentleman, perhaps?"

"Not exactly. But I didn't want him to know where I was
... that is ... not easily. It isn't easy for a soldier to get
about and make investigations so I believe he must have gone
to lots of trouble. This letter ... may I have it, Dr. Dean?
Will you let me answer it myself?"

"Naturally. It's your own business. I confess to a human
curiosity and a professional dismay. This doesn't mean that
you'll be leaving us? I have cases for you more urgent than
this one ..."

He seemed, in fact, far more than professionally dismayed
and was looking down at Jenny with an intensity of which
his almost beautiful face was especially capable.

Adam came striding into the magic circle from the stables.
He was back from his ride. He checked for an instant, threw
a contemptuous and angry look at the two people standing
there, close together and very self-absorbed, smiled disagreeably and was gone. Contempt, anger, and something ... could
it, thought Jenny, be a shadow of his ... fear?

Dean called after him, "Hi, Adam, almost well enough to
go back?" then, to Jenny as the young man strode away without an answer, "Rotten manners, hasn't he?" and added,
smiling not less disagreeably, "I think we'll have to run him
out of Castania. He's overstayed his welcome here."

Jenny did not like this. But neither did she like Adam with that look on his face.

She took the letter and went slowly to the house and slowly up into her tower room.

She did not know what she felt.

But she took all the letters she had written to Nick and, putting them into one envelope, she addressed them to him at Camp Bennington. She added nothing because of this letter of his to Dr. Dean . . . this longed-for, prayed-for letter which proved that his love was deep and true, which might prove that no past shame and no future disclosure would have power to estrange him. She was dazzled by hope of his magnanimity. She was proud, but, "Oh, dear Nick," she thought, "unless my search here is successful, how can I ever marry you? And, if it should be successful . . . how long will it be before I can prove my mother's innocence? When I hear from you again, when you have read the contents of these letters, will you still be true?" and she wrote in her diary, "I am crying. These are the marks of tears. I'll leave them. They are part of the record. Later I may be able to interpret them. Now, I don't know. I don't know . . ."

On the day after she had received Nick's letter, Adam came into the book room at noon, opening and shutting the door with an unusual hard precision. Jenny did not look up from the work she had begun a few minutes before. She was only too conscious of the kiss he had given her on the path up from the beach, of the feeling of his arms. But when he spoke, she did turn and then, for the first time, it occurred to her to be afraid of Adam.

He had not come to dinner the night before but that had happened frequently enough. So she had not seen him since he broke in upon her interview with Dr. Dean in the place that she had chosen for its privacy. The change in his face from the one that had bent above her on the beach, and on the path up from the beach, was startling. It was controlled but the very control made it formidable. A man who can ride such a storm of fury and suspicion in his own soul would be strong for destruction, if for an instant he lost his self-mastery.

He said, "All right . . . what have you got to say?"

He stood against the closed door rather as if he had been impaled there. And the pain of impalement was in his young strange face.

"What do you mean?"

"I mean: why did Roger Dean send you to this house? I mean, who are you spying upon here? And for what purpose? Who reads your diary, your report upon the people and the doings at Castania? What is it you have to say to Dean that makes it necessary for you to hide behind hedges out of ear-shot of the house? Why are you so keen to help me with these books? To shake them out and quickly pick up any papers? Why do you go down dangerous trails to that beach? For that matter, why were you on that beach in April, before you came to Castania? Who was in the house that night when you went prowling downstairs with your flash and got me out of this room on a wild goose chase . . . so that you could come safely, perhaps, to your window above and speak to someone in the garden below the tower? Was that it? Or, perhaps, throw down something to him? Why do you listen to my grandmother's stories? And question the servants? Why are you captivating my mother, winning her affection and her confidence so that she can hardly move without your help?

"I'm not the master of this house. It has no master except the one who controls its mistress but I swear to God, Jenny Thorne," and here he broke free from his impalement, strode across the room and set one of his lean big hands on each of her shoulders, "unless you can give me a satisfactory answer to these questions, you can't stay here. And that means . . . I can run you out of Castania . . . out of Barent. I can and I will, in spite of Roger Dean."

The shame and guilt she could not help feeling for her real role in this boy's unhappy home made her react to his false accusation with a violence almost to match his own. She kept her eyes on his, held her body still, spoke evenly. But the violence was in her body, shaking it.

"Take your hands off me."

He did so but he did not step back. His body blocked her escape.

"I am not Dr. Dean's agent," she told him. "I can't imagine why you should suspect him of needing one. I came here because your mother asked for a trained nurse. What goes on in this house that you watch each other and hate each other and suspect each other? Yes, I've listened to what you call your 'grandmother's stories.' I was forced by her to listen. I couldn't very well refuse. It was the story of her son's death. Why would she want to tell me, a stranger, that? Perhaps you know the reason, I don't. Yes, I heard a step at night ... I told you why I had to go downstairs ... a step at midnight in the hall where there should have been no foot to step. But I did not investigate it myself. I was scared ... a woman does sometimes lose her nerve alone in a dark house at night ... and I went to you. If anyone has been prowling under the tower windows, it was you. You told me yourself you'd seen me writing in what I thought was a decent privacy. Can't a girl keep a diary or write letters in Castania? I'm not the first girl to keep a diary and write letters. I've helped you here in this room by your own request. I've imitated your method of shaking out papers and catching them up. I haven't asked why you're so interested in these old notes. You don't seem to be finishing your father's book but ... that isn't my business. I went down that trail to find out why it scares you so"—the young blood flamed in his face at that—"and it was by the merest chance, because I lost my way, that I got to that same beach—not knowing what beach it was—that day in April.

"Yesterday, Dr. Dean wanted to consult me about a letter that had reached him from a friend of mine. I don't know why he wanted to be out of sight and earshot of his patient ... except that she is nervous and he might have feared that low tones in consultation might worry her. That letter is entirely my own business but I can and will show it to you if it will bring you to your senses.

"I don't have to say that this is the last morning I'll help you in this room. Nor will I stay with your mother unless she insists or Dr. Dean gives me definite orders to stay. I am Dr. Dean's agent, yes; the agent of his attendance on your mother."

In all this, Jenny had not told a single lie and yet she knew that she had been false, as false as any spy in enemy country.

Adam had moved from her step by step until they were the width of the room apart. His face, white and bewildered, smote her heart.

"Adam," she said in a changed voice, "I don't know what you are about, or what you're trying to do but I do know that you are not good material for a sleuth, that suspicion and treachery are poison to you. I wish you would give up this crazy and cruel attempt—twenty years too late!—to discover the person who was accountable for your father's death."

"You said you didn't know what I was about."

"I don't know anything. But I'd be a fool not to guess.

You and your grandmother—yes, you are busy about something that will bring final ruin to Castania."

Adam went to the window.

She saw that the old fear of height was strong upon him and found herself discovering that hate goes hand in hand with fear, that it is indeed love and only love—of country, of home, of friend, child, lover—that can cast out that sick emotion.

When he faced about, sweat stood on his forehead.

"I mean," he said, "to find out who killed my father even if I have to pull down Castania about my ears."

"But why?" Then her voice left her.

"For a reason I can't and I won't tell."

After a moment, Jenny was able to speak again.

"It has to do," she held her voice to its work, "it has to do with your . . . mother."

He went white, came at her. She thought he would strike.

"By God . . ."

"Adam, forgive me. I love your mother. I only want to help."

And that was true, terribly, almost fatally true, she did love Felicia.

He answered chokingly, "That was what I meant to do. I was going to ask you to help me. But how can you help me now? You are Roger Dean's agent."

"But tell me why you think anything so fantastic? I never saw Dr. Dean until I came to Barent three months ago. I can easily prove that. If he was crazy enough to want a spy here after twenty years in the house of his oldest friends, what inducement could I possibly have to do his work for him?"

"There are inducements and there are reasons. And Dean has his powers. Hypnotic. Mesmeric . . ."

"Adam, you are definitely out of your mind."

"Perhaps I am." He sat down before his father's desk and put his dark head in his hands. The big fingers worked together so that she was reminded of her mother's in distress and, following a channel of old habit, went and put her own hand over them.

"Don't, Adam. You're not out of your mind. Don't suffer so."

He lifted his head, stared up at her. Then he rose, turned and took her into his arms. She felt his lips moving against her hair.

"Jenny . . . help me. Help me. I need your help."

Her whole heart wanted to cry out to him, "No. Don't trust me, Adam. Your instinct is right even if your facts are wrong. Send me away. Throw me out of your house. I'm dangerous." But she thought of her mother and of that long, helpless agony. She had set her will upon a quest and had sworn to God that she would not turn back from it.

She drew herself out of his arms. She could not stab a man who held her against his heart—and she spoke almost coldly.

"I will be glad to help you, Adam, in any way I can."

Her coldness convinced him more than any vehemence. A traitress does not, he thought, remove herself from such an opportune embrace.

He said ... and lit his pipe and began to walk about the room, "I need someone without prejudice, not like my grandmother, not like my mother, not like anyone in this house or in this town. I need someone who can bring a fresh eye and a clear mind to the problem. If I could trust you, Jenny ..."

"I can say nothing as to that. That's for you to decide. I know I can disprove complicity with Dr. Dean for any plan whatever."

"If only," he went on, not noticing her remark, "I could be sure."

"Don't speak to me again until you've made up your mind as to that, Adam," she said and left him.

Chapter Eleven

Jenny was so unnerved by her interview in the book room that, when John called her to the telephone a few minutes later, she found that her shaking hand could hardly lift the receiver. It was a relief to hear Roger Dean's calm voice at its most professional.

"Miss Thorne, I've a request to make. I'm in a bad spot here. My attendant, Miss Brace, is ill. I've got nobody to help me in this office and I'm wondering if you could persuade Mrs. Grise to lend you to me for a fortnight. It oughtn't to be for longer than that. Would you be willing to help me out? There would be no pecuniary loss."

"Of course, doctor."

"It's as hot as Hades in here, about ten degrees hotter than it is at Castania where you get the river breeze."

"I don't mind heat. And I'm sure Mrs. Grise will agree to let me go."

She did so agree but reluctantly and, with a long, half-quizzical look up into Jenny's face, she asked, "How much do you like your . . . doctor, Jenny Thorne?"

"He's wonderfully attractive for a man of his age," she answered and saw with some amusement Felicia's smile of ironic reassurance.

As old Mrs. Grise had suggested, it was quite true that Felicia was jealous where any of her worshippers was concerned. She even resented, a little, Beauty's condescensions to the trained nurse. And yet she had been kind, more than kind, to Enid Ambrose who had sinned so deeply against her royalty. Felicia's was no cheap, ordinary, sex jealousy. It was the jealousy of possession and of power. She must have believed truly in Enid's honor, her good intentions and her innocence. Her anger would be rather against Philip, of whose complete devotion she had been so sure.

It was with inexpressible relief that Jenny turned her back upon Castania. Roger Dean's office was certainly very hot but she contrived to keep his shades down and his electric fans going so that he said never before had he been so com-

fortable during a Barent hot spell. His offices, outer and inner, his little laboratory and, above all, the room where he
kept his books and papers, were crying for a woman's care.
Jenny employed her leisure, for the office attendance was
very erratic and the hours short, in cleaning thoroughly.

The room back of the office had once been heated by a
Franklin stove, one of those open iron stoves that hold a
grate for coals far out into the room. It had not been used
for years and neither had it been cleaned, she thought, for
years. Wearing a dust cap and big apron, she went at it, with
brush and cloth. The throat at the back of the grate was vel-
vety with soot. She shook it vigorously and down on her
hands fell a small package of papers charred at their edges
and yellow with time. She thought it was a bat and cried out,
scolding herself, as usual, for her timidity. She was about to
burn up the papers, which were receipted bills escaped by
chance from some past holocaust, when she saw a name and
a date. "March, 1922." Twenty years ago. "To Martin Elliot,
M.D. Debtor for drugs." She ran over them half in idleness,
half in curiosity, because already she had acquired the metic-
ulous habit of the sleuth to whom nothing is unimportant.

And so she came upon a receipted bill for drugs among
which . . . was one for cyanide . . . the poison that had sent
Philip crashing in anguish to his death.

Dr. Martin Elliot! The old doctor, the doctor who had attended Felicia, the doctor whose practice Roger Dean had
bought. The doctor who was dead.

Her heart pounded and her head swam. She put the paper
into her dress, buttoning her uniform carefully over it. She
went through the half dozen other bills closely and put them
as carefully into her purse. In her room at The Dutch House
she examined them, knowing enough chemistry to understand
the prescription. The one she had hidden in her dress was the
only one of importance.

Then she sat up most of the night deciding how to use her
discovery.

In March of 1922, the year of Philip's death, Felicia's old
family doctor . . . and old he had been! over seventy at that
time . . . had lain in a supply of a drug which is useful for
certain physical conditions. The same drug had been used for
the killing of the husband of his patient. The receipted order
had, supposedly, been burned. A murderer, hiding his tracks,
would certainly have seen more closely to that destruction.
She could hardly even imagine that Dr. Elliot, whose name

was so revered at Barent, could have made any criminal use of such a drug. If she could only go through some record of his cases, she might find out for whom he had ordered it.

Well, she had the name of the pharmacist, a Baltimore firm. Why had it not come forward at the time of the trial when certainly there must have been advertised requests for such information? She would go to Baltimore, if necessary, to make an inquiry. It began to seem necessary for her to engage a lawyer or a professional detective. About this evidence there was the suggestion of danger. She had touched at last upon the live nerve of this drugged body of a crime.

She wrote to the Medical Board for information as to that firm. The answer which came to her at The Dutch House filled her with dismay. The firm was out of business. It was burned out of its uninsured quarters, lost heavily, had changed hands and was now defunct. The fire, Jenny supposed, was the reason for the lack of evidence at the trial. It had destroyed the doctor's original order and the clerk who filed it had either a faulty memory or some motive to keep that recollection to himself. It was strange, however, that Dr. Elliot did not come forward to explain his own purchase of that particular drug . . . and its distribution. Perhaps he was afraid of involvement. But his silence could hardly be called the act of an entirely honest physician.

The evidence now in Jenny's possession seemed to her to be of deadly importance. What, she thought, wouldn't Adam give for it? And what might not his own experience, his own memories, add to its value? And Roger Dean? She questioned him as casually as possible about his predecessor. His answers were, as usual, clear, concise and colorless. He had bought the old man out shortly before Philip's death, had taken over his practice, his office and his house. Yes, with all the medical supplies, drugs and so forth. And the books. Here Roger Dean laughed . . . it was, he said, a rat's nest. (And Elliot's record of his cases was the quaintest document imaginable. More of a journal than a record. "Some day, I'll show it to you, if it would interest you." It would, she told him, interest her greatly.)

She took the prescription with her, back to Castania, as an assassin carries a time bomb under his coat. She thought that she could write to Nick and ask his advice as to engaging a lawyer.

For the first time she realized she was in danger, that this quest might put her own person in jeopardy. If the real murderer were still alive and if he or she should discover that she was on the trail, might that murderer not be dangerous even after twenty years?

Felicia was very glad to see Jenny. Her face, flushed and weary with heat, lit beautifully. She lifted her slim hand and lovely sapphire eyes. The girl's heart was touched. Jenny was homesick for her mother. She bent and kissed Felicia lightly and was rewarded by a radiant smile.

"Sweet thing! It's good to have you here again. It's what I always needed, a girl, a daughter. Jenny, while you've been away, Adam has been with me again, almost as he used to be. We've played backgammon and chess. It's you that did it. It's you, Jenny. You've given him just that push he needed, you've got him over the obstacle, psychic or otherwise. He hasn't been mumbling with his grandmother in some horrid collusion. I got Lizzie to report, of course, without letting her know my motive or my suspicion. I just said, 'Tell me if the captain spends much time with his grandmother. I want him to be out in the fresh air as much as possible, not poking round in dark dusty old rooms.' I think, I hope, I pray that he's been diverted from that morbid intention. She is furious, of course, but," Felicia shrugged, smiled wryly, "I'm used to that. As a matter of fact, that's how it's always been ... what makes me happy, makes her glum. The poor old thing has the proverbial mother-in-law jealousy. It used to be Philip, now it's Adam." Felicia sighed. "How horrid it all is! Life. Human relationships. I hope you're alone in the world, Jenny."

Jenny said, "I'm pretty lonely sometimes." She dared not mention her mother, fearing questions, a request for a photograph, perhaps.

"Well, you'll be getting married before you know it." She looked out towards the river and her face fell into sad lines. "And then you'll know what loneliness really means."

"Oh, Mrs. Grise!"

"I'm sorry. That sounded bitter, didn't it? And I'm not bitter ... really. I won't be. But here I've kept you gossiping long past the hour of your cataloguing. Yes, Adam told me about that. He's thinking of finishing his father's book. A touching idea, isn't it? Aviator into author. Hurry, Jenny. He will be impatient. Anna can put away all these things."

Jenny did not tell her that the cataloguing appointments had been indefinitely postponed. She went slowly up the stairs. In the second story hall, old Mrs. Grise sprang out at her.

"Come in here please. I've got to talk to you."

Old Mrs. Grise was mysterious. She shut her door, drew Jenny to the dimmest and most crowded corner of her queer old room. She put one of the dark little hooked hands upon her, pulled her down and spoke in her harshest, deepest voice. "You were interested in that story I told you before you went away, weren't you, Jenny?"

The girl pretended bewilderment to disguise her nervousness, her too vivid interest. You mean . . . ?"

"The story of Enid Ambrose's crime."

"Yes, Mrs. Grise, of course. Though I should think it would be too painful for you to . . ."

"Something very interesting. I've had news of the Ambrose woman."

Jenny could not control her start.

"Ah, that makes even Nurse Jenny jump. Jenny who's as crisp and cool and stiff as her starched uniform. Yes, *she's* alive."

"How did you find out?"

"An old friend of mine in North Carolina saw her in the street of a little town and recognized her. Didn't you get your diploma in a place called Bonnetsville, North Carolina? Well, it's just there my friend saw Enid Ambrose. Said she was still beautiful and looked fairly prosperous and young.

"She—my friend—was going to make inquiries about Enid but couldn't find out where she was living and hasn't seen her since. Stupid not to follow her up immediately. Enid, of course, is using another name. And now, drat it!"—the expletive was venomous enough to emphasize a stronger word—"of course the woman has made her getaway. She knew that she was recognized."

Carefully the listener let out a caught breath. "I should think she must have suffered a thousand deaths."

"Not too many to pay for the one she caused. But what I want to ask you is this . . . while you were at Bonnetsville did you ever see her?"

"You mean . . . ?"

"Enid Ambrose of course. Wait, I'll show you a picture of her. She can't have changed so much, if Elsie Greely knew her at sight. Besides, she's still quite young . . . not more than forty-five."

While Enid's daughter waited with locked lips, locked

hands, locked heart, Mrs. Grise went to a tall highboy and rummaged in a drawer, returning with an immense, bulging scrapbook. In this was pasted every notice, every story, every picture, every paper, every little scrap that had to do with the famous case of 1922.

Jenny could not altogether disguise her eagerness. There was Felicia . . . with her lifted face, young mouth, seraphic eyes. And there, Jenny's lovely mother, a dark dryad with a panic look . . . ("No," said Jenny slowly, "I never saw that woman at Bonnetsville. I'm quite, quite sure. After all, I was living in the hospital.") And there was another woman whom Jenny did not recognize.

"Who is this, Mrs. Grise?"

"Now, Jenny, surely . . ."

"Of course." But it was only from the bridling of the original that she had known. "It's you." She was astonished. Mrs. Grise, in those days, had been young herself. Only a few years past forty; a firm straight little figure with a face, piquant and vivid, a pursed mouth, big eyes. She wore an odd, tilted hat, carried a parasol. An elegant little woman, very self-confident and alive.

"I suppose you think I was an old woman twenty years ago! What idiots young girls are! They think, when they're in their 'teens and early twenties, that they have all the men sewed up in a bag. Then they scream with rage at the 'cradle snatcher,' forgetting that a woman over thirty has more understanding of men in her little finger than they have in their whole meagre bodies. Those two . . ." she flicked the angel and the dryad with the back of a dark finger, "they went simpering about, picturing themselves as the heroines of the story, and, all the while . . ." The old witch, older now even than her years, tapped herself on the concave chest and simpered.

Well, Jenny had learned something from that simper. Something that might prove valuable. "Old Mrs. Grise" at the time of Philip's death had not been an old woman at all. Somewhere between forty-five and fifty. Her son had been twenty-four. She had been far from a mere observer at Castania. She had been not just the jealous mother-in-law. She had been, in her own mind and perhaps in the minds of others, the heroine of the tale. Felicia had her worshippers, Enid of the tower her secret lover . . . but Helen Grise . . . had someone or something to excite and to foster her feminine vanity. Jealous of the two beautiful girls she had been.

Obviously. But there was a sweet-tasting secret memory now on her old tongue. Jenny looked at her with fresh eyes. Yes, she was now a hideous hooked old woman but could she possibly still think of herself as someone desirable? It seemed a fantastic notion but she could not dismiss it.

Old Mrs. Grise was talking. "I'm glad anyway to know where the creature has been so recently. It oughtn't to be too difficult for the law to put its finger on her in case ..."

Jenny asked, dry-lipped, "In case of what?"

"Fresh evidence. Listen, do you know what Adam hopes to find?"

Jenny shook her head. She could hardly see now for the mist of fear across her eyes.

"He hopes to find that note she spoke of at the trial, the one that never turned up. Of course she pretended it would clear her but that was certainly a bluff. No doubt about it! It would probably have damned her. Of course he won't find it—I've been through those books a hundred times myself! And he hopes to find the tools she used to cause that fall which, but for me, would have destroyed the evidence against her."

"After twenty years?"

"Twenty years can't change the truth. No, nor bury it. I've never given up. And now that I have Adam to help me ... young blood, young eyes, young brains! Come, Jenny, you must be with us. You're in close contact with Mrs. Philip and with the two servants. No one would suspect you. Keep your eyes open and your mouth shut. It will ..." she put her purple mouth close to the girl's ear, "it will pay you well, my dear. Very well."

Jenny braced her sick soul. "I'll do what I can. If you'll tell me what to look for and what, if anything, you've found."

Mrs. Grise got up, went to the door, looked out, closed it again and returned. "Anna's deaf but I don't trust that Lizzie. Now, I'll tell you. Adam has found a child's spade. He's looking for a child's saw. They were both good stout tools and might have done the job."

"But whoever did it could so easily have brought tools from Barent or from somewhere else."

"*If* that 'whoever' had not been Enid ... yes. But if she had got herself tools anywhere in Barent ... well, you can see for yourself."

Jenny did see ... vividly.

"So, if we can establish the use of tools ... found somewhere hidden near the scene of the crime . . . we've got somewhere. Adam has seen Josh Hogan. He's got nothing out of him yet but he knows there's something to be had. Hogan's in somebody's pay . . . Probably Felicia's by way of Roger Dean because Felicia's insane on sheltering Enid. She's loyal to her protégés and she'd go to the stake for any dependent. It's only a rebel that she hates. Lady Bountiful . . . that's Felicia. And now you're coming into that category, my child. Be careful of yourself. Above all, not a word to the doctor or to her about any of all this. And better not tell Adam that I've let you in. He hasn't made up his mind whether or not you might be useful to us."

"Hasn't he? That reminds me, Mrs. Grise, he may be waiting for me in the tower room."

"Yes. Yes. Run along. Keep your mouth shut. And your eyes open. It will pep up your job here. I'm sure you're sorry to leave your handsome doctor's office. Never mind. This thing will pay you well. I guarantee that. I've put by a substantial sum for this one purpose. How about a couple of thousand dollars for your share, Jenny?"

"Oh, Mrs. Grise!"

"That makes you open your oriental eyes, doesn't it?"

The eyes were open. But they hardly saw the steps of the tower stairs. Sick, she felt, and old.

There was no letter from Nick. And Adam was not waiting for her in the bright tower room.

Chapter Twelve

Her own room without a river wind was stifling hot. Jenny found herself unable to breathe. She was oppressed in mind and body. Castania was dreadful to her so that she felt smothered with her fear of it and of its inmates. Her heart beat heavily. She dreaded the sound of Adam's step upon the stairs.

So she fled from the tower, from the house, out into the blazing garden where even the tunnelled alley could not keep its shadows cool. She told herself that she would give up her purpose, cancel her stern resolution, escape. She would go back to her mother and to the interminable flights. But even thinking of this increased her fears, for now it was too late for flight. There were other people at work. It was not only in the hope of clearing Enid from shame that her child must remain here, it might be to save her very life. The hounds were up. Jenny had the dry mouth of the hunted.

She came to the place of the arbor, high and shadeless, and looked down at the heat-shimmering beach. To her astonishment a woman stood there, a tall, thin, stooping woman in a sleeveless cotton frock. Stood and stared up at her. Jenny wondered if her own face resembled Adam's when he looked down, startled, from behind his rock.

The woman below stared and spoke. The distance was too far for Jenny to hear her words but she seemed to be questioning anxiously so that Jenny went carefully down the trail until she reached the danger point. The woman had come to stand just below. Jenny could see her face and hear her voice.

It was a strange, remote, pale face, as though it had been bleached; skin, hair and eyes. A woman with strong bones, high-cheeked, a face like an empty box, for there was no expression beyond a half-complacent vacancy.

"Hullo," she called, putting her hands about her mouth, "I've seen you before. And you know me, don't you?"

"I'm sorry," Jenny said. "I don't know you. What's your name?"

"But sure you know me. Everyone knows me. I'm Enid Ambrose."

There was an echo from the steep bank and her calling voice went back from it and away. "E-nid Ambro-ose." Jenny turned to run away from that speaker and saw Lizzie above her, waving her hands and apron frantically.

"Come up here, Miss Thorne, please, quick! Don't take notice of her. She got away from me. It's my niece, Mary." And, as Jenny came, breathless, up to her, she went on, "She will run off and visit me, try as they do to keep her in. She's not bad enough for an institution-like and mostly she's quiet and reasonable. She's been here for twenty-four hours or more now ... and me keeping her out of Miss Felicia's way till I'm near about as crazy as her. She thinks she's Enid Ambrose, the poor, foolish creature. Here, Mary, stop where you are, darlin'. Aunt Liz is comin' round to show you how to get back safe to the house ..."

But before they knew it and in spite of their cries, the poor thing came springing up the trail, flapping across the face of the cliff like a crazy gull, her smiling eyes fixed all the while on the two women above her so that they half felt an angel kept her feet. For there she was, in no time, beside them, she all bathed in sweat and smiling. Lizzie took her by the arm.

Jenny could see now that she was a woman in her late thirties, more vacant than mad, except for that one strong obsession so terrible to the girl.

"You better look at me good," said she, "you don't often see such a pretty and famous lady, do you now?"

The Irish brogue came out as soft as summer.

"Lizzie ... this is Mary Ryan, isn't it? The girl who was Adam's nurse?"

"She is that. She's Mary Ryan but she won't admit it and it drives her to fury if she's told. See now!"

Mary was indeed furious. "Who says Mary Ryan? That poor simple thing. She was just the one that came before Enid Ambrose and sure you know it. She was just ..."

Lizzie dragged her away, talking loudly, drowning out her words and, at the same time, over her shoulder, she flung back, "Don't say a word, Miss Thorne! I'll keep her close now until they've time to send for her. They ought to be here any time now. I'm glad you come across her. Lord knows how far she might have got ... killed herself in the river water, likely, or on the rocks . . . Hush, hush, darlin'. Sure we know you're Enid Ambrose . . ."

But before she was out of Jenny's hearing, the woman turned round and pointed at her. "Good-bye, Enid," she said. "I know who's goin' to meet you in the arbor for his tea. Sure thing I know. Bad luck to your beautiful long fingers!"

Jenny Thorne sat down on the dreadful slab of stone that marked that spot and bent her head to her hands—the fatal hands that everyone remembered. She had what a psychologist might call the graphic mind. After a while, she found herself using those same beautiful hands to draw in the gravel a diagram which represented her situation, the problem of her mind.

There, in the circular central space, it stood, that small spider mind of Jenny's . . . and from it radiated the lines of her webbed research; lines that might be called:

Felicia
Adam
Helen Grise
Roger Dean
Dr. Elliot
Josh Hogan
Lizzie
Anna
Mary Ryan . . .

and always,

Enid Ambrose.

Along each spoke ran the slender threads of her discoveries. *Felicia:* her simply enormous power to charm, her fear of Adam and his grandmother. Her dread of a re-opening of the case; her almost abnormal will to protect her husband's lover; her tyranny as a benefactress, as a possessor, as a saint; her hysteria, her cruelty to an old friend; her wish to win the devotion of Jenny, of her cat, of everyone who came within her influence. And here, too, the small factual mystery of an inexplicable footstep outside her door at night.

Adam: his neurosis, roots buried deep in a forgotten, terrifying childhood experience; his fear of heights, which in sublimation had first led him to climb mountains, to rush down steep places on skis, to fling himself to combat thirty thousand feet above the earth but which, in illness, had come overwhelmingly into its own. His fearful wish to explore the past, to unearth the secret of his father's death. A wish? A furious determination which had something to do with a

gnawing suspicion of his mother whom he adored, something
to do perhaps with a forgotten childish passion for his gentle
governess, something to do with his dislike and jealousy of
Roger Dean. Adam, who did not believe Enid to be guilty,
who suspected someone else and couldn't rest until he had
verified or disproved this suspicion. Adam, who had made
certain discoveries and might at any time make more. Therefore (here Jenny's little diagram-stick underscored her determination), it was important for her, at any cost to her pride
and at any risk to her own safety, to overcome his suspicion
of her, to persuade him to let her in on his activities. He might
even suddenly remember what it was he saw that terrible day
upon the beach.

Anna: a faithful doglike soul, Felicia's most perfect slave.

Lizzie: faithful, too, perhaps, but at the same time critical of
Felicia's "kindness to everyone." Jealousy here too? Of
Anna's more intimate relationship, of Enid Ambrose with the
little boy? Lizzie who sheltered a niece, life and reason
wrecked, it would seem, by that past event.

Josh Hogan: close to the scene of the murder, who had de-
clared under oath that he had heard a speech which the noise
of a passing train must, demonstrably, have made inaudible;
who was grateful to Roger and a protégé of Felicia; who
knew something about tools or garden rendezvous, something
he had not told and would probably never tell. Josh, who had
recently informed Dean of Adam's secret inquiries and had
put his patroness and her agent on guard, thereby destroying
Felicia's purpose of hiding from Dean any suspicion of
Adam's peculiar activities.

Roger Dean: not entirely in Felicia's confidence. Disliking
Adam, quarreling with Felicia. Wounded and angered by her.
Unhappy. For all his charm and his good looks and the fas-
cination which Adam called "hypnotic" a lifelong bachelor.
On Felicia's account? If he loved her would he show to Jenny
Thorne a growing lover-like devotion? This change in him
troubled Jenny greatly. He had a certain power . . . not mesmeric as Adam foolishly suggested, but a power of charm
that was quite indescribable. You felt, when you were with
him, that here was the most important person, perhaps the
only important person in the world, that his need for you was
a hunger that must at any cost be fed. It wasn't that you
needed him but that he, proud and strong and sorrowful,
needed you. And the appeal and the flattery were very strong
indeed. His hatred of Adam? Jealousy again? Or fear? Or

merely prejudice? Roger, who had been at Castania at the hour of a murder the chief peculiarity of which was that it did not necessarily require the presence of the murderer upon the scene. Roger, who like everyone else had been thoroughly investigated and cleared but who might have had access to Dr. Elliot's medical supplies, who could most easily and secretly have obtained the drug and used it. Roger, who since then had been an intimate of Castania.

Helen Grise: her hatred and her jealousy of Enid, and, it sometimes seemed ... of Felicia. An impossible suspect because the victim was her only and beloved son, and because of her desire to discover fresh evidence and re-open a case which, if guilty, she would certainly wish to keep closed. But valuable as a source of motives, of past emotional entanglements. Her will to vengeance. Her vanity. Her inflaming of Adam's will, her cruel enlistment of his weakness. Her hints of a past love affair of her own of which Enid and Felicia had suspected nothing.

Mary Ryan: her insanity. Her obsession. She wanted the lurid glory of Enid Ambrose for her own. Had there been envy and jealousy here too?

Dr. Elliot: who had a supply of the poison and who had been silent as to his possession of it. A fine old doctor, seventy years old, who had attended Felicia ever since she came to Barent as a bride ... a matter of about six years.

Enid Ambrose: (here Jenny's finger paused.) She was eaten away with a growing suspicion that her mother had told her ... the truth, yes ... but not the whole truth. Something had been left out, some vital element. She must soon, she decided, go down to see that mother or arrange for that mother to meet her at some halfway point. There was so much she had not told. There were so many details lacking. Jenny didn't dare write about it all. The story of the sugar for instance. In the trial Enid had described taking the last spoonful of sugar from the pantry bowl ... the only sugar she could find. She said that she usually took sugar in her tea but that she had decided to give it up that afternoon rather than bother to look for more. Philip rarely took more than one cup. Mary was out and so was Lizzie. Both had gone to the house of Mary's mother across the river. It was Mary's mother that had furnished them both with an alibi. Anna was with Mrs. Philip Grise and Dr. Dean. So Enid had contented herself with the small sugar supply, not wanting to call attention to that last rendezvous of hers.

Any one of these people might have been able to arrange
the murder, though of course for its full and sure execution
the criminal would want to direct it himself, on the spot. But
Felicia was a cripple and the man killed was the only and beloved son of Helen Grise.

Jenny thought about it all till her head reeled. Not one of
these was the right figure, not one seemed to fit into the
shape of a murderer, least of all, that darling mother of hers
so timid and grateful and affectionate. Surely a murderer
must carry somewhere upon him visibly the mark of Cain!

In the minds of every one of these possible suspects, in the
background of their lives, in the very air of Castania, stood
and moved some other presence, some faceless, formless, un-
named figure. If she could put her finger on that nebulous
shape, half of her problem, surely, would be solved.

Jenny, who had been busily drawing with a little stick now
slowly obliterated her design. Lines, she thought, that radiate
out from a common center will never meet, never bring her
tortured mind to a point, to a solution, to the crime itself. It
was necessary to alter her pattern. She must see herself at
the bottom of a pyramid . . . inside, at the center of its base.
All about her on every side the lines spun themselves up and
inwards. There, at the top, when she could see so far, they
must all meet.

There was only one method for her to use: a patient one.
She must take each thread by itself, each channel, each fine-
spun ladder and, ignoring all the others, follow it to its end
. . . or as nearly to its end as she could reach. When each one
had been pursued, she would find herself close to, if not immediately upon, her goal. She must no longer let her mind
run confusedly, feverishly, from one discovery, from one suspect, to another. Anyone that knew Philip might have killed
him. And she must now be bolder, take greater risks. She
must confide in these people to the point of eliciting confidence from them. She must not be squeamish or timid. She
had accomplished the first part of her task. She had become
a familiar and accepted figure in this house. She had dis-
armed suspicion, except in the case of Adam Grise. That suspicion must at any cost be allayed. The second and more dangerous portion of her quest must now be undertaken.

She stood up, wet and weak, from her place of torment
and dragged herself back to the house. She faced the lunch
hour with the horrible old woman, an afternoon with Felicia,
a dinner with Felicia, Adam and Helen Grise; . . . afterward

... if she could live so long! ... cool night with its river wind and a merciful loneliness in her tower room.

There and then, clear decision must be made and followed ruthlessly.

Chapter Thirteen

Adam had left Barent.

This news, curiously disturbing, with a taste of desertion in its mouth for youth draws a mysterious and profound support from its own kind, reached Jenny that afternoon when she came to Felicia in the verandah at about three o'clock. She could see at once the effect upon Felicia. Not since the incident of Beauty's truancy, followed by the attack of hysteria, had Felicia been so desperately disturbed. She sat, all huddled in her chair. She always looked fragile and small with her slim bones, light shoulders and relaxed pose, but today she was like the ghost of a long-limbed child. Only the two lines of age had deepened in her forehead and there were heavy shadows all about her eyes.

She spoke sharply, fretfully, at once.

"Jenny! where has he gone?"

"He? Who has gone?" Jenny stammered, stopping just outside the door, book and knitting in the hands which, these days, she kept as much as possible concealed.

Felicia's impatience jerked her fingers in their own delicate manipulation of fine wool.

"Adam, of course. You must know. You were with him."

"No, Mrs. Grise. He didn't come to the book room this morning. And he left no message for me. His grandmother didn't know or, at least, if she knew she didn't tell me. She hardly said a word at lunch."

"She doesn't know. Or at least when I asked her, she said she didn't. Adam left word for me. He thought I was resting . . . simply that he's gone to meet a friend just back from foreign service. In New York? In San Francisco? He didn't say where."

"I'm sorry I can't help you, Mrs. Grise. I know nothing at all about it." But Jenny was wondering while she spoke, "Has he perhaps been told by old Mrs. Grise about Enid Ambrose's recent whereabouts? Has he gone to Bonnetsville to track her down?" Her own anxiety dulled the sharp impact of Felicia's ill humor.

© Lorillard 1974

King Size
or Deluxe 100's.

KENT

WITH
THE FAMOUS MICRONITE FILTER

DELUXE LENGTH

f you have
a taste for quality,
ou'll like the taste
of Kent.

© Lorillard 1974

*Try the crisp, clean taste
of Kent Menthol 100's.*

The only Menthol with the famous Micronite filter.

"Even if you knew you wouldn't tell me, would you? You don't tell me anything. And yet that's why I brought you here."

Jenny sat down on the step in the shade of the wind-shaken awning. Slowly and carefully she took out her work; but when she spoke her voice was swift and clear. It held, for an understanding ear, the sound of her courage and of her alarm.

"Mrs. Grise," she said, "there hasn't been anything to tell. I am probably stupid at this business of investigation. Captain Grise is better. I think his going to meet a friend, just back from the front, proves that he is very much better . . ."

"If he's really gone to meet a friend," Felicia murmured, her head bent low and over her work.

Not heeding this, Jenny went on, "I *have* told you about his fear of heights. I've reason to believe that he's getting over that."

"What reason?" Felicia's knitting stopped.

"You know, when I hurt my leg."

"Yes? You said it was by a fall in the garden."

"It was by a fall," Jenny fixed her wild, brave, secret eyes upon Felicia's, "a fall down the river cliff."

This speech was the first fruit of her plan for a new and bolder campaign and it produced immediate results.

Felicia's face was frozen but her fingers moved like a bird's foot closing.

"You . . . were . . . climbing . . . down . . . the cliff . . ."

"Yes. I found a little path."

"Jenny! You didn't attempt to go down that . . . trail? I didn't know there would be any of it left at all." Her breath was short.

Jenny went on steadily. "Yes. It is still there. But halfway down, just after you get to a big rock, I found a sort of land-slide and, when I stepped into it, it gave way. I fell and hurt myself. Adam must have seen me or heard me. He must have been in the garden and fairly close to the edge of the cliff. He thought I was half killed and he forgot to be afraid. This is important, Mrs. Grise. It's why I'm telling you the story. He leaped down to help me. He carried me up. Until then he'd been going part way down that same trail but had stopped always by the rock. Since then, he's been on the beach very often."

Felicia repeated as though she were learning a lesson by heart, "You fell. The ground gave way. Adam went down

. . ." She turned her wheel chair abruptly, shot herself into the house, into her room.

Jenny did not follow her. She remained on her step and went on with her work until Felicia called, "Come in here to me, will you, Jenny, please?" when she laid down her work and came.

In the sitting room when, in obedience to a gesture, the door was closed, Felicia spoke, looking up with proud sapphire-colored eyes. "What was Adam doing? Why was he near that path? Do you think he really goes there often? Do you think he goes down to that beach? Is it part of this unnatural, insane attempt? I mean, his grandmother, has she been directing him?"

"I think he has been investigating," Jenny answered, "and I don't think he has given up the attempt. I think he is very determined, with or without his grandmother's encouragement, to find out the truth about his father's death. I think, Mrs. Grise, that, like you, he does not believe in the guilt of Enid Ambrose."

Felicia sat for a minute, staring straight ahead of her, that haughty expression stiff upon her face. Then she said in a tone that matched the look, "Please send for Dr. Dean. I want to be alone." And Jenny found herself dismissed.

Jenny felt the importance of this unexpected summons and was tormented by her inability to fathom it. Being told to leave her patient alone, she felt justified, however, in a complete self-effacement and, making as much noise as possible, she went upstairs and watched Roger's arrival from the window of the upper hall. When he had gone into Felicia's sitting room and had closed the door, she took her courage in the two hands of her will, and, ignoring the rules of her profession, the instinct of her birth and the traditions of her education, she came soundlessly down the stairs, out by the front door and down from the verandah. On those velvet nurse's feet she passed the corner of the house and drew herself in among the dense vines close to one of the long French windows that opened upon Felicia's space of turf.

The wind, as always, blew. It moved the vines, the trees, the great white summer clouds. A wraith of black smoke from the railroad crossed the chimneys like a riding witch. There was the perpetual sound of sighing and whispering. But Jenny could hear Roger Dean's cool voice.

He was saying, "Well, Felicia, what now?" and she remem-

bered that this was, probably, their first private interview
since the day of their quarrel and of his distress.

The queen of Castania spoke in a level voice high and
sweet as usual but without warmth. She said, "I sent for you
to tell you that I have come round to your opinion. I must,
I suppose, beg your pardon for my first reaction. Because I
now see that you are entirely right. Adam will have to ...
go."

High, cool and sweet, the sentence ran like ice along
Jenny's veins and the skin of her nape pricked.

Roger said in his driest and most practical voice, "I
thought you'd come to it. There's no reason why you should
put up with his behavior. There's no reason why you should
entertain a dangerous mental case in your house. No reason,
that is, that I can discover. Fundamentally you are a proud
and a sensible woman. There can only be misery for you in
such a tearing open of old wounds. If your tentative remon-
strance has no effect ..."

"Adam has been playing a part with me, making me believe he had given up his attempt. Making me feel safe and
sure."

Roger laughed shortly. "Safe!" he mocked. "Safety is your
fetish. Of course, to have the case opened again would be a
hellish thing for everyone. I feel, wrongly perhaps, for people
are surprisingly tough, that we'd none of us survive. We went
through it once. And that once was enough."

"Oh, yes ... yes ... yes ..." No queenliness in these three
breathless words.

"Tell me what changed your mind about Adam. Tell me
what he's done."

"He has been going down to the beach ... he is trying to
bring back the memory of what ... he saw there."

"Any sign of his remembering?"

"Only that he has gone away suddenly and without leaving
an address."

Here Roger moved and came toward the window so that
Jenny shrank closer to the wall, holding her own quick
breath.

"Gone away?"

"His reason ... the one he gave ... was to meet a friend
just back from overseas service. But he didn't give me his destination. I can't help wondering if, perhaps, he's gone to
consult with a lawyer, to look for Enid, or ... to interview
Mary Ryan."

To Jenny, as evidently to Roger Dean, the last-named destination seemed an anticlimax.

"Mary Ryan? Why, she's only just across the river at Tom Ryan's place. He wouldn't need to be absent long for that. The ferry runs back and forth every twenty minutes. Anyone could find his way to Ryan's Hotspot and be there and back in a few hours. Besides, what good could Mary Ryan be to him? She's as crazy as a loon."

"I know. Poor girl! Poor girl!" This was Felicia at her sweetest and most tender. Jenny felt her heart turn over. The owner of that voice had a power greater than anyone knew. "But, if he talked to her, if she saw him, heard him, it might bring something . . . back . . ."

To the listener's amazement Roger laughed. "What's got into you, Felicia? You've lost your nerve now after twenty years. You act as though . . ." he laughed again in the same bitter and mocking key, "you had a sense of . . . shame!"

Silence followed this until Felicia said in a tortured voice, "Perhaps I have." To Jenny's ear there was audible in this strange speech a question as though she had made a statement that she wished him to say that he believed. But what he did say was, "You have nothing of the kind. You've allowed yourself to go to pieces. Ever since Adam came here, you've been acting like the neurotic he has always been. You're heading for a bad nervous breakdown, and, as I warned you in our last interview . . . which I suppose you haven't forgotten . . ."

"No, I'm sorry. I've been very sorry. Roger! How you have changed!" Here she must have held out her hand and Roger, after hesitation, must have taken it for she said, "Thank you, my dear. That's better. Now we can go on with more courage, can't we?"

He said in a softer tone but still keeping some of its dryness, "Under the influence of this mother-son disturbance you will do or say something that you may be very sorry for. Very sorry indeed. Something that might bring Castania crashing down about your ears."

He was now pacing the room, his footsteps barely audible on the heavy carpet. He had lit himself a cigarette. Jenny could smell the smoke. She shrank down and back among her vines. If he should come to the open window, he must surely see her in her white dress. She went a little farther towards the corner of the house. She could hear his next long speech only in fragments ". . . sometimes I almost wish . . . ready to wash my hands . . . humiliation . . . shameful situation."

Felicia murmured a protest, "Roger please!" with no effect. It went on, ending with an acid exclamation. "Your precious son!"

"But don't reproach me with that now." Felicia's speech was fully audible. "Haven't I just said . . . ?"

He seemed to stop his pacing and stand near her chair.

"How do you want me to proceed?"

"Couldn't you . . . what you suggested the other day? Just temporarily of course."

"I could if you'd stand back of me and if I could get some other evidence."

Felicia in her high voice asked, "His grandmother? And Jenny Thorne?"

"God! It's hot here." Roger exploded suddenly. "Let's get out on the grass. It's shaded now and we might get a breath of air. Oh, to hell with your precautions. I did look out of the windows when I first came in. Might think there was a detective in the house. Shut up here in your rainbow pool you forget time. You are still a child. But, in the meantime, I have grown up. Yes, Felicia. At last. At last. Do you realize this thing happened twenty years ago? Do you remember that twenty years ago you were . . . young?"

Felicia said nothing. Jenny wondered how she looked, sitting there in her strange, draped throne, her perennial young pride of beauty and of royalty so bitterly affronted.

Roger went on, "If it hadn't been for your precious son's insanity, his jealousy and malice towards you and me and the whole world, there wouldn't be a chance in a million of this . . . trouble you so extravagantly fear."

They were moving towards the French window, Roger no doubt propelling Felicia's wheeled chair. And Jenny fled. But, before she was out of earshot, Felicia spoke a name. "Enid Ambrose?" she said. Jenny heard that name and, faintly, the speech that followed it, "You know, don't you, Roger? Or have you forgotten . . . that Enid had a child?"

With that name and with that sentence in her ears Jenny, again in the upper hall, waited to be recalled to her patient; waited in a condition that demanded more self-control than even she could immediately muster. Her thoughts ran about like sparks in paper, only one being clear: "I must really run away. Now, I can only bring ruin to everyone by staying on at Castania. Once on the track of 'Enid's child,' the possible interest of that child in clearing Enid, they're bound to find me out. Unless . . ." here unexpectedly back surged her courage and her hope, "unless, by some lucky find, I reach my own discovery first!"

Courage took her downstairs with a steady countenance enough, at Roger's softly spoken summons.

He stood at the bottom of the flight, a hand on the post, looking up. His face was white, exhausted, but, at the same time, tense.

She went down to him.

"May I talk to you alone, privately, somewhere, Jenny?"

This time she did not have to fear interruption from Adam but she hesitated to return to the former place of meeting.

She asked him, "Where shall we go?" in a vague, anxious tone.

To that he smiled. "We'll go out of the back door down into the 'Narrow Garden'" which was Castania's name for the strip of turf that cut the steep bank just below the tower.

"That's under Lizzie's window."

"What of it? We can move out of her orbit, can't we? You're very pernickety this afternoon."

She followed him out of the back door and along the narrow lawn away from the tower, back from the river end of the house into a little woods, full-leaved and quick with birds. Leaf shadow and split sunlight patched them. Roger Dean unnecessarily helped her over a log and down the slope until they were lost from sight and sound of Castania.

"Now, Jenny," he said, "I want you to listen to me . . . Closely."

She listened.

"Without beating about the bush, I am going to have Adam Grise committed to a sanitarium." He checked her exclamation by putting his hand on her arm. "And I want you to help me."

"Dr. Dean. I can't. I can't. I wouldn't feel justified. He's not mentally incompetent or even nervously deranged."

"I'm probably a better judge of his condition than you are. In any case, it is at the request of his mother, who has the best right and the best reason. Do you know what the young man has been about?"

Jenny shook her head, wondering the while why it was easier to lie with any other member than with the tongue.

Dean let her go, stepped back and sat down on a big rock. He took out and lit a cigarette, she staring at the long skillful fingers, at the bent, shapely head in its silver helmet. He was delightful to look at whatever he did and the appeal of his good looks, of his grace, his gentleness, above all, his controlled pain were strong upon the sensitive and lonely girl. He seemed to cry out at once for worship and compassion—a combination dangerous to the sympathies of women.

He said slowly, "I've told you the story of Castania. You know how the shadow of that tragedy has hung over this place, over Felicia Grise. You know that it is only by a great courage and a great will that she's been able to keep her sweetness and her sanity, her charity and peace of mind."

Jenny nodded, this time with truth in motion.

"Very well. Now, when she is no longer young, now, when she's been through the terror and suspense of war, of having her only son dangerously, almost fatally involved, that son is spending his time, using his privileges as a son of the house, to deceive her, to spy upon her and her household, to dig up the bones of this horrible corpse . . ." Roger spoke with passion, lifting his brilliant eyes, "Do you call that the action of a sane man?"

Jenny said, "But he too is a victim of the war. He should be considered more than anyone. He has served his country almost to the death. Besides, it might after all be the action of a sane man."

He stared at her, his face tightening. "Now what do you mean by that?"

"He might have reason to suspect someone. He might have a sense of . . . of abstract justice. He might even have a sense of guilt."

"Guilt? Adam was five years old."

"I don't mean personally. I mean—what is the word?—vicariously. After all, though no one seems to consider it, a suspended sentence would be a tragic burden, wouldn't it, for a woman to carry about for all her life?"

"Oh," said Roger, flicking the ash from his cigarette with a contemptuous gesture, "if you're thinking of the Ambrose girl, I assure you, Jenny, she's not worth your commiseration."

"Perhaps," Jenny was astonished at the calmness of her voice, "perhaps Adam doesn't think so."

"Don't tell me you think it's normal for Adam Grise to risk killing his mother or wrecking her reason for the sake of a cheap little governess who took care of him for a few months when he was five years old!"

"Perhaps not. It may be that the other motive is stronger. I mean, his conviction of somebody's guilt."

"Now you're talking. But I don't think 'conviction' is just the word for it, Jenny. I think it's a wish. He desires to prove somebody guilty. Yes, that's what he wants."

It was not Jenny's belief and she said so quickly. "He's not malicious like his grandmother."

"So you believe. Let me tell you this." The man spoke with concentrated anger, throwing down his cigarette, grinding it into the earth. "Adam Grise wants to believe that I killed his father. He has always wanted to believe it. And now with the crazy obsession in control of his whole wrecked brain, he's out to prove it."

He stood up and actually smiled down into the pale small faun-face, its eyes the color of sun and leaf and earth. "Perhaps, Jenny, he'll succeed. Perhaps he'll have me arrested, brought to trial. Perhaps he'll have me convicted, sentenced, hung."

"Dr. Dean! Dr. Dean!"

His passion, so controlled and so astonishing, made her move back from him.

"You're ready to believe it, you see! So easily." He laughed, followed her near flight and his hands closed gently one on each of her white starched shoulders. His clean-cut face with its bright eyes bent towards her own. "Jenny Thorne, answer me truthfully. Do you believe it possible that I killed Philip Grise?"

"No. I don't. I don't. I can't believe it's possible that anyone I've seen or known here ... could have killed Philip Grise."

She tried to draw herself away. "But what makes you think," she cried, "that Adam, after twenty years, would want to ruin you, to ... kill you ... his mother's best and oldest friend!"

"Precisely. Precisely for that reason. The truth is, Jenny, that he's sufficiently deranged to suspect that I have been ... her lover."

Jenny managed to free herself. She could no longer bear his burning, white proximity. She went back against a tree, put her hands out a little to hold him off, and said, "Is he right? Is that true?"

"You know Felicia. You know me. What do you think? What do you believe?"

"I can believe that any man could be her ... hopeless, faithful lover."

"Ah! And you can believe in Adam's jealousy?"

"Yes, of course I can. Such things happen. I mean, I know that a son can be jealous of his mother, can hate her lover, if he believes there has been ... guilt or even a taint of guilt ... where he has always wanted to worship innocence."

"So you understand frustrated passion and jealousy better than you do malice or madness. Perhaps you are jealous yourself."

She looked her bewilderment, widening her oriental eyes. "Of ... of ..."

"Of Felicia," he answered and went on, as her narrow, beautiful little face flamed. "There now, I've said it! It's off my chest. I feel better. I want you to be jealous of Felicia, darling. Because, by God, I'm jealous of Adam Grise.

"And not," he went on feverishly, "on Felicia's account. But on yours. You know I love you, Jenny, I've seen you recognize it, with that fugitive, brave little face of yours. And don't dare to answer me now. I'm not asking you a question. You've no right to answer me. It would be sheer impertinence. I'm making an announcement. Take it or leave it. I love you. And I want you to know that I love you. The past is a corpse ... a ghost. Beyond even a madman's power to resurrect. I've spent my life trying to bring back its breath of youthfulness. I've given up. I'm beginning myself to live again. I'm young, Jenny, I'm as young as you are. Younger by far than Adam with his old man's suspicions, hates, envies, secrecies. My youth has been preserved ... in a block of beautiful, clear ice. Yes, I am younger than Adam, as young as Jenny Thorne. I've been loved by other women. I am going to be loved by you. But, mind you, I'm not putting any questions. Except this one: will you help me ... me, *your* lover, not Felicia's? Will you help me to silence for a certain necessary interval this Adam Grise? Think it over."

He did not wait for any reply but turned away from her, as though at a summons she could not hear, and went swinging, tall and lithe and, indeed, young to look at, from their woods and back into the house ... she supposed, for she did not follow him.

She sat down on the rock.

Now that his voice was stilled, it was the wood voice and the river voice she heard, a lovely solace of sound.

Going back to the house at the sound of Dean's departing

motor, for she did not want to be out of the way of Felicia's need, Jenny began to tell herself, "Roger Dean loves me. Roger Dean wants me to be his wife."

She recognized in herself a faint reflection of the glow that had fallen upon her climbing the shabby stairs of Mrs. Clarke's tourist home, the evening after Nick's proposal. Her woman's vanity which had never received its normal nourishment was still alive. She recognized it with self-contempt. The compliment of being desired outshone all the blackness of her recent experience. And yet she was angry with Roger Dean. No, not angry—that was not the word. She was afraid of him, of his passion and of his charm, of his contempt for Enid Ambrose, of his supreme self-confidence and of his will to ruin Adam Grise.

She clenched her two hands, which might yet betray her secret, and spoke through her teeth to Castania's young son before she entered his house, "Nothing will ever induce me to witness against your sanity, Adam. I'll fight to save you from their wickedness, from their malice, their terror and their guilt. Not as murderers . . . not yet, but as secret lovers."

Roger Dean might now be weary of his long enslavement, of insufficient rewards, he might now be ready to break free from Felicia's tyranny, to turn to youth and warmth and health and innocence. But he could not, for that weariness, move Enid Ambrose's child. She was sorry for him and for Felicia. For Felicia, even now, her heart bled. What bitterness there must have been in the life of this beautiful cripple with her reputation for saintliness! For if, at the trial, any hint of clandestine passion between Philip's wife and the handsome young doctor had come out, the missing authentic motive for murder would have screamed itself against both the man, as active agent, and the woman as fellow plotter. She herself, Jenny Thorne—no, Sheila Ambrose—for all her true tenderness towards her mother's benefactress, could hardly keep from a conviction. If Adam had guessed, if Adam knew, would he not inevitably suspect Roger Dean? But in that case would he dare to look for further evidence? Would he dare risk a new trial where Felicia herself would almost certainly be revealed not as a saint, not as an innocent, magnanimous betrayed wife but as a woman tempted by, perhaps involved in, some strange and morbid love affair? It was difficult to believe in this involvement and Jenny did not believe. Roger Dean himself had furnished some proof of Felicia's technical innocence. "His youth had been preserved in a block of beautiful clear ice." Felicia had accepted the man's worship, had fed his romantic devotion with such crumbs as Jenny could not imagine. She had held him, even, by their mutual fear of a discovery. No doubt, they were now in terror of Adam's search. Adam, Jenny told herself, must really be ignorant of what he's doing. He must be on the track only of Roger Dean, thinking that the young doctor had destroyed Philip in the hope of eventually winning Felicia and her fortune. A rich and beautiful young widow, a young and handsome doctor—secret love in his heart, secret ambition in his brain—it was not impossible. It was, as a matter of fact, much more probable than the other solution which involved Felicia herself. And Adam hated Dean. Adam wanted to get the man out of his own and his mother's life. Out of Castania. He resented Dean's influence, Dean's power.

Anna met Jenny in the hall. "Mrs. Grise says she won't come to dinner tonight, Miss Thorne."

"Oh, Anna, I wonder, then, if I may stay upstairs. I've such a racking headache."

"Why, yes of course, Miss Jenny. Why shouldn't you? I can't see any reason. I'll bring you tea . . . supper . . ."

"No, thanks really, Anna. I don't want anything to eat or to drink. I'll just take aspirin and put myself to bed. It's not so hot this evening, there's a beautiful river wind."

Chapter Fourteen

Sometimes the river wind stopped blowing and the house was still. All the whispering and murmuring, the rustle and the tapping fell away from it as flesh from bones and a skeleton silence louder than noise possessed the air. That night, partly because of this silence, Jenny could not sleep.

She had shut herself into her room, written in her diary, considered and reconsidered all the facts at her command. She had gone back over the lives of these people until her own identity was all but lost and she hardly knew if she were young Felicia, or young Enid, Roger Dean or Philip Grise himself.

It was there and on the entrance of that name, that the silence descended upon Castania and it had, perhaps for that reason, kept possession of her weary and excited brain.

Philip Grise . . . she had considered him hardly at all. He had, in her imagination, in her re-telling of the tale, been merely the figure of Enid's clandestine lover, a childish, weak young man, more his wife's spoiled son than her husband, an irresponsible charming butterfly of a boy, whom nobody, not even Enid, had taken quite seriously.

Now it came to her with a sensation of strong shock that he had been taken very seriously by somebody. Some person had wished him the gravest, the most final ill of all. A butterfly had been murdered. Yes . . . someone had taken that butterfly very seriously indeed.

She put out her light and, in wrapper and slippers, went down into the book-lined room below her own where this butterfly had once amused himself.

There were no shades nor curtains for its enormous windows and she did not want to betray her own presence behind them at this hour, so made her firefly way about by the help of her tiny flash, step by step, as far as the big central desk. There she sat down, switched off her light and let the silent emptiness of the room possess her attention like a softly spoken tale.

Philip had sat there hour after hour working or pretending

to work at a book which was to be a history of the Hudson River. The river voice must have talked to him as, more loudly than usual, it now talked to her. That he should have considered the writing of this book at all, that he should, at least, have worked out its plan, collected his references, made his notes, proved a serious and scholarly, even if a dilettante, turn of mind. He must have loved his books, his solitude. A young man, very young, only twenty-four years old, with a crippled wife, content to employ himself thus tranquilly, content, it would seem, until the arrival of a lonely and lovely girl, a sentimental girl; a boy of twenty-four, handsome and eager and red-haired, who had so conducted himself towards his invalid wife that she implicitly believed in his devotion, this was a boy not perhaps to be too suddenly condemned. And perhaps too he had an even better pretext than Enid's seductiveness or his wife's invalidism or his own young male restlessness. Perhaps he had suspected or discovered an infidelity of her own, a tentative or actual betrayal. Perhaps Philip himself had been jealous of that young doctor who came to the house "socially when they needed an extra man" and who had been called in, rather superfluously Jenny now thought, for Anna's throat. Perhaps Philip had hated Roger Dean. There certainly was a man to be taken seriously. If somebody had murdered *him* . . . Jenny, shuddering, thought the motives might not have been so far to find.

When Philip quarreled with Enid Ambrose, threatening to confess the affair to his wife so that Enid would be dismissed, what had been his real motive? To drive the girl into unconditional surrender to his passion? That had been her own interpretation. But there might have been other reasons. He might have been genuinely repentant, anxious to be released, as Roger Dean had thought, from his entanglement, rid of his temptation. All of his notes to Enid she had destroyed and Jenny knew that women's memories, where their emotions are concerned, are not only short but extremely unreliable. It was not that Jenny mistrusted her mother's story but that she could not blind herself to the possibility of self-deception. Philip had been angry with Enid. Felicia's half-guilty protégée had thought it was because of her own resistance, but his motive might have been different and less flattering to her.

If Philip could only come back tonight to that room where he had spent so many long and tranquil hours before passion had mounted the spiral stairs to interrupt and to confuse him

... if Philip could come back and tell her his truth ... how welcome a ghost he would be! What a light his words would throw on the dark tangle of her comprehension.

She stood up from the desk and, her eyes being now accustomed to darkness, able to see the windows and the stars, she went over to them and looked out and down towards the dark river. Then she heard the whispering in Lizzie's room and knew that, again, more secretly, more quietly, the two servants were together and at their difficult gossiping. They must be sitting as far as possible from their shuttered window, muttering mouth to ear, not to disturb her sleep. Perhaps they were talking about Mary Ryan's troublesome visit, of which "Miss Felicia" must not know. Standing there, Jenny could see the broken ribbons of their light and hear the strained interchange of conversation.

There were stars in the black night sky and their light was stronger than she would have imagined possible, strong enough for her now, looking out and down from the dark room, to see, for example, the difference between sky and treetops and even the difference between the treetops and the ribbon of turf just below her tower wall. It seemed to her, as she looked, that something moved there, a shadow detaching itself from deeper shadows, a stealthy living presence of beast or man.

So quietly it emerged and moved along the turf, so close to invisibility, so nearly an integral part of the night, that it was not until it trod the bricks before the house door that Jenny's pulses confirmed her observation with a leap of conviction.

Someone was nearing the river entrance of Castania's big hall; someone was moving on rubber soles, without light, without sound.

Adam returning late, and careful not to wake his mother? Adam, who often prowled the ground at night and might find his way cat-eyed in the dark? It must be Adam, she told her panic, it must be ... But there was that in the stealthy movement of the shadow which sustained her doubt. There had never been a hint of stealth in Adam's big-boned body. It had the grace of strength and youth but it was all bone and muscle, control and steadiness. He could never, she thought, not even behind enemy lines, have slithered through the night like this panther-supple animal below the tower.

Slowly, with agonized pain, she gathered the strands of her courage together in the cold hands of her will. She must this time depend on her own powers, she must herself go down and meet that intruder and detect his identity and call him by his name. She must not allow herself to be a timid girl "alone in a dark house at night." She did not know how long she stood there, fighting her will to escape, to lock her bedroom door and hide behind it, but at last she went out and began to move quickly down the stairs. Motion brought back some measure of her courage. Her blood ran again, her heart beat more evenly. She would be able, she thought, to speak a firm and angry summons . . .

She had made only a few turns, however, when she knew that someone was coming up that staircase from below. The unexpectedness was too much for her and she took at once to flight, ran up the steps until she was behind the turn beyond the study door. Here she managed to control her action and stood still. Her breath was short, she had to tranquilize it; her heart was loud as an engine, she must quiet it . . . and all the while the step was coming up through the darkness. So slow, so soft, really not audible to her ears at all, she fancied, but to an extra sense, an antenna of sensibility, more touch than hearing. It was an incredibly cautious step, clad in rubber soles and bitterly intent on secrecy. A step that was acutely sensitive to her own supposed proximity in the room at the top of this stairs. Could it be possible that someone . . . anyone . . . had guessed her identity and had been terrified by her search, that somebody who had reason to fear her might have decided in a desperate and guilty mind to put her out of the way . . . at night . . . up there . . . in her dreadful loneliness? For the first time an icy and immediate fear, not of discovery but of her life, made her stomach flutter and her feet turn into lead.

There was time for her to get back into her own room and to lock its door.

A light now felt its way up the wall. It could not reach her there behind her turn until and unless its carrier passed the study door. Poised, almost winged for flight, she watched it, saw it waver, saw it disappear. It had been turned in at the study door and the body that held it must have stood still or have followed it for the sound of the step had dissolved itself into nothingness.

This must of course be Adam, who, not wanting to wake her, had gone thus noiselessly into that room.

She forced herself to believe that it was Adam and went quietly down, her hand against the wall to steady her shaking body, to aid her weak knees in their descent. Without it, she could hardly have kept her steps so quiet and gradual. She went down. Now the light in the study was visible, pointed steadily down across the low bookshelves below the windows, traveling along them like a seeking finger. The body that held it was crouched low, but, as she watched it, rose, holding one of the volumes, looking down. The light showed its sleeves and arms, dimly its bulk ... that of a tall, slender man in a loose tweed coat with rough hair, small-headed. Not somehow a frightening figure but an entirely strange one to Jenny Thorne. It had a look of being frightened but of knowing its way about. It ruffled the pages of the book, stooped to return it, taking out another.

Jenny spoke. "Who's that? What do you want?" she said and her voice was clear and loud as a trumpet in the night.

With that, out went the light, the figure leaped and ran. It thrust her violently out of its way and took the stairs like a running demon ... no caution for soundlessness, sheer, desperate, panic flight ... dumb flight. The flight of an extreme terror. The flight of an extreme guilt. Jenny followed. By the time she reached the lower hall, a cool air told her the door had been opened and closed. Suddenly her courage was completely gone. She managed weakly to drag herself to the front door; locked inside, its key in place; then to the back. Locked too. No key. Left on the outside, of course.

She listened. The house was no longer still for the river wind was up again. Not a chance now for her to hear a step so close to inaudibility. Should she rouse Felicia? Call Anna? Run down to the gardener's house? Telephone for the police?

Then she heard Felicia calling, "Who's that? Who's that?" in a high, shaken key and she went over to the bedroom door.

"It's Jenny, Mrs. Grise. May I come in?"

"You can't. The door is locked. All the doors are locked. Wait! No, perhaps Anna hasn't got back yet. She went up to visit with Lizzie. Come in through her room and the bath. What's wrong? You frightened me."

Jenny did not answer until she was in Felicia's room, looking down at the roused occupant of the bed. Felicia had switched on the lamp beside her, had pulled herself up against her pillows. She was flushed, her breath quick, her eyes in a blaze. She looked more than ever like an excited, lovely child.

"Tell me, Jenny. Tell me quickly. What's wrong? Why are you up?"

"Don't be frightened, Mrs. Grise. It's all right now. We're quite safe. But there was someone in the house."

Felicia's hands closed on her delicate silk-covered sheet. "Someone . . ." she panted. "Someone . . . Then Adam has come back!"

"It wasn't Adam. That's what I thought at first. And it wasn't John. Or the gardener. I was at my window." Jenny would not confess her midnight expedition to Philip's study, "and I just *almost* saw somebody coming along the Narrow Garden . . ."

"*Almost* saw?"

"Yes. It was like a piece of darkness moving away from other darkness. And then I *almost* heard . . . steps on the bricks and someone at the back door of the hall. Wasn't that locked?"

"It should be, always . . . yes."

"This man must have had a key. I . . . I was coming down . . ."

"Oh, Jenny! Little Jenny! You shouldn't. You mustn't. So little and so brave!"

The beauty of that tender voice almost brought to Jenny's eyes the foolish wetness of self-pity. She hurried on, "I started down the tower stairs and then, somehow, I *knew* that somebody . . . that it . . . it was coming up. I couldn't exactly hear but I knew there was a step. I wasn't at all brave. I put out my light and ran. But, beyond one of the turns . . . above that little landing, you know the one, perhaps, before the study door . . . I stopped myself and waited.

"And presently I saw the . . . his light. It didn't come farther. It went into the study and . . . the man went after it."

Felicia waited. Just as a child waits, breathless, for the climax of an exciting tale.

"So then . . . then I got myself down and I saw that there was a man in there, looking at a book. It wasn't anyone I ever saw before. But perhaps you may recognize him."

Felicia, whiter now than her sheet, whispered, "Tell me! Tell me!"

"He wore a loose brown tweed coat and, I think, an open-collared white shirt. And . . . and he was thin and tall. He had rather rough hair. I couldn't tell the color. That's all I could see for, when I spoke, I just said the way you always do, 'Who's that? What do you want?' or something . . . he put out the light and went by me and down the stairs like a demon. I mean, a rush of evil and of fear. Horribly fast. Hor-

ribly afraid. By the time I got to the lower hall, the back
door was closing and he locked it on the outside. I tried both
the doors. The key was in the front one but not in the back.
But it was certainly locked. Oh, Mrs. Grise, let me phone for
the police!"

Felicia put out her hand, felt for Jenny's as though through
a fog and laid the long fingers close about her wrist. "No,
Jenny. No. The police must never again come into this house.
Not into this house. Besides ... I know now who that man
was."

Her hand went back to join its fellow on the sheet and she
sank down deep into her pillows. "There's nothing to be
afraid of. That is, there's nothing to be afraid of if you hold
your tongue. If you tell nobody in all the world."

"But you will tell me, Mrs. Grise!"

Felicia's blue eyes searched Jenny's face. She smiled faintly
and shook her head. "I wish I could. I wish I could."

"Does Dr. Dean know?"

"Nobody but me knows. Nobody but me will ever know. I
wouldn't for the world have told you that he existed, Jenny,
but, since you've seen him, seen my . . . ghost, my spectre,
my familiar, then, there's nothing for me to do but trust you
to the extent of asking you with all my strength to keep the
secret ... the foolish, frightening secret of my life, oh, it's
not tragic . . . not wicked . . ."

Jenny whispered, "Was it he ... who killed ... your husband?" at which Felicia gasped, "No! My God! No. No.
Never say that. Never think that, Jenny." She dragged herself
close. "Jenny, my darling little nurse and friend, I do love
you and I feel that you love me. Don't you? A little?"

Jenny answered tremulously, "Yes. More than a little . . ."
and tasted tears in her throat.

"I'm very lonely. I've been hurt so much and so often. I've
been so many times betrayed. But you're young and sweet
and you have the nobility not only of your nature but of
your profession. What a nurse learns in the intimacy of her
work is sacred, isn't it? It must be or nobody would ever
have a nurse at all—least of all—Felicia Grise. I brought you
here for a special mission, a very confidential mission, and
you accepted it. Didn't you, Jenny?"

"Yes, Mrs. Grise, I did."

"You wouldn't have stayed here at all unless you'd been on
my side, unless you'd been willing to pledge yourself to help
me loyally, in silence. I know you've kept your word. I know

you haven't told Roger Dean the real reason why I wanted you here at Castania. And that has made me very sure of you. Now, Jenny dear, brave little nurse and friend, I know you'll keep this queer visit, this queer visitor, a secret. Just between us. Just between you and me, Jenny. In all the treacherous, unfaithful world. Look at me, Jenny ... not with that wild, secret, runaway look, but with the honest one, the open one, the brave one. Smile at me. You've been scared half to death, I know. I promise you, on my honor, it won't happen again."

"He was looking at the books," Jenny whispered. "He was looking for something—up there—in the tower."

"I know, I know. Please, Jenny, forget it all. What can it possibly mean to you? What difference can it possibly make? Soon you'll be leaving Castania, leaving Barent, going away from our stupid old mystery, our sorrow which was buried and almost forgotten until Adam, in his derangement, brought it to life. It can be of no significance to you, Jenny Thorne ... any of it. Why should you care that Mrs. Philip Grise, poor old woman! has more than one secret in her life? More than one problem she hasn't been able in all these years to solve? Isn't that true, Jenny? Tell me."

Jenny was under a double spell: Felicia's and her mother's. She chose her path by the light of immediate emotion, of immediate expediency ... for how could she explain her willingness to stay on, her interest in all these events?

"Of course, I promise not to speak about this ... this man, Mrs. Grise. Not to tell anyone what I saw and heard. But don't you think, perhaps, we should have John or ... a night watchman ... ?"

Felicia actually laughed. "Silly! You just don't believe me, do you? Didn't I tell you I knew all about this man and understood his visit? Didn't I tell you he wouldn't come again? Believe me, if I'd had any common sense I wouldn't have allowed him to come this time. Now, Jenny, please, you must go back to your room. Quietly. As quietly as you came out of it. And when you've had time to get back, I'll ring for Anna. Then we'll all go to sleep. I will and so will you. And you won't be frightened any more, ever. Promise me again." She drew herself up and put her hand on Jenny's arm. "Promise me," she said solemnly, "on your honor. Before God."

Jenny's pale young lips moved faithfully. "Unless you release me, Mrs. Grise, I do promise to be silent. On my honor. Before God."

Felicia shook her arm tenderly and sank back. "Now, you go up and when you're well out of the way and in your own room I'll ring up Lizzie's room. All's well, Jenny, believe me. All is well."

She said it with a ring of conviction; with a reassuring confidence.

And Jenny believed her. She was foolish enough to believe her. She did as she was told . . . went up to her own room and shut and locked her door. She felt safe with Felicia's assurance ringing in her ears. Yes, she actually felt safe!

Chapter Fifteen

A thin man in a brown tweed coat, a man in an open-collared white shirt; a man with narrow feet in sneakers.

Jenny found, next day, footprints, one at the edge of the turf. The night intruder, it would seem, had come up the bank from the river by a flight of hidden rock slab steps, she had not before discovered. These were overgrown by a thicket of small low-growing shrubs, ending close to Felicia's turf, almost at the spot where she spent her sunset hour of remote uninterrupted meditation. From there the steps led down to a little cove with a dilapidated bathhouse. The deep water here was hidden from the railroad, which passed far out from point to point on a trestle that left the water beneath it alive. Here, it seemed, Adam had been taught to swim by the father who, in Enid's account, had not liked children, had had to be coaxed to spend any of his time with his own little son. Anna had volunteered this bit of information in a postscript to her muffled talk about Lizzie's niece that morning.

Jenny had found Felicia's maid making up the tower room and had risked a casual seeming question.

"Tell me, Anna, did they come for Lizzie's niece?"

"Oh yes'm. Poor Lizzie. She was that thankful. It's only happened once before. The girl's aunt and uncle look out real good for her. It's only on their promise and the way they've kept it that the poor girl has been left out from asylum. She's harmless but usin' the name of the poor lady that was supposed to kill Mr. Philip kind of made her seem more dangerous . . . if you know what I mean."

Jenny knew and said so. "When did she begin to be like this, Anna?"

"Oh, it come on gradual, after the trial. Though to tell you the truth, Miss Thorne, she always seemed kind of flighty like to me. Everyone liked Mary. She was a happy-lookin' kid them days with red cheeks and great big laughing eyes and a dimple so deep that Mr. Philip used to say, 'Look out,

Adam, someday you'll fall into Mary's dimple and we'll never find you again.' Adam was such a little fellow them days." Anna sighed. "Mary was like another child, always laughing and playing tricks but she begun to overdo it like. That's one reason I guess why Miss Felicia got the child a proper governess."

"Overdo it?" prompted Jenny listening with all her ears.

"Yes'm. Practical jokes like. She hid Mr. Philip's clothes when he went swimmin' down to the little bathin' beach where he taught the two of them to swim, Adam and Mary, that is. He said, Mary must be able to take care of Adam asea and ashore. And then she took to hidin' things; queer little tricks like a monkey or one of these here tame crows you read about. People thought she was funny first off but it got to be annoyin'. Old Mrs. Grise, now, took Mary's part . . . well, you know how it is with womenfolks in a house—they's always sides for and against.—Well, me, I begun to suspect the poor thing wasn't just exactly matoor. Nor she wasn't. She begun to be quite wild after Miss Ambrose come here. She didn't like Miss Felicia gettin' in a governess over her head like. Oh, she was jealous all right.

"We was goin' to send her away" . . . Anna often used this pronoun, so closely did she identify herself with her beloved mistress, "when," she sighed, "there come that awful crash." Philip's death to Anna was always "that awful crash." "It kind of sobered Mary up. She got right quiet and steady and was a good straight witness more sensible than you'd ever suspect now. And after the trial she went back to her folks real quiet and subdued. And the next thing we heard from Lizzie was that she'd do nothin' but read about the trial and think and talk about Enid Ambrose. For a long while it was 'she' and 'her' then she seemed to be confused like and begun to talk about 'I' and 'me' like she was Enid. It was all sort of gradual and harmless, no violence nor nothin' except she'd get mad if you corrected her." Anna sighed. "Seems as if that trial did mischief to most all of us. My hearin' was always poor but it wasn't till after that I begun to get real deaf. Up until then Miss Felicia was like a girl. Pink in her cheeks like the lovely free young lady she used to be! I thought she was goin' to get well."

It was rarely that either of the two women was so communicative and Jenny felt advantage must be taken of her opportunity. How, she wondered, without breaking her promise of last night, question Anna about a thin man in a brown tweed coat?

"It's a wonder to me," she said, "that Mary would come so far as this . . . all the way across the river . . ."

"Oh, she can find her way about all right. She's as sane as anyone except only on the one subject."

"How long does it take you to walk to the village, Anna?"

"About thirty minutes fast steppin'."

"There's no nearer stores or Post Office to Castania?"

"No, miss. Glaston, the next town, is far up the river as Barent is down it and a picayune place."

"The neighbors always use Barent, then."

"We haven't got what you'd call neighbors, miss. The hospital's closest."

"Do they take care of any mental cases there?"

"Not that I know of. They've got an incurable ward like, donated by old Mr. Grise, Mr. Philip's father. But they'd be bodily diseased like, I guess. Dr. Dean would know likely. But Lizzie wouldn't put Mary there. She'd keep her with her own folks across the river."

The man in the brown tweed coat . . . a conspicuously warm garment even for midnight in this weather, had come up from the water by way of the bathing beach . . . where a narrow rubber-soled print betrayed him close to the water's edge. He might have come by a boat or he might have come afoot over the rocky point that separated this cove from the larger rocky beach of Philip's death. A chronic patient would hardly be allowed to wander about at midnight even if he was strong enough, but Jenny could not rid her mind of the hospital ward, donated by old Mr. Ferguson Grise for incurables.

She would ask Dr. Dean.

She said, "A jolly playmate like Mary used to be must have been just what little Adam would need most, Anna. He with no brothers or sisters . . . ?"

"Yes'm," said Anna, suddenly curt, gathered up soiled linen, broom and carpet sweeper and went out.

That decision to question Roger Dean was not so simple to carry out as it once would have been. There's nothing static she discovered in human relationships. She thought back to the time only a few weeks ago, May, and now it was August, when she had first set eyes on these people of Barent and Castania. Roger, tall, formal and courteous, coming into his sitting room to look over a candidate nurse . . . Felicia . . .

radiant at the open threshold of her sun-filled hall, and
Adam, curt, arrogant, turning his back upon her that first
evening in Castania's living room. To them all she had been
Miss Thorne, a stranger, and an employee. While to her they
had been possible suspects, her mother's enemies, material
for espionage. Whereas now ... Roger a determined man
who had made up his mind to marry her. Felicia, a beloved,
helpless yet powerful reality. And Adam ... Adam ...

Here in Jenny's diary ...

"Adam is back. Adam is here. Adam is in the house again.
I heard him coming up the tower stairs ... my stairs ... our
stairs ... like a strong wind. His coming, after that dark
night wind of guilty flight, had a clean strength."

At the sound of those steps she stood up from her search.
Following the queer visitor's example she had been looking
into Adam's child books beneath the windows ... and there
stood Adam himself at the threshold, glowing, smiling.

"So you're at it again. That means, I hope, that you've forgiven me and are glad to see me back. Or are you? I'm here
as a sort of human worm. There's nothing like getting away
from Castania to clear a man's head. Jenny, I was, as you
said, out of my mind. You couldn't be anyone's agent, least
of all that slimy doctor's. Come here and give me your hand.
I'm not sure I want to go on with this darn cataloguing but I
want that hand. Plenty. And quick."

Jenny came over to him and gave him her hand. He took
more of her than that. His mouth was on her own again, his
arms around her.

"There! I feel better. How about you? Better or worse?"

"Both, I think," said Jenny, getting herself back, putting
the width of the room between his excitement and her own.
"Better because you don't suspect me any more. And worse,
because ..."

"Because what?"

"Of so many things," she told him sadly, "that I can't tell
you about. Why do you want to stop cataloguing the books?
I was ... I am ... sort of ... intrigued."

"You must be ... even nosing through that child's library.
Find anything?"

"No."

"Father wouldn't have been likely to put notes in those
books, silly! Well, if you're interested, we might as well finish
the job. I'd like to suggest a change in method however."

He had pursued her to the windows and teased her there with his deep-set eyes.

"I suggest we work together on the same side of the room, on the same section, the same shelf, and, if possible, the same volume. No? I stand corrected. Back to where you were, Grise."

"Tell me about your trip?" she asked to break a busy silence which beat upon her ears.

"I met Tommy and some of the other boys. Told them I'd be back with them soon."

"Adam, have you seen your mother yet?"

"No. She is always resting at this time of day. I came right up here . . . to you."

"I hope you'll see her soon. I hope you'll spend the whole afternoon with her alone. On the verandah."

He turned with a book in still hands.

"Why, Jenny?"

"Because she is terribly worried about you and alarmed. Because this . . . this effort of yours to find out what she wants everyone—you especially—to forget has driven her to the point of . . . of accepting a suggestion, a piece of advice . . ."

"Look here, Jenny." He threw the book violently down on the desk, strode up to her. "What are you trying to tell me anyhow?"

"I'm not trying to tell you. I'm trying to warn you, Adam. You accused me of being Roger Dean's agent but what I'm doing now is informing against him. Adam, he believes that you . . ."

"Go on. Why stop? He believes that I am . . . dangerous."

"He believes that you are in a condition . . . a mental condition that would justify your mother in giving him authority and evidence to—to have you—locked up."

His lips repeated without sound "locked up" and added aloud, "In an insane asylum."

"In a sanitarium perhaps."

His teeth drove into his lip. He became possessed with a fury so white and stiff and still that it was like the centre of a tornado. It made Jenny shrink and hold her breath. She whispered, "Don't."

He began without moving, or wiping off the blood that burst from his bitten lip, to speak in a low rapid voice. "Put me in an insane asylum. Dangerous. By God, it's what I am now. I'm dangerous, Roger Dean, to you and to your plans and to your secrets and to your dirty, slimy, hiding life.

"If I don't strip you bare to the dirty skin of your soul and lash the life out of you, I'm no son of a murdered man. Mad? Yes, by God, I'm mad. I'm mad the way Hamlet was mad. 'A little more than kin and less than kind.' He's hidden behind petticoats all his life. He's going to get out from under them now even if they get torn to tatters too. Here, Jenny. Let me out of this. Mother wants to have me put out of the way, does she? She thinks I'm dangerous . . ."

And with that his rage broke into an agony of hurt love, broken trust, beaten pride. He went first to the desk, blind, stopping there over his hands, then looked up at Jenny helplessly.

"Get out," he said, "for God's sake." Tears were pouring down his face.

And she went closing the door as gently as she could.

But out there on the small landing something held her, something drew her. She could not leave. Not knowing that she had moved at all she found herself back in the sun-filled room beside him with her hand upon his head.

"Adam. Don't. Your mother loves you. She is afraid. When people are afraid, they don't know that they are cruel. Please go to her, talk to her."

"There's no one," he gasped, "no one,"—and with that he got up and caught her, holding her head down against his breast. She heard the labor of his heart, felt his kisses on her hair. They did not speak. She did not have a word in her mind nor in her heart. They were interrupted in their silence by a calling up the stairs. Old Mrs. Grise's voice, "Adam, are you up there? I want to see you please."

And Adam, letting Jenny go, was able to smile.

"There's a friend," he said. "Yes, Gran, I'm here. I'm coming. Don't take those crooked steps." He went out to the landing. "I'll be right down. See you in your room in about five minutes. O.K.?"

She croaked, "O.K." and they heard her at the stair's foot close the door. Adam, returning, said, "I'll go down and talk to her, Jenny. Then I'll see mother." He controlled a spasm of his racked face. "Perhaps I can persuade her that I'm fit to be a free man. I'll tell her in any case that I've given up my plan. I've got to hoodwink Dean and, as long as Dean's in mother's confidence, I've got to hoodwink her."

"Then you mean you won't really give it up?" Jenny faltered.

"No. I'm going on ... and through. I don't care where it gets me nor what it does to me ... or to them. To tell you the truth, Jenny, I don't give a damn for anyone in the world but you. Maybe you've guessed that. Good-bye for now. I'll be seeing you." He went down a few steps, stopped and his warm voice came softly up to her, "God bless you, darling."

Jenny, in a shaken tone, called back, "Don't be afraid of them. Take control of your mother, Adam. Be the master in your own house."

There was a short laugh and, again, the closing of the door.

Chapter Sixteen

It was Jenny's free afternoon and she wanted Adam to be alone with Felicia. She walked to Barent, thinking she would go to Dean in his office. That would give the interview an impersonal setting, favorable for her intentions. She went, bare-legged and sandalled, wearing her coolest frock. The lights on her hair sparkled in and out like fireflies as she moved from sun to shade. "A spy in enemy country," she told herself with grimness, "has to use every advantage. A woman spy deliberately wins men to find out their secrets. If I am loved by Roger Dean, I have power I ought to use for my purpose ... for the sake of my mother, who is the one person to whom I owe allegiance, truth and loyalty. Adam will be relentless now. He will work day and night. And his grandmother's influence upon him is strong. It is a race between us and he has the inside track. I must take what I can get. I must. God help me to be cold and firm."

She was neither. Well she knew that she was neither. She summoned her mother's image. She remembered Nick. To Nick she clung, blindly! Nick of the blue eyes and the sane mind. Nick of no violent rages, of no clammy or sweating brow. Nick with no haunting fears, only love. Steady and loyal love.

If she should get his letter today, the one assuring her that nothing in her mother's past nor future could change his devotion, his desire to have her for his wife? Adam's voice repeated his "God bless you, darling" and she was cold under the hot August sun. For this was August, the first day of August. It had been April when she signed her name in The Dutch House register. Four months since she had left Enid Ambrose. The image of that mother had almost been effaced by the image of Castania's heroine, the lovely young governess who had beguiled Philip—no matter how innocently—to his death. That Enid was with her day and night and yet that Enid was still a mystery.

"Yes," thought Jenny, "it's time for me to see mother again. Now, I can really see her for the first time in my life. I can look into her heart, her mind, her soul. When I see Enid Ambrose now she won't be hidden from me because of being my lovely sad strange mother, a fugitive. Now she'll be Felicia's Enid and Philip's Enid and the Enid whom Roger Dean despised ... Poor Enid Ambrose! Again she'll come before a judge and jury ... all of them in my face and be tried for her life." But this time, Jenny swore, she will be acquitted, she will be sent out free. Her name will be her own and she can have a home. No matter, really, what happened to Jenny Thorne; Jenny has no importance. She was never a real person at all. She is only a shadow of the past, a sort of ghost. She has just one reality, her power to discover truth, her love that casts out fear. And for Jenny, as it was not for Enid, that love must be a good and honest love.

Yet already she was guilty, a traitor to her mother and to Nick. For she had let Adam kiss her, hold her in his arms. And in those arms she had been no spy. Here, she was all but struck by a car emerging from the entrance to the hospital. Dr. Dean ground on his brakes and swore.

"Look out for yourself. For God's sake ... You, Jenny! Are you trying to be killed? Where are you going? It's too hot for walking into Barent."

His face when its startled fear had vanished was vivid with pleasure at the encounter, vivid and beautiful. It was a face with a sort of translucence, emotion working upon it from within like light on parchment. "Get in. As long as you've scared the wits out of me you should make me some amends. Off for the post office, I suppose."

"Yes."

"Good! I can drop you there. I'm on my way for a visit. Perhaps I can pick you up somewhere later and bring you back to Castania."

Jenny got in. She could think of no excuse and his delight had its appeal to her woman instinct to give more delight. But she was uncomfortable. She had especially wanted to avoid this sort of tête-à-tête. She did not know how to start her questioning about the incurables; could think of nothing else to say.

He spoke first. "Heard from your pursuer lately?" he asked. "The young North Carolina doctor who's kept in by army regulations?"

"No," said Jenny. "I've been expecting a letter but it hasn't come."

"Maybe you weren't sufficiently encouraging."

"Maybe I wasn't," Jenny answered truthfully, thinking of the dreadful burden of the amassed letters she had sent to Nick, enough to silence him forever. How could she dare to hope that he would still care to win her to be his wife?

"He makes you unhappy, that lieutenant doctor, doesn't he?"

"Yes."

"Poor little Jenny! Why not forget him? There are people nearer by, you know."

She put her hand on his and felt him start.

"Please, Roger Dean. You don't know what a riddle my life is or . . . or you wouldn't even dream of getting yourself mixed up with it. I wish . . ." Unexpected tears came to her eyes so that to brush them away she withdrew the hand under which, after the start, he had sat still.

"I wish I could depend upon your friendship. I do dreadfully need a friend."

"It's a hard thing to come by, Jenny, when you're a woman 'beautiful and young.' I can't be your friend, my girl. Don't cheat yourself with the hope. I'm not much given to that sort of relationship with women anyway."

"It's what I need," she murmured. "It's all I need."

"Forgive me, Jenny. That's a lie. And you know it's a lie. You may need a friend but only because you think you already have a lover." He spoke in a steady low tone. "Young Adam Grise."

She looked him full in the face—

"Adam," she said, "is not my lover. We are going into Barent. Put me down now, if you please."

He stopped the car. "You're angry. Oh, what a wildcat! So there's something in it! You are white and red and white again and your mouth is tight either because Adam is your lover or because he isn't, and you want him to be. You see I'm something of an analyst myself. I've known a good many women in my life, known them rather well. Why shouldn't I be able to see through Jenny, twenty-two . . . and not half so mysterious as she thinks she is? All right . . . All right. You may get out . . . don't kill yourself, will you? And I wish you'd do something for me, nurse."

She stood at the curb, staring, astonished by his change of tone, its absence of feeling, malicious or affectionate.

"My office is just round the corner from the post office. A woman is coming there this afternoon whom I shan't have time to see. No patient. A visitor who announced herself by telephone. It's Sarah Wingate, Miss Sarah Wingate. She'll account for herself. And amply. Will you just receive her for me? Let her look about and sentimentalize for a few minutes? Too much of a chore . . . to do for a man who isn't your friend?"

"Of course not, doctor. I'll go in. She will be there now?"

He looked at his wrist watch. "Any minute. There's nobody there at present. Thank you."

He gave her his key, started his engine and was gone.

Chapter Seventeen

Jenny presently admitted a large pink-faced hot woman in a brightly flowered silk dress to Dr. Dean's waiting room. She stood with her hands folded together looking sadly about from under a flowered hat. Jenny, assuming her most professional manner, asked, "Are you looking for Dr. Dean? I'm afraid you're too late for office hours. He has gone out on a case. His regular attendant is not here now—but I'm a trained nurse on one of Dr. Dean's private cases. Perhaps I can do something for you. There is no one else here this afternoon at all."

"Oh," sighed the big woman gustily, "I know the regular attendant's not here. I wanted to be here alone, if I could be, miss . . . so's I could sort of put myself back."

"You were here before?"

"Yes, indeed, I was Dr. Elliot's office assistant. The old doctor—perhaps you've heard of him . . ."

"I certainly have. He must have been a wonderful man. Many of his old patients miss him, talk about him."

"I'm glad to hear he's been remembered. But it was a long time ago. Twenty years is quite a stretch. I was young then. I'm here for a day and couldn't resist dropping in. I wrote to Dr. Dean and he told me to feel free. He might be in and might not. I rather hoped he wouldn't be, miss . . . I felt so badly when Dr. Elliot retired and sold out and went away. Just couldn't reconcile myself to him giving up. So wise he was and so capable."

"Was it because of his age, Miss . . ."

"Wingate. Sarah Wingate."

"And I'm Jenny Thorne."

"It wasn't so much his age physically, Miss Thorne. He was in good shape. It was his memory. It was getting awfully poor. I'd noticed it myself. I had to keep reminding him and he had to jot everything down . . . the least little thing. So, a few times, he made some pretty bad slips and that scared him. He was an awfully conscientious man."

She went over to the office, opened the door with reverence and looked in. "Seems as if he must be there now looking up so mildly from his desk. God bless him! He was certainly a beloved physician."

"What a shame his memory failed him. Did he get into any trouble, Miss Wingate?"

"Nothing as bad as that. There were a couple of things that worried him. He gave a wrong prescription to a little Mrs. Carter. Nothing dangerous luckily. A mild laxative instead of a tonic. Then once he lost a whole supply of drugs. That is, he thought he'd laid a quantity of certain drugs or a drug—I'm not sure which—on a shelf in the inner office but when he went to lay hands on it . . . well, it just wasn't there. And he never could find the record of that order. Though we both looked everywhere. So he just came to the conclusion he'd forgotten to order it."

Miss Wingate then went across the office to the door of the small storeroom that held its cold and empty stove.

She looked wistfully at the self-lined walls.

"It's neater, I must say, than he'd let me keep it for him. They say this Dr. Dean's a fine physician." She muttered to herself, "Yes, I was certain, myself, that package was there. I don't rightly remember. But I was always sure it stood right there"—she lumbered over to set her big pink finger on the spot—"and I thought somebody might have stolen it. But," here she turned to Jenny, "you know, I never said a word. I didn't dare. I never even whispered it to doctor. Nor to anyone. I dare say it was wrong of me. I never could make up my mind, but all that's water long ago passed under the bridge now, thank heaven."

Jenny's heart had begun that now-habitual pounding. She wet her lips for the question. "If it had happened when the famous Castania trial came on . . . it would have worried you all right, Miss Wingate."

Miss Wingate's face lost all its pink.

She put a hand uncertainly to her mouth and her eyes moved uneasily from side to side. She came out of the inner room and closed the door.

"I see you know your Barent, Miss Thorne. That's pretty old history now."

"They still talk about it, though. The powder in the broken teacup was cyanide, you know. And I should think if there'd been such stuff here at that time, to your knowledge, you'd be in a pretty tight spot. Of course, you wouldn't dare mention it, not being at all sure of your own knowledge and with no record to back you."

Miss Wingate looked almost ludicrously relieved. "I'm glad you think so, Miss Thorne. That I did the right thing. But it's weighed on me dreadfully at times. You see, as you say, I wasn't sure enough and there was nothing to offer in proof of a statement. I looked everywhere and couldn't find an order or a receipt or a bill or anything. Of course Dr. Elliot was awfully vague and careless those last days. He really was."

"And you had no suspicion at all of course; nobody having had a chance to get in here and take stuff naturally."

"Well," she shook her big head, "it wasn't so much nobody having a chance as everybody having a chance. Anyone who had the run of Dr. Elliot's home. The rooms are all connected up . . . and he was casual about locking things away. Some old familiar patient who got left a few minutes in this inner office or some working woman or tradesman. It's not a thing you'd feel like giving names to, naturally."

"Certainly not. But if the old familiar patients visiting his office at that time were from Castania I should think you *might* have felt uneasy."

"Say, you're really interested, aren't you?"

Jenny, in considerable discomfort, said she was, that a hung case was always "sort of intriguing."

"Well, of course, I couldn't help but think of it myself. But the trouble was, most all of the Castania folks had been in here one way or another. Lizzie and Anna dropped in a couple of times for Mrs. Philip's medicine and old Mrs. Grise had her nose blown out . . . she had sinus trouble pretty terribly at that time. And . . . yes, Mr. Philip himself was in here several times and stayed a long while talking to the doctor . . ."

"He's hardly a subject for suspicion," prompted Jenny for Miss Wingate had fallen into a long and brooding silence, with a finger stuck deeply into her heavy cheek.

"The Ambrose girl herself brought little Adam in . . . he was a kind of nervous kid, had nightmares."

Jenny's heart protested. No. No. Enid was never in this office. Not in those fatal days before the crime.

Aloud she asked weakly, "Did Dr. Elliot keep a record of his cases?"

"Yes. He did but it was more like a journal and I believe he burned up about twenty volumes before he left. Such a shame!"

Jenny was astonished. "Why on earth did he do that?" she

added. "Dr. Dean has one volume though, Miss Wyngate. So he says."

"Has he really. I'd dearly love to own that. I believe I'll ask him to let me have it. Dr. Elliot must have overlooked it ... you see ... that's how he was, poor man! And a doctor can't feel safe if he doesn't trust his own memory."

Jenny thought, "Neither a doctor nor any of his patients."

Sarah Wingate, who had forgotten her sentimental intentions in alarm at her own inadvertent confidence, came out of the inner room and shut the door, as though she would have liked never to open it.

Her face was all puckered with doubt and with distress.

"I can't think how I happened to tell you all this and I hope you won't take it very seriously, Miss Thorne. I think I've made it sound more important than it was. You being so interested and clever about questioning, as though you half knew about it all already. It was never more than just a sort of vague worry ... and Dr. Elliot never got on to it at all. By the time of the trial, he was moving out and the deal with Dr. Dean was being completed. I don't think he ever associated the possible disappearance of the drugs ... if there ever was such a package ... with the Castania tragedy at all. It was only me that had the notion and it was silly of me, I guess. But once the idea got into my head, it stuck there and it has worried me off and on ever since."

She sighed heavily. "I guess I'm glad I did speak about it after all. It's helped to clear my conscience, you agreeing that I did the right thing not to talk."

"You had no evidence, nothing but the most unfounded suspicion. You couldn't actually remember seeing the drugs and you never found a scrap of paper about an order. So ... what else was there for you to do except ... forget it? And I hope you will forget it now, Miss Wingate. And stop worrying. After all, you know," Jenny actually managed a light soft laughter, "it happened twenty years ago! And nobody was sentenced. So you haven't *that* on your mind."

"It was a hung sentence, I know. But it must have been a dreadful shadow on that poor thing's life. I wonder what's become of her. Oh dear! She was such a beautiful girl. And so gentle. And that Philip Grise was a nice fellow too. Very friendly and pleasant. Not at all the sort of boy ... for he was a boy, wasn't he? ... to come to a violent end. Well, I suspect I'd better be moving on. I've got to take a train tonight. It's been a real pleasure to know you, Miss Thorne. I hope we'll meet again. And you won't say anything about all this, will you? I oughtn't to've mentioned it, I know. I still don't quite see how I came to do it. I was sort of talking to myself and . . . you seemed to enter right into my mind. An odd thing really, wasn't it? Good-bye and thank you. And please forget everything I babbled about. There's nothing in it, you know. Just a piece of moonshine."

"I'm sure you'll agree that there's no reason why I should think of it a second time, Miss Wingate. Twenty years ago! I don't belong in Barent, anyway, and won't be here very much longer. I was just idly interested . . . a fellow professional interest, you might say. And I hope I helped to clear your mind on the subject."

"Oh, you did. You did."

Alone again in the outer office, Jenny sat down quietly with its ghosts.

Enid holding by the hand a little nervous boy.

Old Mrs. Grise, in young maturity, vain, impatient of her sinus infection, flirting with the old doctor, curious, peering about from under a smart tilted hat.

Anna and Lizzie . . . Jenny could not imagine them younger or different, the one sturdily, the other irritably fulfilling a commission for "Miss Felicia."

Philip, curly-haired, narrow-waisted, in an open-collared shirt . . . here a thought stiffened Jenny's fluency, a cold thought. An idea that took slow misty shape like the substantiation of a spirit. That night visitor had had the look of Philip in his portrait.—She had not time to see more than its premonitory outline, feel the cold spirit wind across her flesh, when the phone on the attendant's desk across the room rang shrill and loud. She ran to answer it.

A voice said, "Is this Dr. Roger Dean's office?" and her heart stopped.

She saw, through the window, that Dean was about to come into his inner office. He had parked his car and was climbing to the pavement.

"No," she murmured.

"I can't hear you," said the anxious voice.

"Dr. Dean is out. I'm his nurse. Can you leave a message?"

"Jenny! It's you. Thank God! This is Nick speaking. I was trying to find out if you could be reached by phone at . . . what's the name . . . the place up the river . . . ?"

"Oh, no, Nick. Please!"

"O.K. I've got just three minutes before I have to report. I won't waste a second. Listen, Jenny. You must leave Barent at once. Go to Hotel Wilson, West 11th Street, a small quiet place. Wire me when you get there. I'll come the first free day. Soon."

"But, Nick . . ."

"Be quiet. Don't you know you're in danger of your life? I've read all your letters . . ." Here Dr. Dean came into his inner office, closing the outer door. Nick's voice rushed on, "What's blinding you, child? Why have you set up your opinion of a romantic schoolgirl against the considered and experienced judgment of a devoted mother and a physician who cares? I can't talk . . ."

"But, Nick, you forget . . ."

"No more time, Jenny. Do what I say. Promise me . . ."

"I promise to wire you . . . Oh, Nick!"

He had hung up. Dean came into the room.

He stood for a long minute looking down at the flushed uncertainty which she was not at once able to disguise. "Your captain doctor has quite a lot of sense," he said then, smiling. "Forgive me. I took up my receiver instinctively in there. I heard only one sentence . . . his diagnosis of your danger at Castania and it supports mine, Jenny, doesn't it?" He bent over her, set his hand on hers which was made into a tight fist on top of the desk. "Now maybe you will agree that when a devoted mother believes, against her will, that her one and only son is in a serious mental condition and when she is confirmed in that belief by her family physician who, better than anyone, knows the history of that family . . ."

Jenny began, "But Nick didn't mean . . ." and bit off her speech. For her own interpretation of Nick's sentence . . . the mother and doctor in question being Enid Ambrose and Nick himself, was not one she could safely repeat or explain to any of Castania's inhabitants. She substituted a lame, "Oh, I see. Yes," and stood up wearily.

"I'll take you up the road as far as the hospital entrance, Jenny," said Dean. "I've an appointment there at three o'clock."

Jenny got into his car. Her mind in the last few minutes had done an about-face. Dean was probably right, Nick had meant Felicia and Felicia's doctor. It was by all odds the most rational explanation of his warning and of his state of mind. In reading her own letters, all at one time, in detachment, without prejudice, he had seen clear evidence of

Adam's insanity, the danger to herself of that lonely tower of
hers, of those hours of uninterrupted tête-à-tête. That was
what he meant by her "romanticism." A young aviator, handsome, heroic, pitiful—yes . . . she had sentimentalized Adam's
situation and her own. Whereas Nick, with cool professional
detachment and experience, had been able to diagnose the
rages, the suspicion and the fear, the abnormal determination
to re-open the case of his father's murder. And Nick had understood that at the moment when Adam should suddenly
discover that the one human creature he had decided to trust
and to love . . . was the daughter of Enid Ambrose, who had
come to his home and won his confidence with the sole purpose of accusing someone in Castania of crime . . . at that
moment——

"Roger," she heard herself saying in a small cold voice, "is
there . . . has there ever been in the Grise family history . . .
a taint of . . . of insanity?"

Dr. Dean said, "Ah," in a tone of satisfaction and stopped
his car. "Here's where I must drop you, Jenny. Your . . .
lover told you to trust me, didn't he? Did you tell him that I
had lost my head over you? No. I see you did not. Is that a
good or a bad sign, I wonder? Ah, now you jump down in a
hurry . . . well, I'll think it out and let you know. Perhaps a
quick blush and a quick get-away are compliments from a little female faun . . . Oh, there she goes." He was laughing.
She heard his taunting and pursuing voice, "Are you wondering why I'm not jealous? I'll let you find that out for yourself."

She checked her flight, by which she was suddenly bewildered and shamed, crossed the shady footpath and sat down
on a low creeper-covered stone wall. She thought, "I'll give
myself just one week more. I'll try out every clue to its end.
I'll favor nobody. There will be no more prejudice, no senti-
ment. I'll be ruthless. I'll be quick. And, on the seventh day
of August, win or lose, I'll leave Barent. I'll go to New York
and I'll wire Nick. And . . . when he comes . . . I'll let him
take me into his safe, safe arms." She sat at peace, in a stillness of heart, unreal, incredible.

After that dazed instant, she looked down at her wrist
watch and rose.

It was three o'clock. The ferry crossed from Barent to
Cragge every twenty minutes. She had time to get down to
the slip, to reach Cragge, to visit Ryan's Hot Spot and have
a talk with Mary or her guardians. As Mrs. Philip Grise's

trained nurse she had a motive to hand: her patient must not be disturbed by visits from the crazy woman who called herself Enid Ambrose. A protest in the name of medical authority. "Tom Ryan's Place." . . . Jenny was already on her way.

The town of Cragge was a larger and uglier edition of Barent. It boasted factories along the river front and several slums and shopping districts which as they climbed the hill merged into the heights of better shops and residences. Jenny's inquiry for Ryan's Place brought a stare and a dubious assent.

"You're sure you want Tom Ryan's Place, miss? It's a saloon, a kind of a tough joint."

N-no, perhaps she didn't. Where did Tom Ryan live?

Nobody knew. But at last, moving slowly along one of the wide dirty dock streets, she came upon a newsboy who directed her. "Ryan? Sure. He lives up Hill Street, a couple blocks from the saloon. A little frame house with a yard next to the Swan's Wing Laundry."

Now, Jenny was fortunate. She passed the Swan's Wing—a very dark-complexioned swan—saw the small frame house and, under a big hickory tree in its yard, sat Mary Ryan, herself. Alone. She was shelling peas from a tin basin into a yellow bowl.

There was no other living creature in sight except a hen scratching for her chicks in the faded grass. Jenny came through the gate and softly called, "Enid Ambrose, may I visit with you for a little while?"

The tall, faded woman lifted a face grown bright with pleasure. Not often before, Jenny surmised, had her assumed identity been honored. She swept back her greying blond hair with a big hand and smiled almost fatuously up into Jenny's face.

"Sure. Glad to see you. Oh, you're the white lady, aren't you, that was up above the beach?"

"Yes. I'm Mrs. Grise's nurse, Jenny Thorne. Lizzie told me where to find you, Miss Ambrose."

"Not 'miss.' Mrs. There's my little girl."

"You have a little girl?"

"Sure. Her name's Sheila. And what's the name for a mother that leaves her own child to care for somebody else's baby?"

Jenny sat down on a circular bench at the base of the big tree. Mary was in a low wooden chair.

"Let me help you," said Jenny and took up a handful of

green pods. "So you didn't like Mrs. Enid Ambrose, did you, Mary?"

The poor, bewildered thing stared, then giggled. "We had a good joke on her, didn't we? Only when I saw who was on the beach I got scared . . ." She was looking down at Jenny's fingers. "It didn't turn out right, did it, Enid Ambrose?"

Jenny bravely moved one of those tell-tale hands of hers and put it firmly, urgently upon Mary's aproned knee.

"Tell me who you are," she said, "Tell me truly who you are and who it was you saw there on the beach."

Mary Ryan was staring now with all her eyes and, it seemed to Enid Ambrose's daughter, that she was entirely sane, remembered actual events and distinguished real identities. A quiver of grief passed over this real, suddenly awakened face.

"Mr. Philip! Oh, my Mr. Philip!" Mary moaned and covered her face with both stained hands. The tin basin of pods clattered to the ground.

"Tell me who you are?" Jenny softly urged.

"I'm Adam's nurse," sobbed the poor woman, "and that was my afternoon out. I know you well, Enid Ambrose, but I never thought you'd come back here to question me. It wasn't my fault that Mr. Philip fell."

"Of course it wasn't, Mary." (It's my hands, Jenny told herself, and they were cold in the warm sun. How to give them skill to hold this brain for a few minutes longer to sanity.) "Of course it wasn't your fault. Who was it then, that made Mr. Philip fall?"

Mary said, "They let me have the little spade and the little saw, didn't they? And it was all planned to be funny. Why did it turn out so bad?" She let fall her own hands disclosing the wet, simple face that had once been so rosy and dimpled and blue-eyed. "I'm Enid Ambrose," she simpered, pinching at her apron foolishly and bridling, "and I'm the one he loves. I'm so pretty that everybody loves me . . ." she bent close to whisper, "even that handsome young doctor, see? That's why Mrs. Grise spies on me. 'Tisn't for Mr. Philip's sake. She don't know the first thing of Mr. Philip's tricks . . ."

Oh, God help me, Jenny prayed, to make sense out of this jargon. It's all here, the motive and the act, the true story—but my head goes round. Who can believe or understand a crazy woman's memories? But here are new elements, new suspicions.

"Who gave you the little spade and saw?" she urged.

"What tricks didn't Mrs. Philip Grise know?" and got nothing but a queer sly look.

"Weren't you on the beach that day?"

Blind alley. Mary's face went blank. Someone had opened the door of the small house behind the big tree and was coming out.

Mary hastily picked up the fallen basin, gathered the peapods and began busily to shell them.

Mrs. Tom Ryan, Lizzie's sister and Mary's aunt, was not unlike Castania's dark-eyed cook, a few years younger. Crisp and stern and clean, she charged this visitor who had come uninvited.

"Who are you, please? Why are you talking out here to my niece without letting anyone know?"

Jenny rose. "I came to see you, Mrs. Ryan ... if it is Mrs. Ryan."

"It's Mrs. Ryan all right but if 'twas me you wanted to see why didn't you ring at my door first off?"

Jenny said, "It looked to me as if the house was empty"— a shot in the dark that made a lucky hit. For Mrs. Ryan really had been out.

"Well," said she, "will you come in now and state your business?"

"I'm Mrs. Philip Grise's trained nurse," Jenny answered and her hostess stood still for they had already started housewards. "I came to ask you if it wouldn't be possible"—she lowered her voice although they were at a considerable distance from Mary—"to prevent your niece getting away and disturbing the Grise household?"

"Oh, my goodness! As if I didn't do my best. It's the first time it's happened in over a year ..."

"But you leave her alone like this, outdoors. She might just as well as not be on her way across the river now. It's very bad for Mrs. Grise, not to mention your sister. Mrs. Grise is far from well. Luckily we were able to keep Mary's presence from her but that was only luck ... I hate to trouble you, Mrs. Ryan. Truly I do. But I know that Dr. Dean ..."

"He don't know she got off, does he?"

"No. I think not."

"Thank the good Lord for that! Well, you see how I'm fixed. It's hot. I can't keep the poor thing shut up forever. Nor can I help but leave her alone now and then ... the man called for the trash just now and I had to go out back for fifteen minutes or so ... It's not once in an age the poor thing takes it into her head to wander. Come on now, Mary. I'm going to give the lady tea. You'll like that and a bit of cake."

Mary looked obstinate and as though she had not heard.

"She wants me to call her Enid but I just won't give in though it would make things easier. Sometimes I think she's getting back her senses and then she seems worse." Mrs. Ryan took her niece by the arm and led her up the path, she going along very meekly and into the neat stuffy house, all shut against the heat and a few degrees cooler for that airlessness.

Mary went with her aunt into the kitchen to help get tea while Jenny played company in the stiff crowded parlor well filled with furniture and knick-knacks.

When the women came back, Mary was sent to sit in the back room at the table beyond an open pair of folding doors, where she was easily visible but not one of the tea party. Mrs. Ryan sat close to Jenny.

She seemed to be a more communicative person than Lizzie and Jenny decided to be a gossip.

"Mrs. Ryan, what a sad, sad thing this has been for everyone . . . I've heard the whole story of Castania and I'm so sorry for you all. And what a narrow escape for your poor Mary. Isn't it lucky that the dreadful thing happened on her day out?"

"It wouldn't have happened any other day, that's flat, nurse. For it was planned for Mary's day out. But, my goodness, it's so long ago. Fancy anyone troubling to think about it . . . and a young thing like yourself."

"I'm like that . . . sort of curious and interested in people's histories. After I got to know the folks at Castania, I went and read up the case . . . Yes, I did, really. And I felt how lucky it was for Mary Ryan that she had her alibi out here with you."

"Yes," the voice was automatic, "it surely was. Her being with us all the day from noon on."

Well Jenny knew she could not expect to shake the twenty-year-old evidence, the story Mary's aunt had given at the trial under oath, the story Mary had told before her feeble mind gave way.

But she made a desperate move.

"Just now," said Mrs. Philip Grise's gossipy nurse, "you know . . . isn't it queer? . . . what Mary said?"

A paler face and a rapidly blinking look. "Mary . . . who can follow what she says . . . not worth repeating, miss . . ."

"She said just now—and actually she forgot her obsession and knew who she was and she took me for the Ambrose woman—yes, really she did—and told me she had seen someone on the beach that afternoon."

"Well," said Mrs. Ryan, flushing now and sharp and straight, "it wasn't your business to talk to her on any such subject."

"Oh, but she started it, taking me for Enid Ambrose."

"What's on your mind, miss, if I may be so bold as to ask?"

Jenny set down her cup. "This is on my mind," she answered slowly. "I am quite sure, Mrs. Ryan, that your niece was on the beach below the summer house that afternoon. I am quite sure that somebody put her up to playing what she thought was a rough practical joke and that this joke was the cause of Philip Grise's fall, if not of his death."

Mrs. Tom Ryan was on her feet, her thick face ashy with anger and with fear.

"You're no trained nurse," said she, her hand on her breast. "You're a female detective and you're here to get evidence of something and why anyone should open the case now after all these years, and hire you for the job and get you into Castania in the disguise of a nurse, I wouldn't know, but I know one thing ... you won't be allowed to spend another night there ..."

"Hush, Mrs. Ryan. You haven't thought this thing out, have you? Not all the way. It might well be, mightn't it, that I have been engaged by Mrs. Philip Grise herself ..."

"Oh, my God," said the poor woman, shrinking down in her chair and twisting her hands together. "It's to do all over again. But they must be crazy ... those folks over yonder ... they all came clear ... to dig it up now and only God knows what'll turn up. Well, anyhow ..." she straightened, was firm again, "you can't bully me into admitting anything but the truth. 'Twas Mary Ryan's day out and she spent it here with me. Whatever other notion you'd taken into your head ... that's the truth, the whole truth and nothing but the truth."

"Thank you, Mrs. Ryan, I'm sure it is," said Jenny gently and was rewarded by a breathless, "Oh, I do thank you for saying that, miss. I do indeed."

"And you're mistaken about my situation, Mrs. Ryan. Believe me! For a moment I was angry with you and so I let you think I had been engaged to do detective work ... but truly no one has given me such work to do. I am honestly a trained nurse. I couldn't help being interested in this old story and I confess I questioned poor Mary and got some rather weird and contradictory answers from her, but that's no proof that I've a plan to make any use of the poor woman's self-contradictory statements, even if I could. I've behaved very badly to you, I know, and I hope you'll forgive me. I came here to warn you very seriously ... to frighten you a little perhaps into realizing how serious a matter Mary's wanderings might be for her as well as for other people . . ."

Lizzie's sister was so relieved by this plausible explanation, so eager to accept it, that Jenny had no more difficulties and was able to finish her tea, to thank her hostess and to get away with no apparent renewal of suspicion or alarm.

But she was weak with her own reaction and climbing up to the empty top deck of the ferry, she sat there, breathing deeply of the river wind. Her mind was weary of the problem. She was ripe for surrender. Not even for another seven days could she keep at her quest. No, she must throw away the rusty keys of this old locked door, and go back to her mother and accept the tragedy ... All her trip had won for her was further suspicion, more clues to follow ... more threads to the complicated dusty web . . . She sat staring down at her own hands which had called Mary's wandering mind for a few moments back to its realities ...

What use could she make of this experience, if she had the energy to use any experience at all? Here she threw back her head against the woodwork, lifted those hands to her eyes and shut out all the painted west.

There is a genie dwelling in the subconscious mind who silently collects the fragmentary materials of a bewildered consciousness and working upon them in darkness suddenly thrusts them up in a coherent and intelligible shape. So it happened to Jenny's weary brain. Alone there on the upper deck, blind to the beauty of her friend the river, utterly defeated in her intense sacrificial purpose, there came to her, as though someone had thrust a key into a hanging hand ... one sentence. "My Mr. Philip." This Mary had spoken during her moment of rational recollection and she had used it with warmth, with yearning, in emotion as fresh as yesterday. Again that haunting vague neglected image of a debonair philanderer came bodily upon Jenny's stage, and again she thought, sitting up straight, opening her eyes, "Why would anyone, any of these people want to kill Philip Grise? Everyone's spoiled darling ... everyone's 'My Philip.' Not his ten-

der-minded, half maternal wife, unsuspicious of his infidelity
... not a young ambitious physician just settled in the neigh-
borhood, only just introduced to Castania's important little
world ... not the dark-eyed and honest girl who loved him
and who loved and worshipped his noble wife ... no one
could have wanted to kill Philip, not mother, wife, mistress,
desired or rejected, not the physician. It was the entire lack
of any credible or sufficient motive that had hung the trial.
Very well then. There had been two people in that arbor.
There had been two cups of tea. May not Enid herself have
been the intended victim? May she not innocently have given
Philip the deadly mixture ... perhaps at the last moment
confusing the cups. Philip's presence with her that afternoon
might well have been a secret from the rest of Philip's household. Perhaps Philip himself ...

From Mary's incoherence, one thing emerged with fair
certainty, someone had planned a practical joke ... someone
had induced a moronic nursemaid to borrow Adam's little
saw and shovel nearly to sever a rail and to dig away the
earth under the arbor corner. Old Anna had said, "Mary was
always up to tricks." A moronic nursemaid half insane already with jealousy of "my Mr. Philip's" new distraction ...
for hadn't Anna said that Philip had taught Mary and Adam
to swim, played with them the while his wife believed him to
be averse to the society of children ... even his own child?
Motives for Enid's destruction might not be so far to seek.

She had quarrelled with Philip. Perhaps in the lost letter
she had herself threatened to call his bluff and go to Felicia
with the story of temptation and of love, tearing the veil
from Felicia's eyes. Philip was dependent upon his wealthy
wife. The day before Philip's death Enid had made, perhaps,
some discovery ... the affair with Mary Ryan or something
even worse ... and in the lost letter she had threatened him
with disclosure. This had not been brought out in the trial because then poor Enid was concerned with shielding her dead
lover and her living benefactress. All the explanation lay in
that letter which may have been destroyed but which several
people—Adam and a strange night intruder in a tweed coat,
yes, and Enid herself—believed to be still hidden somewhere
in the tower library.

Jenny must indeed find that important paper ... Enid's last
message to her lover ... within the next twelve hours and,
failing that, she must leave Barent at once, go back to her
mother and force from her the truth. The whole truth. And

nothing but the truth. That truth had not been told before a jury sitting twenty years ago to examine two beautiful young women sacrificing their heart's blood each for the other.

Loyalty to Felicia and Philip's death had sealed Enid's lips, holding back something, some cruel and sudden discovery, some knowledge that had almost driven her to tear that rainbow veil from Felicia's eyes, to break down the wall about her garden enclosed . . .

Had the secret anything to do with the night visitor in the tweed coat . . . Felicia's mystery . . . ?

He had searched the shelves beneath the window—well, that signal would not be neglected. Let her search them again, that very night.

Chapter Eighteen

The wind could not blow too loud for Enid's child that August night. She went late to bed, for after dinner, as a departure from the usual procedure, Felicia insisted upon a game of bridge and they sat down to play: Old Mrs. Grise, Adam, his mother and Jenny Thorne. It was difficult indeed for Jenny to keep her mind on the cards. But her partner, Adam, played a brilliant concentrated game, old Mrs. Grise was keen and Felicia, uniformly correct. It was obvious to Jenny that Adam had, that afternoon, contrived to lull his mother's suspicions and to convince her that the danger from his morbid activity was done. It was obvious too that old Mrs. Grise noticed a difference in the relationship of mother and son, was uneasy, curious. Jenny, trying to remember signals, tried at the same time to put herself into the place of Philip's mother.

According to Felicia, Helen Grise had been vengeance incarnate, had sworn to hunt down the wretched victim that had escaped the law. Nevertheless she had allowed all these years to pass without an overt act, without even, it would seem, making any attempt to discover Enid's whereabouts. Only when Adam, coming back nervously disorganized by war, had stirred the embers, did Mrs. Ferguson Grise's will to vengeance regain its force. It seemed to Jenny that it was rather a wish to control Adam, to triumph over Felicia's past championship, to keep her own hands upon the threads that was now inspiring her intense interest. Quick darting looks she threw from one absorbed face to the other, trying vainly to catch Adam's grave eyes. What goes on here? said her dark anxious face. Why this calm? This atmosphere of reconciliation. Why am I not included in the signing of the truce? As though she feared more private consultation, she outstayed the bedtime of the others, was the last to leave the downstairs hall. Jenny, looking down and back, saw her below Philip's picture, in queer tense vigil for a long five minutes before she turned, switched off the light and began slowly to mount the stairs. Jenny lingered an instant with the

143

knob of the tower door in her hand until the old woman had emerged into the upper hall and entered her own room. Adam was in his quarters; Jenny could hear him walking about, running water, preparing presumably for bed. Felicia was quiet below there in Anna's hands. The queer old house, but for its eternal wind, was still enough. And that wind grew stronger as the hours of August darkness, star-watched, went by.

For four more of those lonely windy hours, the girl in the tower room sat brooding, dozing, waiting. It was two o'clock in the morning, Orion aloft the roof, when she crept out in stocking feet, flash in hand, and down the winding stairs. She made not the slightest noise, kept her light on the floor, crossed the landing, entered the study and closed its door. Under the big bay window, the man in the tweed coat had searched the books that belonged to Adam's childhood. This was where Jenny would now look and thoroughly.

Everyone in Castania knew that there had been a letter that had not been found with the other notes in Philip's pocketbook. Everyone knew that once in the trial Enid's courage had faltered and she had said that the contents of that letter would argue strongly in her favor. That Philip had read this letter Jenny alone knew because Enid had told her, had said she was glad nobody but Philip had ever seen it. Had said besides that Philip had not destroyed it, that it must be somewhere in the study hiding place. But further at the trial or in her confidences to her daughter, Enid would not go. She would not mention the hiding place nor would she divulge the contents of the letter. Dynamite they must have been, would still be, for anyone intent on reopening that case. Deadly and dangerous to the safety of the real murderer, whom Enid had sacrificed her lifelong peace to save. "You will get no help from me, Jenny," Clara Thorne had said, white and rigid, "in your wicked purpose. I'll have no portion in it. If you go to Barent, you go against my will and with none of my support. I've told you already more than I would have told if I had guessed what use you might make of it. Without fresh evidence you can't possibly reopen the case with any chance of success. You're just putting me again into peril of the law and destroying the poor patched up peace of my Felicia."

Felicia's poor patched up peace! It was her own son who had first planned to endanger it, because of a long repressed suspicion which had poisoned his very soul and which he felt he must at any cost allay. Every member of the Castania family, except poor crippled Felicia, must have undertaken the search for that missing paper. Adam, now, would keep at it until he was sure that the letter was not in any one of these thousand possible hiding places!

Jenny's spotlight fell across the books at the place where she remembered the hands and the bent head of that mysterious intruder, whose visit Felicia said she understood and who, she had promised, would return no more. Her agent perhaps for this search.

"Alice in Wonderland," "Alice Through the Looking Glass," "The Red Fairy Book," "Leather Stocking Tales" ... "The Wizard of Oz." Jenny went through each of these using the technique Adam had instituted, ruffling the pages, shaking down the open volume. She lingered over "The Wizard of Oz" because it had been a favorite of her own childhood. So often read aloud to her by that gentle girl who had been Adam's governess. It had no extraneous contents, but she pleased herself by turning its well-worn pages and even reading a sentence here and there. She came to Finis and noticed that there was no fly leaf at the back. It seemed to her that she remembered one in her own similar copy. No leaf had been torn out. But, on minute repeated examination, it seemed to her that a leaf had been pasted to the back cover, delicately along the edges. Yes ... and at the top it was not pasted. She slipped her finger into the narrow pocket carefully. A thin, thin sheet of note paper, the airiest of the air mail sheet, was in this improvised envelope. She drew it out with difficulty. Her hand trembled. She saw a writing as familiar to her memory as was the lovely hand that had once written it. Her mother's fine close script. The paper had been crumpled once, smoothed out carefully and re-inserted in its hiding place. Philip had read it, failed to destroy it, for some reason of his own, and had returned it to its secret post office. The Wizard ... how inevitable a title for romantic, clandestine lovers! Why had nobody guessed!

It was a pencil letter, long, closely written, a trifle blurred and dim. But legible. Now Jenny forgot wind and stillness, house and night. Orion rode without influence across the tower. The river was a friend whose whisper went unheeded. She read:

"I said I'd meet you in the summerhouse on Mary's next afternoon out as usual, Philip. For the last time. You'll find this in the Wizard's hole and perhaps it will make you change your mind about seeing me again. In any case, I'll be in the garden with little Adam at five o'clock. If you do come, you'll find me there. But, believe me, Philip, nothing you can say or do will change the new decision I have come to. You know that I have a will of my own; it is now set as hard as iron. For, you see, Philip, I *have found you out*. Mary Ryan has told me her story . . . I found her crying. I tried to comfort her. She turned upon me. She has been nearly out of her mind with jealous misery. And I've discovered what Carrol has been doing with your connivance. Oh, Philip, it is more than I can bear to believe. But I have to believe it. My treachery has been wicked enough but it is less than yours. Felicia must know. You threatened me with telling her about our 'affair'—oh, it makes me writhe to write that word.— Well, now I call your bluff. I am going to tell Felicia myself. She has lived too long in her ivory tower, in her walled garden, loving and trusting and being sure of everyone's devotion. I am going to tell her the day after our last meeting and it will make no difference if you don't come!—I'm going to tell her everything I know, and it is a great deal . . . about her 'worshippers'!

"It may free her from you for some finer relationship. Nothing . . . no temptation would make Felicia false but if she knows how false other people have been, how doubly false you are . . . and I include myself, my own weakness—in this accusation . . . and I will tell her that I have loved you and that you've broken my heart, as well as hers, and crucified my pride! She shall know about my treachery, which was great though not so great as if I had agreed to be your mistress! And I will tell her of the vain folly of another man she includes among her worshippers . . . and when she has her eyes open, and knows you all as I have learned to know you, perhaps she will turn us all out and begin her life again. Oh, Philip, I know that without her you will be very poor but, perhaps—oh, I dare to hope a little!—perhaps without her mothering and spoiling, forced to work for your living, on your own, you may become the sort of man that a decent woman can respect and love. You say you love me. I wonder if that's true. Here is a way to prove it, Philip.

"I hope Felicia will indeed be ruthless with the whole treacherous crew of us. Oh, Philip, what disgust I have for you, what loathing and . . . what shameful love! I am more unhappy tonight than I thought it possible for a human being to be. I've lost Felicia . . . I've lost you.

"I am so bitter. So humiliated. To be made a rival to Mary Ryan. I deserve my punishment and you deserve yours and you shall have it at Felicia's hands, so help me God. And may He, indeed, have mercy on your soul.

"I am doing it for the sake of that soul, Philip.

"Your most unhappy, most determined Enid."

Jenny returned the Wizard to his place on the low shelf and, carrying her precious trove, went softly out and up into her own room. There, with closely drawn curtains and shaded bed lamp, she read and re-read the letter which she believed might have cleared Enid and condemned another.

That other, Jenny now felt certain and believed that any-one else would feel certain, must be Philip Grise. He had found the threat of ruin in his Wizard's Hole, and, for some reason none would ever know—a sudden interruption per-haps—had first crumpled then restored it to its pocket. With-out seeing Enid again, he had gone "to the city" and, whether on his way from Dr. Elliot's office or by other more distant means, he had obtained the cyanide and had put it into Enid's cup. First, no doubt, he had tried to shake her resolu-tion. That failing, he had done his deed. There must, at the last instant, he being suddenly distracted, have been a substi-tution. Yes, Clara Thorne had said something about a scant supply of sugar and going without it herself by giving her share to Philip. He must have sugared her cup and she had quietly transferred it, taking his own. Josh Hogan's discred-ited report came to Jenny now with the ring of truth. Loud with his own terrible awareness, Philip might well have cried out, "Enid, *you* gave me this!" Philip had drunk the poison which he had prepared for her. And she, knowing this, Feli-cia perhaps suspecting it, had worked together to keep clear Philip's name! Perhaps if Enid had been sentenced, then at the last bitter moment, the poor governess would have pro-duced the evidence contained in that lost letter. But Felicia had managed to save her and that poor governess had chosen to bear the burden of a hung sentence rather than blacken the name of Enid's dead husband, Adam's dead father, Helen Grise's dead son. In gratitude, Felicia had given Enid and her child their livelihood! Jenny wept, half in worship of her mother, half in doubt. All these years, the knowledge had lived in that lonely haunted brain. Yet she had kept the secret. Even from her own child. And was that true justice! None more innocent than Jenny and no one bound to suffer more. Well, at last she would be free of her mother's patient submission to ignominy. *She had the letter!*

But what to do with it? Dynamite in her hand, beneath her pillow!

No sleep for the head that rested above that high explosive. At sunrise Jenny had come to at least one decision. She went over to her little table and wrote a letter to Nick.

She told him about her discovery. Gave him, in full, the contents of the letter, copying it down, word for word. Asked his advice. She owed him the "whole truth."

"Now that I've found this evidence," she wrote, "I feel that my work here is almost done. From now, I will need a lawyer. Oh, I know there are a dozen loose ends . . . the identity of Carrol—the man in the tweed coat—Mary Ryan's crazy speeches . . . the digging and the sawing part of the crime . . . and, no doubt, many others as important. But here is what was lacking in that trial, a motive! I believe that Josh Hogan was closer to the arbor than he said but did not like to confess to eavesdropping and then was caught in his own falsehood. He had sworn to his whereabouts and couldn't go back on his oath in face of the factual experiment.

"In any case, Nick, I will come to your small hotel and meet you. But I'll wait until I have your answer to this. I assure you I'm in no possible danger . . . The only dangerous inmate of Castania died inadvertently by his own hand twenty years ago. I must decide what I am to do here. I've been taken in and affectionately treated. I think, Nick, that Adam really loves me. And Roger Dean has asked me to be his wife. I have Felicia's partial confidence. But not one of them knows who I am nor why I came to Castania.

"It does seem heartless treachery to go away and from a distance spring upon them this horror. Yet, what else, to clear my mother, can I do? I feel now that I've killed Philip for the second time. I feel I may be guilty of Felicia's death. I can understand mother's sacrifice. Felicia inspires that sort of devotion.

"Waiting for your reply will give me a few days of grace. Perhaps I can discover who Carrol was or is. I can make peace with my conscience. I can, at least, definitely refuse Roger's offer and show to Adam some change of face or manner that will chill his growing interest in me. I feel like a vain idiot writing this, but it is the literal truth, and I'm ashamed of it; it's like the success of one of these female spy-sirens. Just for a few hours you worried me but, no,

Nick, Adam is not dangerous. I've never been so sure of anything as I am of that.

"I'll give this letter to John just as he leaves Castania for the post office. He puts the letters into a leather bag and mails them as soon as he reaches Barent. I'd go with him but tomorrow . . . no, this is already today . . . is the day after my day out and Felicia will want me . . . or will want to seem to want me . . . we still have to keep up our pretense as Adam has never yet guessed I was brought here to watch and to help his 'nervous condition of combat fatigue.' Rather, I think to watch the form it took.

"I shall tell mother nothing yet.

"So, write when you have decided for me what I must do next . . . and wait for me to come with what patience you can. Dear Nick, I haven't said a word to you about my deep and loving gratitude. You must understand it without words. You've been wonderful—generous. I am touched past any expression by your loyalty."

She sealed and addressed this most important missive, hid that other in her own dress and went down, white as her uniform, to breakfast.

When Anna had left the room—it was Anna who waited upon them at this hour—old Mrs. Grise said, "Well, Miss Jenny Thorne, you've not done much to earn your thousand dollar bonus, have you?"

Jenny fairly jumped. She had forgotten, actually forgotten, the dreadful little talk in that hideous second story room.

"But, Mrs. Grise, there was nothing I could do about it really."

"Well, since he found the little spade, Adam has found nothing he was looking for . . . that's flat! He's got his mother scared half to death and it's about all he's accomplished. Isn't it? Isn't it, Miss Jenny?"

"I don't know."

"Sometimes I get wondering about you, Miss Jenny Thorne. You've got some queer ways of your own, you know. Take our fascinating doctor, now . . . Are you on to him or aren't you? Tell me that and I'll have a line on you."

"On to Dr. Dean! I don't understand. Hush, there's Anna!"

"Anna's deaf," grunted the old woman crossly but, "We're through, you don't need to wait."

Then, as Anna went out, "Yes, Jenny Thorne, you do too . . . understand. That is if you're as smart a little trick as I believe you are. You know our doctor is one of the world's great unsung lovers, eh? The women he's loved! The women who've loved him! I suppose you'll laugh—girls are malicious and stupid creatures—but there was a time when young Roger Dean—and if you think he's handsome now!—neglected the wiles of two girls of your age and with more than twice your charm, Miss Jenny, for one Helen Grise.

"A woman over thirty can be very fascinating to an intelligent younger man. And Roger, if I'd said the word, would certainly have been at my feet. He was at my," she whispered, "lips . . . let me tell you."

The wrinkled purple morning mouth! Jenny felt a strong repulsion and contempt.

"I'm sure he was," she heard herself murmur, "I'm sure he was very much in love with you."

"He'd have been glad to marry me if I'd have had him for a husband. That was before he lost his head over Felicia. You must have seen *that*, Miss Jenny, even if your eyes are always half closed. Oh, I admit, you've been a fresh distraction. No man of Roger Dean's temperament and charm can be content forever with a platonic passion; if there is such a thing as a platonic passion. Well," she pushed her bent body up from its chair, both dark hands pressed down on the cloth, "maybe it's not a good topic for the breakfast table. Too early in the day for gossip. You look rather seedy today, child. Didn't you sleep well?"

"No. The wind kept me awake."

"It was high last night. But what else have we here every day and every night but wind? And a great blessing it is in August weather, don't you think? Well, you're off to visit Mrs. Philip, I suppose. It looks to me as if she and Adam had made it up. I think Felicia was on to him, don't you? Don't you think she was on to him? Oh, you've a letter to mail. Give it to me and I'll let John have it with mine."

"Oh, thanks. I'll give it to him myself. He's at the door now." And she went out quickly, caught the man just as he was climbing into the station wagon at the front door, heard him start his engine and went in to Felicia's high sweet calling.

Felicia wore the look of a prisoner straining at bonds.

"I didn't sleep a wink last night, Jenny," she said feverishly.

She was not in bed nor on her couch but seated already in her wheeled chair with its collapsible hood and rainbow draperies. "I thought the morning would never come. But, tell me, what's wrong with you, Jenny? Didn't you sleep either?"

"No."

"It was that dreadful incessant wind. I get so tired of its blowing sometimes that I could scream, 'Stop! Stop!' And then, when it does stop, I'm scared. Castania isn't used to stillness. But, Jenny dear, I don't really believe it was the wind that made you wakeful last night. Come close to me. Give me your pretty hand, I promise I won't think of resemblance." She shuddered strongly. "I was silly enough once to imagine. There. That's right. Now I can see you—Jenny. Do you love me?"

How often, Jenny wondered, had she asked that, lifting those seraphic eyes, smiling wistfully with pale-rose delicate lips. Who could resist Felicia? Even her half-helpless body had a fragrant clinging warm appeal.

Jenny writhed in spirit, answering "Yes."

"You've done so much for me. Your commission has been most perfectly performed. Adam has never guessed I brought you here for his sake. And it was truly just what he needed ... your cheerful sympathetic companionship, your exquisite quiet skill. Yes, Jenny, my Adam has come back to me. He's given up that purpose of his. Yesterday afternoon for hours he sat with me. He talked to me, gave me his confidence. Jenny, part of that confidence—don't turn your face away— has to do with you."

"With me?" Genuine astonishment, quickly followed by dismay, blanketed her sense of treachery.

"Are you so surprised? Jenny, your time here is—should be—nearly up. I don't feel justified in keeping on a trained nurse, these days, for nothing but my pleasure in her dear company. But if you and Adam ... Ah, now you have some color in your face. You've guessed what Adam said to me."

"If she knew my real name, if she knew my purpose, how would she be feeling towards me now?" Aloud Jenny faltered, "If Adam has told you that ... that he's lost his head a little ..."

"No, Jenny. Nothing like that. He told me that he loves you with all his heart and that he wants you to be his wife."

Voice, hand and body shaking, Jenny said, "He hasn't told me that, Mrs. Grise."

"Your fingers went cold then, Jenny. You're not looking at me. What does that mean?"

"It means, dear Mrs. Grise, that, even if Adam really told you that and meant it, I could never in the world marry your son."

Felicia drew her hand away in order to push herself up higher in her chair and her face went white as linen. "You could never marry ... *my son.* You mean that the son of Mrs. Philip Grise is branded by a history of ..."

"No, no, Mrs. Grise," cried Jenny, "not that. Don't think that, please. It's not at all what I mean." She stood up and went over to one of the windows to stare out at the murmuring river. A mist lay over it and the pale hills beyond. The grass was heavy with moisture, warm haze rose from the land. "Mrs. Grise," she said and the difficult words pained her throat, pained her heart more than she could have thought possible, "I am going to marry another man."

Stillness so dead that, like the cessation of Castania's river wind, it brought a sort of fear. She turned quickly. Felicia sat there, an image of grey stone.

"Mrs. Grise!"

The grey thin lips moved. "You are going to marry Roger Dean." Then with a sort of cry and a great scarlet change of countenance: fire in her cheeks and eyes, fire running through her limbs, "You're *not!* You're *not!* No woman can marry Roger Dean. And well he knows it. If he has made love to you ... and I believe he has ... I've guessed it ... seen it ... I know him very well ... it means nothing, Jenny. Don't trust to it and don't, for God's sake, return it."

"Hush. Hush. I didn't say that I was going to marry Roger Dean."

Felicia went limp. "You're not?" Sweat made the soft curling hair cling to her temples. "He hasn't . . ."

"Yes. He has asked me to marry him but I am going to refuse him."

"Oh, God!" moaned Felicia, eyes closed, head back, rocking from side to side. "Roger! Roger! Poor tortured soul. Even the wretches in hell keep asking for water, don't they, Jenny? That's part of their punishment." Then, upright and open-eyed again, "But what of my poor little Adam? Why can't you ... why won't you ... love him?"

"Dear Mrs. Grise, please take it all more calmly. I'm frightened. You are so passionate. How can I tell you?"

"Very well. I'll be calm. See, I'm calm now. You can tell me everything, if you will, Jenny. Only let it be the truth. I've asked for it so often and so uselessly for so many years."

"I think you should be told it," whispered Jenny. "I think that I should tell you the truth. Wait! Let me think. Listen, may I go out into the garden alone for half an hour?" She was trembling with the temptation to confess herself. She simply did not dare stay one minute longer. She waited for no permission, opened the French window above the little ramp Felicia used to reach her square of turf, and fled.

Chapter Nineteen

Under the mist, the alley held the freshness of morning but Jenny had no awareness of its pearled loveliness. Bird song or flower perfume went all unheeded. She came, so deaf and blind, to the coping that held the bank's edge and sat there, bent over her locked hands, rigid with thought.

Felicia should be told. Life owed to Felicia its truth. She had suffered too long in isolation; her ivory tower, a mere torture chamber for suspicion, fear, remorse.

Did she really love Roger Dean? Or pity him? Or fear him? Had he some hold upon her? Had she knowledge unshared by anyone in all the world? Knowledge perhaps of a "Carrol," put away as incurable—for protection—but, before Philip's death, involved with Philip in some shady transaction, some secret use of Felicia's generous funds? Was it "Carrol" whom Felicia had protected through these years? Her "own foolish but not shameful secret"? A brother, a cousin, even perhaps a father, whose guilt she had suspected or known? Had her own unmarried name been Carrol? Jenny, on the very brink of success, was in terror of a self-betrayal. Why would she, Jenny Thorne, a trained attendant, question anyone about a name never mentioned in her hearing? How could she give an air of naturalness to such an inquiry?

She heard, for all her deafness, the rapid rhythms of galloping hooves, turned, rose, saw, past the fruit trees that bordered the vegetable plots, a horseman. He slowed, came towards her along the path. Adam, on his grey mare. He had seen her, swung to earth, and, bridle over his arm, trailed over to where, having moved a few steps from the cliff edge, she now stood.

He said nothing, nor did she. Under the steadiness of his eyes, a strange serenity came over her. The fret and tumult of her problems fell away. She was no longer Enid's daughter Sheila; no longer Jenny Thorne, Felicia's trained nurse and at the same time Castania's spy. She was someone as simple as

154

the first woman in a garden, the woman of another Adam. Her head was light, her mind as clear as glass.

He let fall his reins and, not moving his eyes from hers, took one step forward and held out his arms.

Jenny, looking up, wide-eyed, walked into them.

And there they stood almost in the spot of Philip's death. And there they kissed not as before, but deeply, in full and grave surrender. There was no place in her now for the glow of satisfied vanity evoked by Nick and Roger Dean. There was a peace such as a lost child feels coming again into its father's arms, a tranquility of running water dissolved in a deep tide. These arms, this body, these lips were Jenny's home. She had never had a home. She melted into Adam's shaken strength ... for he was shaken by his own thirst, her answer and their ecstasy.

It was a memory of Nick that tore her free.

He let her go as soon as he realized her wish to stand apart and she moved, dazed, to the edge of the cliff, the while he led his horse stablewards. When he came back she was prepared for agony.

"Adam."

"Yes, darling." He sat down quietly by her on the great slab of rock but did not touch her. His narrow shining eyes held enough of an embrace.

"It's all wrong."

"What's wrong, my sweet?"

"We can't."

"Why can't we, Jenny?"

"Because ..."

"Don't tell me now you don't love me," his warm voice mocked her, "because I happen to know better."

She bent her face to her hands.

"I think I do love you. I think I do."

"Say you *know* you do and we'll be in full agreement."

"I know I do."

"Well—as the old woman said in criticism of Niagara Falls—'What's to hinder?'"

She couldn't even dream of smiling.

"I love you, Adam."

"I love you, Eve."

"But I can't marry you."

"Why not, mysterious woman in white? Married already? We'll divorce him."

"Not married ... but engaged to be married."

"What rot! And you a southern girl! Why do you bother to mention it? Where's the ring? I'll send it back."

"Adam, you must not treat this lightly. I'm ... suffering ... so ..."

"I won't. I'll be as heavy-handed as you like. Do you want me to kill him for you?"

Her strong shudder and eerie look about her took the color from his face.

"You're thinking of that ..." He was serious enough now. "You won't marry me because of ... what happened here?"

Better he should think so.

"Because of what happened here, Adam."

"In God's name! Must I die because my father died?"

"You wouldn't die, Adam."

"Here or at the front somewhere ... If you are such a devil, I assure you that I will."

"I'm not a devil."

"Either that or an angel, Jenny. Take your choice."

"It's not because your father ..."

"Then ..." Now he was ashen and spoke hoarsely. "It's because you've learned something in this house, something that makes you suspect ..." the hoarseness dropped to a thread of voice, only just audible, "my mother."

"Oh, Adam, no. Why should you think anything so terrible, and so untrue as that?"

"Because I've *had* to think it. It's been twisting the heart out of me for years. If she loved Dean ... if he had ... those two ..."

"Hush, Adam. If they'd been lovers ... for twenty years, you know that, by now, they would be married."

"No." His colorless quiet voice went on. "Not if they were afraid. People might begin to talk. Question. Surmise. Remember, it was a hung case! Fresh evidence, Jenny, a motive, someone interested, perhaps the poor Ambrose woman herself ... or her child."

Out of a long silence, "Or her child," said Jenny.

And with those words, with the tone she used in speaking them she did indeed pull down Castania about her ears.

The big quiet body beside her turned itself slowly. Adam gave her a narrow look, stood up, still looking hard.

"Jenny Thorne," he said.

"No. That's what I thought until a few months ago. Stand where you are. Listen to me. Let me tell you ..."

"Wait a moment," he said.

To her terror he started down the cliff trail, stopped at the great boulder and stood there. When he came back and she let out her caught breath, she saw that there was blood upon his lower lip. He sat down again, not beside her this time, but opposite on the turf, knees drawn into his big tightened hands. He looked at her but the embracing light was gone. The grey eyes were cold. Back of them stood something that had the color of death.

"Go ahead," he said. "Let me have it."

"Last April," she said, "I graduated from the Hospital at Bonnetsville, North Carolina. The day after my graduation a ... a young doctor I had seen a great deal of asked me to be his wife. I ... cared for him. I was grateful to him for loving me. I was happy to think that I'd be his wife. I came back to our lodgings to tell my mother ... Clara Thorne she called herself since I was old enough to know her name at all. I found her packing.

"She is still very beautiful, Adam. I love her. I would die for her. She's suffered bravely, silently for twenty years. But that evening I was angry. So often we'd moved on for no reason I could understand. She always said it was her health, doctor's orders. She said it now.

"I told her I was not going to run away again. Nor was she. I was going to stay at Bonnetsville and be married. Then she knew that the time had come when she must tell me the truth about her ... past. And she stood there with her back to me facing a mirror and gave me the facts. Just the bare facts as she remembered them. How she came to Castania, how she worshipped Felicia, how she fell in love with Philip Grise, and he, with her. Her shame, her struggle to be good. Their quarrel. His insistence upon her giving in to his clandestine passion. The notes they exchanged, the rash ones of her own that were found upon Philip's body and used against her at the trial ... yes, something about one that she wrote and that he left undestroyed in a certain hiding place, and that might, if it had been produced, have witnessed in her favor. She did not tell me why she did not use that information again. But that letter, Adam—which I am sure you have been searching for—contained the suggestion of other motives than any possible ones of her own for a ... murder."

At this word both speaker and listener went white.

"She told me of her gratitude to Felicia, of Felicia's great generosity both in her defense and in the parting gift.

"I was so crushed I had no feeling at all but just the one

she's always had, to run away, to hide. Someone at Bonnetsville, she said, had seen and recognized her. I shared her sense of helpless panic. But when we were on our way to Savannah ... I don't know why she chose Savannah, probably she didn't know herself ... my courage came back. You see, I knew that she was innocent. I couldn't and I wouldn't accept her miserable surrender. I told her that I was going to Barent, that I would stay there until I found out the truth if it took me all the rest of my life. I dedicated my life to proving her innocence.

"She was terrified. She refused to help me by another word, refused again and again to tell me what she had written in that hidden letter, or where it had been hidden. But she'd already told me something ... Yes, Philip had read it and had not destroyed it. Unless someone since had found it, it was still there somewhere in the tower study of Castania. But she would give no further hint, no clue. She would die a thousand deaths and let me die them before she'd disturb her poor Felicia's peace."

"Her peace!" said Adam bitterly.

"I left a letter for Nick, breaking our engagement, telling him my mother's real name and the one awful fact of her history. I gave him no hope of seeing me or of hearing from me again. No address. I made a final break. I knew he was going to camp very soon and wouldn't be able without great difficulty to hunt for me. But, Adam"—here she gave him an awed patient look—"he has found me. He still wants to marry me. He is that sort of man.

"After I'd told my mother and held out against her pleading I took some money of my own and came to New York. There I read and re-read the old newspaper account of that trial and I got a letter of introduction from The Centre to Dr. Roger Dean.

"I was not Roger Dean's agent, Adam, as you once suspected. I am my mother's agent, the agent of her innocence.

"Can you blame me, Adam? Be honest. Be just. Can you, as the son of Felicia and Philip Grise, blame me, the daughter of Enid Ambrose?"

He did not answer. He asked a question of his own.

"What have you discovered, Miss Ambrose? Or will you risk telling me that?"

She felt the knife close under her heart and pain tightened her breath. But she managed to shape an answer.

"I came here for a purpose. Until I've finished the work I set myself, I can't risk ... anything."

"And you imagine that you can stay on here ... in my mother's house, in my home ... and keep on with this work of yours? You have a fantastic imagination, Miss Ambrose. But then I will admit the situation is fantastic." Looking about him, he smiled strangely. "Here we sit, Philip's son and Enid's daughter. And this time you are at the edge of the cliff."

She knew then what physical fear really meant.

Nick had warned her.

Roger Dean had warned her.

She stood up.

"Not yet," said Adam, rising in front of her. "There's one more thing."

She saw Anna coming, saw her big awkward body bobbing above the peonies, and the rhododendrons and the box, Anna like a guardian spirit. And she was calling, "Oh, Miss Thorne, please do come quick. Miss Felicia, she's taken awful sick."

Chapter Twenty

Adam stepped aside and Jenny ran. She quickly out-distanced panting Anna in a return to the house. There in her room lay Felicia, faint and gasping, blue-lipped, upon her couch. She seemed barely conscious, her eyes half-closed, but, as Jenny put fingers on her pulse, she gasped, "Roger! I want Roger!"

"He's been sent for, Mrs. Grise," Jenny answered quietly. "He's on his way."

The pulse leaped and was almost gone.

Jenny poured a dose of spirits of ammonia, putting the edge of the glass between the pallid lips. Felicia swallowed. In a minute a tinge of color returned to her mouth and cheeks. Jenny, having sent a word of reassurance to Adam by the weeping Anna, sat down beside Felicia until the doctor came. He was very pale but had complete professional composure. Jenny left him her place. He used his stethoscope, asked for water, shook out a pill, gave it to Felicia who had lifted her heavy lids and faintly smiled her recognition. He sat quiet then beside the couch, holding the delicate limp hand, looking down sadly at the ghostly lovely face.

Jenny went over to the window seat and sat there, waiting, watching. She saw Felicia's feeble gesture before Dean spoke.

"No necessity for you to stand by now, Miss Thorne," said he. "She's going to be all right. Keep in call, will you? Why not stay on the verandah? Anna can send for you, if needed." In saying this, he did not look at her. His whole attention was focussed upon the patient who was now feeling her way back to the world of living men.

Jenny dared not disobey orders, dared not go so far as her own room, but her need for privacy had become a torment. She went out onto the verandah and sought its furthest vine-covered end. There in one of the great wicker chairs, its back turned against intrusion, she put down her head in her hands, against her knees, and fought with weeping.

Adam's face . . .

Adam's ice-grey eyes . . .

No one but Adam mattered now. What had she done to him? What must she still do to him?

The time passed slowly. She won back her composure, and was able to stand up and to show a quiet face and body when Roger came out at the front door.

"Are you there, Jenny? Ah! Mrs. Grise is asleep. She's all right. She had ..." He paused and his beautiful set face fixed Jenny with its sternest look. "She had a shock."

Jenny faltered, "Did she say ... did she tell you what ... sort of shock it was?"

His smile, Jenny thought, was the bitterest gesture she had ever seen. With it he lifted and let fall his hands still looking down at her with steady sternness.

"You betrayed me, didn't you?"

Jenny's face burned.

"Was it a betrayal, Roger, to tell Mrs. Grise that you——?"

"I think you know it was." He went to the railing, leaned down there on his hands. As though talking to himself he said, "I'm in a trap. Its teeth gnaw into me ..."

Jenny came timidly to stand beside him. "Isn't it because you love *her*, Roger, and have always loved her ... because something has made ... marriage with her impossible?"

"Nothing, that I know of," he said icily, "has given you an excuse for analyzing our emotional situation here at Castania."

"Only," Jenny stammered half in tears again, "only the fact that you asked me to ... to be your wife?"

"In God's name, when did I ask you that?"

"But, Roger ... am I completely crazy? Out there, back of the house; in the woods; only two weeks ago ..."

"I told you that I was jealous of Adam Grise on your account and that some day you were going to love me. But I asked you only one thing ... that you would help me, *as your lover*, to rid the house of Adam Grise. Is your memory beginning to be more accurate?"

"You were trying to win me over to your side against Adam by pretending that you ... cared for me? Was that it, Roger? How glad I am that I wasn't inclined."

"Ah, but you were inclined. And I did not pretend."

"I don't understand you, Roger."

He laughed.

He simply took her into his arms with a fierce tightness and forced down his lips hard upon her own. It was a terrible embrace ... like nothing that Jenny had ever before experienced. She fell away from it in blind fury and fear.

"Perhaps that will teach you something," Roger said, "Something about women and something about men you didn't know before. Something your captain doctor will never teach you. Oh, I could whip the life out of such women. Cruel. And blind. To tempt a man dying of thirst, with both hands tied behind his back! Holding out water ... lifting it to his mouth ... dashing it away ... !"

"You're mad. It's you, not Adam, who is dangerous."

"I've been dangerous. And I may be dangerous again. But not now. And not to you. Here, let's stop this, I've had enough."

"If I mistook your intentions," she heard herself saying with a breathless shaken voice, "I beg your pardon for misquoting you. And I am glad indeed I was mistaken. I did not look forward to rejecting you. But I did admire, I did respect you. It never occurred to me that I ... that I was tempting you. And rather than hurt Felicia ..."

He looked startled, put an uncertain hand to his head. "Someone else said that to me once in just your voice," he muttered. "History seems to repeat itself. It's like a wheel that goes round and round. I think," he laughed, "I must have lived and ... loved too long. Good-bye." He ran down the steps, climbed into his car, was gone.

It had been impossible to believe that this was Roger Dean. Oh, she had hurt him. He was cut as though by a whiplash. His vanity of a "great unsung lover" was bare and bleeding. How quickly, she thought, a man's love can turn to hate and anger and a will to punish!

Adam, in the garden ... had it been anger or sheer pain in his grey eyes? And Roger here ... Was there no tenderness, no fidelity in the face of wounded pride? She thought of Nick and her heart swelled. It was gratitude to him she would cling to and live by, forgetting all the terrible, wonderful rest.

It was lunchtime. The gong was sounding. She did not know whether to look in at Felicia or not but decided that it would be wiser to wait for a summons. In the dining room she learned to her relief, from red-eyed Anna, that old Mrs. Grise had not yet come back. John had taken her to Barent. That's why Anna waited at table.

Jenny ate what she could, told Anna to call her if needed—she would be in her own room—and dragged herself up the winding tower stairs.

It was nearly five o'clock when Anna came asking her to go down now to Miss Felicia.

Mrs. Grise smiled up at her from her chair. She was still very pale but otherwise seemed to be quite herself.

"I'm going out presently for my 'quiet hour' on the terrace, Jenny, but first I want to make my peace with you." She held out her hand. "You told me this morning you'd come back and tell me the truth. I waited. You didn't come. Perhaps you don't know what anguish such waiting is to a prisoner like me."

"I'm terribly sorry, Mrs. Grise. I couldn't think just what to say and, as I think you know now, I quite misunderstood Dr. Dean. I'm not very experienced in flirtation."

"And Roger is an extremely accomplished flirt?"

"I think he must be. He certainly made a fool of me. Lucky, isn't it, that I didn't really care." (But she did not believe that he had made a fool of her or that he did not care.)

"Very lucky for you." Felicia looked sad. Shadows came back to her tired face.

Jenny felt remorseful. "I was a worse fool to talk to you about it, Mrs. Grise. It wasn't really fair to him either."

"That was my fault ... hounding you about Adam, bringing in Roger's name. Poor Adam! I think he's probably no more experienced in flirtation than you—say you are."

Jenny winced. "I suppose I deserve that. I should have been more careful. But I'll be going in a few days. If you are well enough . . . perhaps tomorrow."

"I'll be well enough. I am well now. Those attacks are not so serious as they look. I have a nervous heart and poor circulation. I am besides temperamentally inclined to a sort of hysteria. I agree with you that it would be better for you to go away. I'm afraid Adam's disappointment will undo much of your good work. But, in any case, your being around where he must see you constantly would only make him worse. So, Jenny, when you comfortably can be ready, yes, you'd better go."

She doesn't love me any more, thought Jenny, hurt. But how can I wish her to love me?

She murmured an embarrassed phrase of gratitude, regret.

Felicia said, "I'll not be coming in to dinner and I'm sure Mrs. Ferguson wouldn't mind if Anna carried yours up to your room. Would you like that? You are so pale, poor little Jenny!"

Jenny would indeed like to have her dinner alone and, after she had seen Felicia seated in her hooded sanctuary to face the river and the western hills, she went up to her own high troubled room and began to pack.

She would stay at The Dutch House, she decided, until she got Nick's answer to her important letter, then she would go to New York. She would probably have to engage a lawyer, if Nick had not already done so. Now that Adam knew her purpose and her name, he would be forewarned of what might come upon Castania. He might even suspect that she had found the paper, which they both had so long and feverishly sought. In that case—Nick's warning again blew a cold breath across her heart.

When the dinner tray had come and gone, she locked her door. And yet, behind the lock, she yearned for Adam's step on the stairs, for his knock, a summons in that warm strong voice of "Jenny . . . Jenny . . . Let me in. I love you. What does anything matter but our love?"

That would be a sane Adam, an Adam she could not fear. Love casteth out fear.

Oh, she had failed. She had failed. Even if Enid's name was cleared still she had failed. Fear had won out over love. She was running away from love . . . from Adam. She had not saved him, given him his triumph over fear . . . She wandered from window to bed and there she threw herself down and was free at last for weeping.

Chapter Twenty-one

When her weeping had worked its merciful cure of exhaustion, she slept. Heavily. Without any preparation for sleep. And awoke, as one does wake after such a profound stupor, wide and suddenly.

There was a flicker of summer lightning outside her uncovered windows and with the instinctive response of her training to any necessity she went to shut out a storm of rain. But at the sill she saw only a clear night of stars, the stillest night. No wind at all. Only the wide murmur of the river. She could not tell the time, her watch had stopped but, seeing Orion, she guessed it would be very late; or rather early, close to dawn.

She began to be puzzled by the flicker of light and, leaning out, held her breath to look and to listen. Was there a faint sound of some sort, a faint suggestion of less-than-darkness from the study below? Would it be again, in spite of Felicia's promise, the man in the tweed coat, the night intruder who had the freedom of the house?

For some reason, that might have been desperation or a secret loss of personal hope, Jenny felt not the slightest fear. It did not seem to matter what became of one Sheila Ambrose, alias Jenny Thorne. The ecstasy of love was not to be her portion, only a steady and grateful security. The rest of her life would be long enough for that. For now, she might well taste the full flavor of dangerous adventure.

She removed her shoes, took her light and went again down the tower stairs.

Above the turn she snapped off her light and felt her way in darkness across the landing to the study door. It was shut. For one instant she hesitated, then flung it open, stepped inside, closed it behind her and, all in one motion, switched on the ceiling light.

The figure over there by the low window shelf first leaped then crouched. A thin and narrow pair of shoulders, loosely coated in brown tweed, a curly head bent almost to the floor, a pair of long thin hands spread out across the head so that

165

both bent arms concealed the face. On one of the fingers of these hands shone an enormous sapphire ring.

Jenny came forward a few steps before she could find a voice to speak the name.

"Mrs. Grise. Mrs. Grise! It is . . . it can't be you!"

At that down fell the hands and arms and the figure pulled itself slowly to its feet.

Felicia in a man's coat and trousers, a man's open-collared shirt. Feet in sneakers, a sash about her waist. Felicia, taller than Jenny had ever imagined, her legs being very long in proportion to her upper body. Felicia white as paper, her eyes huge. Felicia, able to stand and to walk.

She reached the desk, dropped into its chair, set elbows down and put her small head into her hands. Again the tell-tale sapphire gleamed.

"So now you know," she said.

Jenny kept her distance.

"You can stand. You can walk. How long . . . ?"

"For twenty years."

"It isn't possible."

"What, in this world, is not possible?"

Jenny now moved to stand beside her and she raised her head, and looked up wearily into the girl's incredulous flushed face. Jenny began to stammer, "But that n-night . . . the night I found him here before . . . and he ran past me out of the door and then . . . *you* called me from your room. And I found you there in bed?"

"How long does it take, Jenny, to run round the corner of the house, get in by my French window, tear off these clothes and be in my bed? You took longer to investigate than you think . . . front door and back . . . and a little while when you wondered just what you ought to do. You found me flushed and breathless, didn't you, Jenny? And put it down to fear. Nobody but someone that has built up a belief as I have and hid behind it, knows how difficult it is for people to discover the unreality of what they have long believed."

"But, Mrs. Grise . . . for twenty years? How could *you* endure . . . ?"

"Hundreds of people, Jenny, have led spiritual double lives. I've led a physical one. Anna is deaf, my room is thickly carpeted. At night I've paced my floor, have gone out, wandered along the river beaches, through the woods. Sometimes in daylight I've left that hooded chair of mine on the edge of the river bank and fled down into the woods. It was a risk, but no one has wondered at my insistence upon strict privacy; no one yet has broken in upon me and found my chair without an occupant. I have not grown careless—I've chosen safe times. It's only you ..."

"Why? Why?"

"Why have I done it? Must I confess myself to you?"

"You've trusted me. You told me once that you had a secret."

"Can't you imagine why, Jenny?"

But Jenny's imagination was so terrible that she could not put it into words.

Felicia went on. "If you were afraid of life, if you wanted to save yourself from ... shame, if you wanted to keep the world's respect and, what's much more important, your own, can't you imagine using your ... invalidism as a sort of shield?"

"For twenty years!"

"During all that time, I've allowed no doctor to examine me."

"At the time of your husband's death, you were able to walk, Mrs. Grise?"

"Ah, now your imagination is at work. I see that I shall have to confess myself to you."

She leaned back in the chair, laid her hands along the desk edge, looked about her. "This is where Philip worked," she said. "This is where he met with and made love to Enid." Her smile was crooked and not sweet. "And here—in this room—somewhere, is a letter that might help to confirm or to contradict." Suddenly she was erect and proud. "Yes, Jenny. I was on the beach below the arbor a few minutes before Philip's death. For several weeks I'd been getting back the use of my legs, practising in secret, keeping the knowledge to myself. Because ..." pride could not keep a rush of sudden shamed blood from her face, "I wanted to see with my own eyes, myself unseen, what was going on in this house. Do you blame me, Jenny?"

Said Jenny wearily, "I can't seem to blame anyone, Mrs. Grise."

"I'd been kept for so long walled in, hedged in, apart. Everyone's life, everyone's real character was a secret to me. I saw people only when and as they wanted to be seen. I was treated like a holy ikon or like some sort of caged pet ... half-worship, half-pity. I was useful and important because I was rich. Everyone was dependent upon me. I wondered always how much anyone really cared. I had a hunger for the brutal and naked truth about these people who were apparently my worshippers.

"So, when I found I could move about, come out secretly from my cage, and down from my niche, it was like being given the helmet and the cloak of invisibility. I meant to keep the secret only until I had satisfied some of my hunger for reality ... but I kept it like an iron mask for twenty years. And the reason for that, Jenny, was fear."

"Nobody ever saw you?"

"Not to know who I was." Felicia threw back her head and made that rocking motion Jenny had seen before. "Except one person ... only one person, Jenny."

She waited and added very low, "I can't tell you about that."

Jenny thought, "It was Mary Ryan!"

"I'd come there from my hooded chair down the path and through the woods, as close to the arbor as I dared, because ..." again shame dyed her face and closed her eyes, the two deep wrinkles stood up on her forehead and her fingers stiffened on the desk edge, "I wanted to see who was with Enid in the arbor. She had passed the window carrying a tray set up for two and I thought that Philip was in the city. So, I came out on that beach. I didn't want anyone to know that I'd come out to spy on the governess and the man I thought was her companion there in the arbor. I hid my face from the person who saw me there and picked up my robe and ran. I got back breathless to my chair. I wheeled it in. Roger Dean was with Anna. He'd brought her to my room to tell me about her throat. And almost at once came Enid running. I can hear her now: 'Felicia, I think he's dead!' "

"Enid Ambrose told you how it happened, didn't she?"

"Yes."

"And you believed her?"

Felicia opened the closed wet eyes and looked at Jenny straight.

"No," she said.

Enid's daughter shrank.

"Why not?"

"Because I am sure that she was shielding somebody."

"*You?*"

"My God, Jenny, do you know what you're saying?"

"I know what I'm saying. You were on the beach. You'd kept your ability to walk a secret. You've given me a sort of explanation but I doubt if it would hold water in a law court. You were looking perhaps for your freedom without the mortification of divorce . . . you had . . . a lover . . ."

Felicia rose. She looked, indeed, very tall.

"Is that what you have been imagining here . . . in my house?"

"Only a part of what I had been *thinking*, Mrs. Grise. You did your best at the trial to save Enid Ambrose from a death-sentence or from imprisonment for life, because you *knew* she was not guilty. And because you knew who was guilty. And, for some fantastic, some quixotic reason she played your game. She let herself be saved by you from one kind of death and preserved for another. You gave her money to live out a life that might perhaps have been better not to live at all. She accepted that for the sake of her child and perhaps for the sake of yours, whom she loved. She was a very loyal girl."

Felicia had forgotten herself, was standing now with all her eyes on the slim girl in rumpled white: narrow and strange face incandescent; her tilted hazel eyes on fire. The hands Felicia had recognized were clenched and trembling, held down close to her sides. She had that look of a drawn angelic sword.

"Jenny Thorne?"

"Yes. That's the name I've lived by for twenty years. You're not the only one to lead a double life. It wasn't my name before then, Mrs. Grise."

"Who . . . are . . . you?" Felicia's eyes had moved now to her quivering hands.

"I think you know."

"You came here . . . ?"

"To find out the truth."

"You're not afraid to tell me that."

"No. I'm not afraid," she said, still white with her will to save her mother. "When you love anyone, you're not afraid."

Felicia was broken. Her head bent. "Your mother told you . . . ?"

"Nothing but what everyone knows. When I told her my plan, she cried and begged me to give it up. She wouldn't help me by a word. She wouldn't hurt her 'poor Felicia.' "

"So, while you worked with Adam—in my employment and by my advice, you were looking for the letter! She—Enid—didn't tell you what she'd written?"

"She told me nothing. Yes, I am in a way a detective. I've

no consideration and no mercy for anyone but my client, Enid Ambrose."

"But," a flash of triumph on a lifted face, "you've found nothing."

"I have found Enid Ambrose's lost letter."

Felicia sat down. "And Adam?"

"He did not find it. I did. He doesn't know . . ."

"Give it to me."

"No. It's safe from you and from anyone in this house or in this town. By now it's in the hands of a lawyer."

"What, in God's name, did it tell you?"

Felicia had stood up again, tall and trembling.

"If you will sit down, Mrs. Grise, if you will listen quietly, if you will promise not to be violent or passionate, I will tell you almost exactly what it said."

Felicia collapsed. She was goddess and queen no longer. She was prisoner in the dock. She stood with haggard eyes before her judge.

"I think I can recite that letter almost word for word," said Jenny; "it went something like this—

" 'I said I'd meet you in the summerhouse for the last time. But this letter may make you change your mind. Perhaps you won't want to see me again. But I'll be in the garden house and if you do come, you'll find me there. But nothing can make me change my . . . my new decision. Philip, I've found you out.' " As she spoke Jenny's eyes were fastened on Felicia's face but, through all the recital, that face was as fixed and pale and inhuman as a star. " 'Mary Ryan told me her story. She's been half crazy with jealousy. I've been treacherous enough but not so treacherous as you. I can't let it go on. I am going to tell Felicia. She's lived too long in her ivory tower, loving and trusting and being sure of everyone's devotion. I'm going to tell her everything I know about her worshippers. And I include myself. I'll tell her that I loved you and that you've broken my heart. I've betrayed her confidence but not so badly as if I'd agreed to be your secret mistress, Philip.

" 'When she knows us all as I do perhaps she'll turn us out and begin her life again. Without her you'll be very poor but perhaps if you are forced to work for your living you may learn to be the sort of man a decent woman can respect and love.

" 'You say you love me. Here is how you can prove it. I hope Felicia will be ruthless with the whole treacherous crew of us. I'm very unhappy, I've lost Felicia and I've lost you. I am humiliated. You made me the rival of Mary Ryan. I deserve it all.' And, at the end, she wrote, 'May God have mercy upon your soul' and signed, 'Your most unhappy, most determined Enid.'"

Felicia, with her fixed, star face listened to the end.

"And what do you think the letter proves?" she asked in a tone so peculiar that Jenny stared.

"To me it proves that your husband, Philip Grise, meant to kill Enid Ambrose before she could tell you the truth that would ruin him, and other people, and that, by some last minute accident, he drank the poison he had prepared for her."

At that, to Jenny's horrified amazement, Felicia threw back her head and laughed.

Of all the reactions she had imagined possible this one of cool, detached amusement was the most shocking to her and her quick recoil must have told Felicia this, for the incredible sound abruptly stopped.

"Listen to me. The letter proves nothing. It rests entirely on the word of Enid and there's no evidence whatever as to Philip's intent to kill. If you had known Philip, you might be laughing yourself. The motive Enid's letter suggests to you is no more valid than the motive suggested for Enid's equally possible attempt at murder. And even that last phrase 'May God have mercy upon your soul' suggests that the writer had condemned a man to death."

"But you don't believe . . ."

"*Believe?* I *know.* I know that Philip was killed by poison. No one else was killed. What sort of a case would any lawyer make of a dead man who had murdered himself by accident twenty years ago?"

"He might clear my mother."

"He would clear nobody on the evidence you've quoted. The case would be hung again." She sat brooding, then her face changed to resolution and she rose.

"You say you've sent the letter to a lawyer. You'll get an answer presently. What else will you do?"

"I can also send in your story, Mrs. Grise. I can let the world know that, at the time of Philip Grise's death, a saintly invalid was not only able to walk but to be on the actual scene of the . . . crime. And I can let my lawyer and the world know about your twenty years of secrecy, of hiding from justice."

"Yes," said Felicia, "you can do that." Then wearily, "I'll go down now, back to my room. It will soon be daylight. Until you choose to—to betray me or until I think the right moment has come, I'll keep my secret. Good night, Sheila Ambrose, or rather, good morning. You're leaving Castania sometime tomorrow, I suppose?"

"Yes," said Jenny.

She stood aside to watch the tall, lithe figure move gracefully away. Its head was high, its step free and silent. It had the grace of a wild beast and some of the essential furtiveness of all wild things. It did not look back but went with no sound down the tower stairs.

Chapter Twenty-two

At breakfast, old Mrs. Grise was silent. Jenny imagined that she was, perhaps, offended by her solitude at dinner of the night before but, at lunch—(for Jenny had been unable to get her doctor on the telephone or John or a taxi-cab for Barent so had perforce to wait for the transportation promised at the hospital for five o'clock ...) Mrs. Grise was affable and extremely talkative.

She chattered about "old days, old times" and Jenny kept her ears pricked for a mention of the name of Carrol. She even dared to ask Felicia's maiden name to learn that it was Gray. After that single query she was hardly allowed to speak a word. Mrs. Grise, as the descriptive phrase has it, ran on and on. To no purpose. For it had all to do with her early married life, when Philip was a little boy and they lived most of the time in Albany, neglecting the tall queer house on the river. She said, at last, when Jenny rose, "Well, child, it's been a pleasure to have you here whatever necessity there was for your service—and I never could see that Mrs. Philip needed more than Anna's attendance—I'm glad it brought you to Castania. Now the tower room has been aired and put to use. Perhaps it won't be haunted any more by our unhung murderess. I believe I'll come up there to say good-bye to you. Do you know, I've not been up those stairs for twenty years."

"Oh, don't come, Mrs. Grise. It will only make you un-happy, upset you. I'll come into your room, if I may, before I leave. Dr. Dean is coming for me at five ..."

"So ... the doctor is going to carry you away in his chariot! King Pluto! I shall be anxious to hear the sequel to this medical romance."

"There hasn't been any romance, Mrs. Grise, so there can't be a sequel."

"Now! Now! Miss Jenny Thorne, I've eyes in my head. And I've seen Felicia writhing. Even her saintliness isn't proof against that old green-eyed demon. And a dog in the manger, I always think, is the most green-eyed monster of them all." She chuckled deeply, following Jenny's flight into the hall. "As for Adam, what have you done to him? He's disappeared from view as though a wizard had waved a wand over him. Or a witch perhaps? Since yesterday morning, nobody's seen hair nor hide of our temperamental captain."

Jenny, on the stairs, stopped. "You mean he hasn't been home at all since yesterday morning?"

"No. He brought back his horse from the early gallop, our gardener-coachman says, but since then, except for one quick run up and down the stairs, he hasn't set foot inside Castania. Lizzie saw him go up and heard him come down. Oh, we're not too anxious. He's a most erratic boy. Perhaps he's gone off on that North Carolina scent—I told him about Ambrose being seen by my friend in Bonnetsville. It wouldn't be impossible for him, if he got down there on the spot, to find out where she ran off to, would it? Would it, Miss Jenny Thorne? What do you think? She was always a conspicuous sort of thing in her own strange, sinister way."

"No," said Jenny, "I suppose it wouldn't be impossible. Perhaps that's where he's gone."

She went on up the stairs . . . lead-heavy of heart and foot.

Adam, vengeful, on the trail of her mother, Adam, who would return evil for evil. Countering her espionage with kindred sleuthing of his own. Adam with so much more strength and power, money and prestige than ever she could muster.

She thought of Roger . . . Roger, with Felicia's permission and with evidence of her own, might stop Adam, might put him "out of the way" where he could do no harm to her mother or to himself. If Felicia knew that he had gone to Bonnetsville she would be as desperately anxious to stop him as Sheila Ambrose.

Jenny would see Roger Dean that afternoon. His hatred of Adam had deeper roots than the queer freakish jealousy or the queer freakish passion he had felt for her.

But heavier than lead . . . iron and basalt and granite was her heart. To lock up Adam, free-striding, head in air, to break his strong male pride, to twist his already tormented brain out of all possible return, perhaps to its complete sanity . . . could she do that? She who had run for shelter into his arms? Even for her mother . . . could she do that?

"Oh God," Jenny prayed, looking out of her window towards the steadily faring river, "what shall I do? Everything hurts me so terribly . . . and can so terribly hurt other people. And I am so alone. Nick . . . Nick . . ." she called to him in a whisper in varying tones but the summons brought no comfort. She was leaving Castania to go to Nick but, for very wretchedness, she could not weep.

She had given the sunny library below one long last wistful look, standing on its threshold, not going in.

What peace and what terror, what guilt it had known, what love and hate, anger and fear! Yes, old Mrs. Grise was right. The tower was haunted but Jenny's presence far from exorcizing its ghost had added only another.

She must, at any cost, prevent that farewell visit from Mrs. Ferguson Grise. Be ready at four o'clock. Go downstairs with her bag, stopping just for a few minutes in that ugly room to say good-bye.

Felicia had sent her no word. She had not stirred all day. She would perhaps let Jenny go in silence. Or ... was there some sort of final danger lurking in that beautiful rainbow room behind the closed and silent door?

Jenny breathed deeply against a weight of dread.

She was not yet free of Castania, not yet safe. There were hurdles to pass: Felicia, Adam, Roger Dean ...

A house of murder is forever a house of fear.

She finished her packing then sat down to write a page or two of final hieroglyphics in her diary. This had been neglected for two days, twenty-four most important eventful hours. Her pen was busy and her head bent, her attention fixed so that a knock at the door brought from her a vague "Come in, Anna," Anna having promised to help her "finish off." But, to her dismay, it was not Anna. Quickly she shut and put away her diary. It was old Mrs. Grise, breathless, smiling and laden with a tray. Jenny sprang to help. She could not but be touched by the queer old thing's effort.

"I always take my tea at four every afternoon," she panted, helping Jenny set down the tray on a hastily cleared table and drawing up for herself the chintz-covered chair while Jenny took the small straight one. "And I thought you might like a stirrup cup before you went away. I don't know what's got Felicia. There hasn't been a squeak out of her all day. And Adam's not back yet. So we just can't let you go without any farewell or little ceremony of gratitude and good will, can we? Can we, Miss Jenny Thorne?"

"It's awfully sweet of you. I do appreciate it. I take it clear, please, with just a little sugar."

"That's how I take it too." Mrs. Grise poured and handed Jenny her cup, busying herself at once with her own.

Jenny took it up. She stirred the sugar, looking down. She was embarrassed by this visit and was thinking of what she could say. She felt that perhaps the old woman had some further tale to tell, some information important to Enid's daughter that might yet throw light.

Through the clear liquid a face grinned up at her. The face of a jolly clown. The cup she held was an odd one, decorated as though for the amusement of a child. Her mother's voice began to speak, ghostly in her ears. "He had a favorite cup, a child's cup, given him by his grandmother when he was a little boy. It had a clown's face at the bottom. He simply refused to drink from any other cup. I'd brought it out to him . . ."

But this was Philip's cup! And it had been there in that arbor on the fatal day. But it had not appeared in the trial. It had been seen by nobody. Presumably it had been broken in the fall. Hadn't it been supposedly in a hollow piece of this very cup that the poison had been found?

It did not seem to Jenny then or later that she made any conscious plan but she stood up quietly, said, "Wait a moment, I think I hear someone" and, before her guest-hostess could know just what she did or said, she went quickly over to the door, took out its key, slipped through it, closed and locked it on the outside, still carrying her cup of tea.

Steadying it in both hands she fled down the stairs, went into the small room that held the telephone, set down the cup beside her on the floor and dialed a number.

"Dr. Dean's office."

"May I speak to Dr. Dean?"

"Sorry, Miss Thorne. He's at the hospital."

Of course!

Gasping, Jenny set down the instrument, dialed and took it up again.

"Dr. Dean? Dr. Dean?"

"Yes, Miss Thorne. Yes, he's here. I think he can come to the telephone. It's urgent? Very well. Hold the wire, please. I'll get him."

A minute like a hundred years then, "This you, Miss Thorne?"

"Yes. Dr. Dean. Could you come to Castania? Now, at once. Quick. Oh, quick. Right away now. You can't come too fast. A matter of life and death, Dr. Dean. Oh, Roger! I can't say, but for God's sake, come." She was looking back over her shoulder and sweating melted ice.

"I'll be there."

She did not wait but went out and up the driveway to the top of the steep hill, still carrying that cup of clear warm tea with its solution of delicate white sugar, not letting spill one drop.

Dean's car came to a stop and she climbed in. By that time, she had her treasure wrapped in a clean handkerchief.

"Don't ask me anything now, please. Take me to the hospital," she said.

"What have you got there, Jenny?" He was pale, his face set tight.

"Something I want Mrs. Graham to analyze for me. At once. Drive slowly please. Something—terrible."

Roger Dean said not a word. He did not so much as ask a question with his eyes, but his face was as grey and as grim as a stone image. He drove and, fifteen minutes later, Jenny with her own hands handed her wrapped specimen into the hands of the analyst. Afterwards, Roger took her into a small room where she sat down to wait. She put her head in her hands, shaking it at intervals as though to refuse information that was not asked for.

After pacing about for a while Roger went to stand before the window. She could see his fingers working together linked at the small of his white-coated back. The time passed.

Dean wheeled about. "You're not going to tell me anything?" There was a sort of snarl in the question as though his patience would break into nervous violence.

She said, "I can't. Please trust me. I can't. It may be nothing."

"Tell me at least ... someone is very ill?"

"No."

He flung up his hands, walked fast up and down, went out. He returned only a few seconds before the little grey-haired expert came in with her report. The spectacled quiet figure closed the door of the room carefully. She was very grave and very white.

"Dr. Dean and Miss Thorne," she said, "that cup of tea contained enough cyanide to kill a dozen men."

Jenny took the paper from her hand and she and Roger both bent over it. He said, "Mrs. Graham, I'll have to ask you to leave Miss Thorne and me. We must talk privately. And not to speak of this. At least for a while."

"Yes, doctor."

"*Now*, Jenny . . . in God's name . . ."

Jenny told him and he heard her through, growing paler as she spoke. At the end he said, "We'd better get back to Castania as quickly as we can. I don't know what we'll find there, in that cursed room. Wait! I'll send for a couple of orderlies."

They flew along the highway under the larch trees down that steep hill. There stood the queer, tall house unchanged, toppling above the river against the steady pressure of the wind. "Don't crumble now," prayed Jenny. "Don't disappear. Wait until we know, remember Enid Ambrose. This is her day, her hour."

They came quietly, without ringing, into the house and went up the stairs into the tower, round and round, Jenny ahead. She turned her key in that silent door and pushed it open.

The room beyond was quiet, filled with sunset light. Without human voice or motion.

Old Mrs. Grise lay back in her cushioned chair. She looked like an old woman who was glad to drift from nightmare into dreamless sleep.

On Jenny's bed, two fully covered sheets of paper told her story.

"Enid Ambrose is guilty of the death of my son Philip," the old woman had written in a clear gothic script. "She gave him the drink I had prepared for her. She deserved to die but Philip did not. She had come to a peaceful home and made everyone subject to her spell. It was a *beauté de diable:* the servants, little Adam, Felicia, Philip and *my* Roger Dean. None of them was free of her. Mary Ryan and I were the only ones that kept our heads. When Philip told me that, in a letter to him, Enid had threatened to carry wicked tales of our behavior to Felicia . . . for example that he had made love to Mary Ryan, that he and I together had laid aside part of her extravagant household money for ourselves—and why shouldn't we, after all? Was it absolutely necessary to be dependent upon her for the rest of our lives? If I saved the money hadn't I right to it? . . . When I heard this, I decided that she must go. Before she had destroyed us all here at Castania.

"Philip had told me that he would be in New York for all that week. Enid always took out her tea to the summerhouse on Thursday afternoons. After the servants had gone out . . . all but Anna who was sick with a sore throat . . . I went down into the pantry and hid all the sugar except a small amount in a little bowl Enid used for her tray. I put the poison in that bowl. I'd had it in my room for weeks. I stole it from Dr. Elliot's inner office—he'd never know. I tried to burn up the receipt and the order but someone came in so that I had to stuff them into the throat of the old stove. They might even be there still! You see, I'd been hating the girl for a long time.

"A few days before that I'd almost fallen over the cliff. Leaning against the railing of the arbor I found that it was rotted almost through. I looked down. The corner of the arbor balanced over space. The digging away of just a little earth there would make it tilt. That gave me the idea. Mary Ryan hated Enid. The poor silly girl thought that Philip had really fallen in love with her and she was crazy jealous of Adam's new governess ... So I talked her into borrowing Adam's little saw and spade and playing a fine joke on 'Miss Ambrose.' She would saw through what was left of the railing and dig out beneath the arbor, working after dark, so that Enid would fall down the cliff. She hated Enid. Anyone sitting in that place—and it would be the place where Enid, taking her tea alone, would sit—and receiving a sudden shock would certainly be thrown against the railing and down the cliff. If she did not fall, I thought, it would be easy for me to push her over and it would look like an accidental death. I saw from my window, that afternoon, Enid going to the garden with her tray. I didn't see that she had cups for two people. I followed her but couldn't get close to the arbor because the gardener we had then was snooping about, trying to spy on Enid. He was much nearer than he said at the trial. He did really hear my poor Philip's last speech.

"But I was near enough to hear Enid's great cry, after the train had passed, to see her rush down the path, followed by the gardener. And when I came to the arbor and looked down ... the side of the cliff had indeed fallen away. I saw my Philip lying dead.

"I found his cup, half empty, and hers, full. I saw what had happened. She had given him all the sugar since there was not enough for two. I half broke her cup, put Philip's tea in it, hid his cup ... for it was one he loved, one I had given him and I couldn't bear to destroy it. I've had it hidden in my room for twenty years ... and then I took that evidence and the story I had to account for it ... to the authorities. The post-mortem bore out this analysis.

"I hated Enid before. Imagine how I hated her after she had killed my son. If it had not been for Felicia's folly, Enid would have been sentenced to death or imprisonment for life. But she escaped me.

"When she sent her daughter here to work in secret against our safety, to help poor blind Adam, whom I was watching, whom I would never have allowed to find the truth ... it came to me that it would be justice if Sheila Ambrose drank her death out of that same cup of Philip's. I didn't know who Jenny Thorne was at first but I began to suspect her soon and when she sent a letter by John, I went to Barent and got the mailbag from him and opened the letter. She had found Enid's last letter with her accusation of Philip and of me. She was sending it to a lawyer. She was planning to reopen the case. So I knew the time had come.

"I had plenty of the poison left. I took tea to her room. After it had done its work, I was going to take away the tea things—nobody knows I've gone up and I've never visited the tower rooms for twenty years!—And after that—I'd push the girl's body out of the window and the verdict would and must be suicide—what else?

"I don't know how the girl detected me. But I know she must have suspected something for she has gone out with the teacup in her hand. She has locked me in, and she has not come back.

"I am waiting.

"If she comes back alone I may have a chance to carry out my plan. But if there is someone with her ... I'll take the poison myself. It works very fast.

"I don't care what happens to me. I'd rather be with Phillip ...

"CARROL GRISE."

"Carrol!" said Roger. "That's the name Philip used for his mother. It was her middle name. To everyone else she was Helen. She was thinking only of Philip at the last."

As they came silently, with bent heads, down and out from the tower Roger stopped in the upper hall and said, "Who will tell Felicia?"

Jenny's brimming eyes and shaking lips besought him. "You, Roger ... please!"

He stood in bitterness. "All these years," he said, and Jenny knew he was speaking to his own hungry heart rather than to her ears, "she has kept herself from me because of this. In her heart she was glad of Philip's death and she knew that I too must at heart be glad—she sometimes thought perhaps that I was guilty—because we loved each other . . . Oh, for all my weakness and my folly I have loved Felicia. I've tried to break away . . . I've tried at the cost of any shame or suffering. But she has held me. And that, to her, was guilt. She felt herself to be at heart a murderess." He turned to Jenny, wet eyes in an ashy face. "She is the sort of person that must be wholly innocent or wholly guilty. And she has taken guilt upon her soul. So she has punished us both—me, for a suspicion—herself for a desire. Jenny, why do I tell you this? You know nothing of me but my weakness . . ."

"I understand."

"Do you? I hope then that God will. Come, we'll go together. Felicia's out there on the grass. This time her quiet hour will be interrupted."

They went down and through the sitting room out from the French window and towards the hooded chair. Roger called her name softly, "Felicia!" looked . . . and stopped.

He breathed out, "Jenny! Jenny!" and she caught at his arm, thinking that he might fall.

The chair was empty, its draperies had been carefully laid back. At first sight anyone would think the chair occupied by a sleeping figure. To Roger it was more frightening than any death. His face had the terror of witchcraft.

"Let's go down the bank," said she, still holding his arm. "There's a path. I see her footprint. Roger, I must tell you—I found it out only last night . . . she has been able to walk for twenty years."

Chapter Twenty-three

Adam Grise came back to Barent that afternoon by train and, leaving his bag with a driver, mounted the hill and made his way out to Castania afoot. So he came into the garden through the orchard as the sun was beginning to go down.

The birds were done with courtship, busy with their broods. Adam reached the place of the arbor and went on to the edge of the high cliff.

He had come back from the city but he did not want yet to go into the house. He had an appointment with himself. The famous New York alienist to whom he had delivered himself for a final and exhaustive test had given him a clean bill of mental health. But he had also given him a warning. "You have a high and dangerous temper, Captain Grise. You had better learn to control it." Adam, remembering the fear on Jenny's face, a fear, which had sent him to take this test, said, "Yes, sir. That's right. I will." "You have also another source of danger to your nerves. There's a locked door in your memory. You have a wound there somewhere that you have not yet found the courage to remember. If you find the way to call upon that courage, find the resolution to lift a latch, push ever so little, that door will open wide and you will be able to look what I may call your draped figure of fear right in the face. A little courage. A little resolution. But don't force yourself. Make up your mind and your will calmly and strongly to be done with this obsession. Finally."

So now, this evening, he had made his way to the cliff. "A little courage, a little resolution." He walked on.

At the place of the boulder he came to a full stop. There was again that fog before his eyes, that wetness on his forehead. But, this time, he was patient. He stood there in the fog, not fighting his fear or his blindness but enduring them. He was in no hurry to drive his steps down the trail towards the sunlit beach below him lapped by its ruddy little waves. He wanted not to go forward but back. Slowly. Turning his mind again to the events that had foreshadowed the wetness and the fog.

On that afternoon, then, twenty years ago ... a warm afternoon like this one and a sunset on the river ... Yes. It was coming. It was coming. He had seen Enid go out into the garden with a tray—a tall girl, chestnut-haired, in a blue dress—walking carefully, looking past the tray to the ground before her feet. And he had promised himself a share in that small feast, a slice of bread and butter or a bit of cake ... So far Adam was able to go back, to feel back through the fog.

Now, he remembered ... he had been told to stay indoors, up there in the second story nursery, until Miss Ambrose came back to put him to bed. But that little Adam, now emerging, strongly possessing the consciousness of the grown Adam ... that little Adam had been quite capable of rebellion and of truancy. He had tiptoed past his mother, awful in her radiant, veiled contemplation, he had scurried along the alley—vivid now was the memory, the very shadows flicked him again as he ran ... And he had come within sight of the arbor. And there ... yes, there, he had seen his father, young Philip Grise.

Philip Grise's grown son saw him again as he had been, tall, smiling, ruddy-haired in town clothes. Yes, Adam remembered his very stance above the slim up-looking governess busy with her cups on the rustic table, and Adam remembered his own disappointment, the wilting of his ready hope. No use to go begging now. Dad would send him back to his bed, tingling.

So little Adam had paused there, in alarm and distress, at the top of the trail ...

But that wasn't the end ... no, the story was going on. He had stopped but, because of his appetite for naughtiness, for forbidden fruit, which was sharpened by its rebuff, he had made up his sturdy mind to go down the steep trail, to get himself to that beach, to play at the edge of the river. Perhaps he would find the spade and saw Mary Ryan had taken from him.

To this point, the memory was clear. Adam had recaptured the story.

He knew, from hearsay, that he had somehow got himself down to the water for he was on the beach when all the world, led by frantic Enid, had come running and someone had tried to quiet his terrible screaming. But, from memory, he knew the first steps down the path, the very feel of the gravel under his sandalled feet. The first steps ... but, from the instant where those careful short steps had taken him out from the screen of the big boulder to a view of the beach, there lay again the blankness and the fog.

On that path somewhere, out of possible view of his father's fall, there was a ghost, a vanished incident, something that would seem important, perhaps, only to a child of five, something so almost insignificant to maturity that no grown brain would have the tiny implement for its recall. And yet this afternoon, that tool did seem to lie within grasp. It had the very shape of Bluebeard's key. With one more effort, with one more resolute concentration, it would, it must come back. This was the day. The hour ...

He forced open his eyes, took one step past the boulder and standing stared. His head had turned of itself towards a wooded ridge beyond the beach and now the fog had lifted from his eyes. Sweat on his forehead dried.

Someone was coming out from the trees of that ridge, a tall someone, all in lacy white.

Adam's big hands tightened at his sides. It was happening again. Mad he must be, in spite of the alienist's opinion, for the forgotten event was returning not merely to memory but actually, it seemed, to all his living senses. For that was in truth the figure of his fear. That was the thing that had stopped his heart twenty long years ago ... coming down and out, slowly, from the trees.

It came. Now it came. It reached the little strand. It went picking its careful way among the stones and, when it reached the very place beneath his post there again, as it had twenty years ago, it stopped, held its long draperies in its hands, lifted its blue eyes and saw him where he stood.

It was Felicia.

It was his mother.

His mother who could not walk had come to stand beneath him at the moment of his wickedness. His angel mother had feet like every other human creature.

And he waited again in cold new sweat for the awful thing that would soon necessarily follow. He waited staring, shaking, nearly out of his mind, and then ... she smiled. She held out to him both her arms. "Adam darling," she called and it was her high sweet clear beloved voice, "John told me you were coming and I've run out to meet you. Look ... I can walk. Don't be afraid of me, my pet. It's simply wonderful.

Come down quickly. Don't be afraid. I can play with you here on the beach. Won't that be fun?"

Captain Adam Grise did not know how he reached her side. His body and his mind were possessed by the spirit of a little boy. But he did know, child and man together, assuagement. Reassurance he knew as wide and sure as Heaven. The healing of a wound, a terror turned to peace.

Then he was beside her, holding Felicia in his arms and she clinging to him and in tears.

Neither knew at that time what had happened above them there in the old crazy tower. Their minds had gone back twenty years and were at grips with memory.

"Now," Adam said, "I have you. You won't escape me. Tell me the truth. What were you doing on the beach the day my father died? How long have you been able to walk? I've heard you at night pacing your rug, trusting to Anna's deafness behind your locked door. I've stood by that door many a night listening and shaking and afraid to knock, afraid to ask, afraid to know what was in my murdered father's rooms. Tell me the truth, mother, and don't be afraid."

Felicia said, "I *was* afraid . . ." and after that stood silent for so long that he drew away from her to look into her face.

"No," she said then, "don't move. Let me stay here in your arms . . . as long as you will keep them round me. It gives me more strength. I can talk more easily. Adam, if they had known I was able to walk and had kept it secret and was here on the beach that day they would have arrested me. They would have questioned me under oath. I would have had to tell them and everyone would have known that I," her voice dropped almost to inaudibility, "that I loved Roger Dean. That I did not love Philip. Not really. He was my child and he adored me. I like to be adored. That has been my real worst sin.

"When I first found that I was going to be able to walk, I hated to give up my invalidism. It was not only an escape from competition and from ordinary responsibility but it was a sort of power. It kept me free from Philip's intimacy and from Roger's passion, which, I knew, was sin. And so I waited and practiced secretly and thought I would soon tell."

Another of the long pauses in which she seemed to gather her memories and her strength. He did not again disturb her but stood still, holding her warmly with reassurance in his body and with faith.

"Then I discovered that Roger, my Roger, was making love to Enid and I was insane with hurt pride and with jealousy. It was a shameful jealousy for I wouldn't give him what he wanted, I wouldn't divorce Philip for his sake nor give myself to him in secret; and yet I couldn't bear his looking elsewhere for his happiness. But that shameful jealousy was too strong for me."

The sound of the little river waves, clapping briskly under a wind, made chattering applause for a long two minutes. Felicia drew in a deep breath and went on painfully. "Please remember, Adam, how young I was ... how young we all were ... Roger and Enid, Philip and I. Younger than you are now, so much younger in experience of sorrow than you are now, my poor Adam.

"That day when I thought Philip was in New York—he had told us he would not be back—I saw Enid. Do you remember Enid, Adam?"

"Yes, mother."

"I saw her carrying her tray out to the summerhouse. And I saw that she had two cups. So I imagined that she was meeting Roger in the summerhouse. I couldn't bear it. I had to see for myself ... hear for myself ... know the truth about them. So I left my chair—as I had done several times before and how many times since!—and got myself to the beach."

"Go on, mother. I'm here. My arms are round you. Don't be afraid."

"I got myself across the ridge and down to the beach at the foot of this trail and there I saw you, my baby, standing and staring down at me with such fear on your poor little pale face. For you did not believe that I had feet like other people. You had never seen me stand or walk ...

"And when I cried out and hid my face and ran from you ... and when you came down the trail, crying 'Oh, mummy, mummy, please don't run away' (I'll never stop hearing you, Adam!) still I ran. I didn't want anyone to know I came there on the beach, to spy on a governess and her companion. So I didn't see your father fall. I got back to the house just in time, wheeled myself in to find Roger with Anna in my sitting room and hardly there when poor Enid came gasping out Philip's death.

"You see how it was then, Adam. I couldn't speak. And when this dreadful charge of murder was brought, so quickly, by his frantic mother—oh, she was out of her mind—I don't think she's been quite sane since ... she was certainly a mad-woman that afternoon. She would have torn me to pieces like a tigress ... I was terribly afraid. And I thanked God, being so wicked and so cowardly, that you had lost your memory of that whole afternoon. They questioned you but you didn't know anything. And I dared to thank God!"

Here she drew back and gave him a look beseeching him for comfort but he said nothing.

"I have suffered, Adam. I've suffered almost enough. This long martyrdom. Wasn't that almost enough? To keep my secret all these years, to pretend helplessness; only deaf old Anna knew and she didn't know all of it. She didn't know how freely I could move and go outdoors in Philip's clothes at night for air and freedom, for movement under the stars, with the wind in my hair and face. Jenny discovered me a few nights ago. I was trying to find Enid's lost letter. You frightened me so terribly with that search. And, all these years, to deceive Roger, to deny him, not to marry him, to warp his nature and my own! But I thought we both deserved that long punishment for even though we weren't guilty of the actual deed—and there have been horrible times when I suspected him—and he me—we were both guilty of wishing for freedom from Philip's claim on me. Oh yes, at heart and in our minds, we had been guilty. Could I let him take me with blood on both of our hands? And could I keep us both from that final sin if he knew that I was not an invalid? It was my only safeguard. And his.

"When you came back this spring, Adam, and when I began to suspect that you were trying to dig out the truth, when I found that you were coming here to stand on the cliff, afraid, you a mountain climber and an aviator afraid to go down this little path, baffled, frustrated, I knew at once what was wrong. I knew that it was the lost memory of that afternoon, the shock you'd suffered at seeing your mother stand and walk and shrink from you and run away. It was buried so deep in your poor mind. You didn't want to fear me or to hate me. You didn't want to believe that I had anything to do with your father's dreadful fall. Oh, I knew. It has been a fight for me because I am a coward and a liar and a sinner worse than anyone. After what happened last night I knew that I must soon find you again on the cliff—where Jenny told me you went every afternoon—and I must do for you what I'd failed to do before, the natural thing, the mother thing. I must hold out my arms and beg you to come down; and be glad to see you. When Roger thought it might be wise to ... to send you away somewhere for a while ... to cure your obsession, I knew then that the time had come for me to take the burden of my sin and to free you. I knew the cure.

"So, when John came just now, running—for we've been anxious about your silent absence, Adam—to tell me you were in the garden just above the trail—I went out to the bank edge and I've come. With God's help, I've come. I don't care what they do now, what Philip's mother does. I don't care if they arrest Roger and me and accuse us of a crime. I only care for you, Adam. Tell me, darling, are you well now? I do ... I do love you. Perhaps you'll believe me now ... at last."

She wept with wildness, clinging to him as though he might try to tear himself away.

He heard the sound of steps, branches rustling, he spoke softly, stroking her hair.

"Hush, mother. It's all right. Don't cry. You have cured me. Indeed you have. I've lost my fear. And I'll take care of you now and nobody is going to hurt you ..."

At the increasing sound she turned and saw Roger coming down the ridge path to the beach. The dazed wonder on his face changed to an even deeper amazement. Adam released Felicia. "There he is ... your Roger. Go to him and make your peace, and mine."

It was strange to see those two prisoners of conscience now draw towards each other in the fading light, ashamed, reluctant, magnetized, asking no further questions of each other or of fate until she put out her arms and went into his own letting her fair head fall to his shoulder.

When Jenny, coming with Roger down the ridge path through the trees, saw Adam with his mother on the beach, she said, "I'll leave you here. You won't need me any more, Roger," and fled. Back to the house she ran, found John and quickly persuaded him to take her to the station in Dean's car.

A few hours later she was in New York city.

Its crowds, its tumult seemed tranquility itself after Castania's recent frenzies and she took her small room in the hotel of Nick's recommendation with the sensations of a hermit retiring forever from the world.

After a while, however, she sent a wire to Nick then went

to her bed and slept, less like a hermit than like a tired, heartbroken child. The next morning was spent in a long, triumphant letter to her mother. Enid Ambrose was cleared. Enid Ambrose could come back to life again. "It will take some time, I suppose, to get things legally straight but Mrs. Grise's (Carrol's) confession will be published and you will be publicly acquitted of any possible complicity in crime. So now, my darling, I hope you will forgive me. I haven't hurt your dear Felicia. And I must admit to you now that I love her ... queer ... beautiful, coward and liar that she is! I think, in spite of all their bitterness and anger and suspicion that she and her faithful, unfaithful Roger will come together. They'll have a lot to forgive each other. That will help. He is no hero of a romantic tale, as he would love to be. Nor is Felicia the heroine, a role she certainly cast for herself. Oh mother, what is the worst sin? Is it vanity? Or the will to power? Is it cowardice or is it selfishness?

"Adam and I (yes, I am going to reproach you now, just once, for the first and the last time)—Adam and I were the real victims of what you and Philip and Felicia and Roger and poor demented Carrol did. We took the worst of the punishment and will have to take it, I'm afraid, until the end. God give us both endurance and some future chance for happiness."

She wrote and cried. Then washed and dressed herself in her simple tailored best. The phone rang. "Captain Landis to see Miss Thorne."

Jenny came down into the lobby and saw Nick near the desk. He had changed. Thin, brown, very straight, handsomer than ever in his uniform. She had a thrill of possessive pride and another thrill of warm and grateful affection when he came to her, took her hand and shyly, gravely kissed her on the mouth.

"You look all shot to pieces," he said, "and no wonder. I've been worried to death about you. No letter since our talk over the telephone! I'm glad to see you still alive. We can't talk here. I've got a taxi. Let's drive about a while then ... how about dinner at a quiet restaurant and the theatre afterwards? I've tickets to what they tell me is a good show. Suit you?"

"Perfectly," she said. Question and answer seemed to outline the shape of her future.

In the taxi she told him that the case of Philip Grise's death was closed. That a letter she had addressed to Nick was stolen on its way. That this letter had no longer any importance. That there was another letter . . . a confession . . .

He gasped aloud and gripped her hand when she described that scene in her tower room . . . the kind ceremony of farewell—the clown-faced teacup. "My God, Jenny! Didn't I warn you? A house of lunatics!"

"But you had the wrong lunatic, Nick."

Said Nick drily, "One is about as dangerous as another. Even your doctor friend showed some alarming symptoms."

"People caught in a trap like that can't be altogether sane, can they, Nick? Not sane, that is, like you and me, for instance."

Sane, thought Jenny, as they ate in the quiet restaurant, Nick certainly was. And extremely practical. He ordered with precision. He hardly looked at her. His manner was very grave and kind. She began to be puzzled. This was not the Nick of Bonnetsville. But then, she admitted, neither was she the Jenny of that distant place. So much had happened since . . . so bitterly much had happened to her. Perhaps to him.

All through the play which they both extravagantly applauded, she was thinking, wondering, "imagining." When they got again into a taxi to go to a night club and dance . . . ("We've never danced together, have we, Nick?" "Haven't we, Jenny? I guess you're right at that.") . . . she sat far back in her corner out of the reach of the street lights that flashed across his linked hands and gravely watchful face. It was the city that he watched, not Jenny Thorne.

"My dear," she said. It was a tone she had never used to Nick before and it roused him sharply.

"Er . . . Jenny?"

"You don't love me."

"Jenny! Darling!"

"Something has happened to you while I've been away. You've changed."

"You're imagining things."

"No. You're loyal. You won't go back on the girl you asked to be your wife and who said she would marry you, you would not throw her over because of what she found out afterwards about her history. But, Nick, now that all that shame, that disgrace, has been taken away from my mother and myself, you don't need to sacrifice . . ."

"Jenny. Jenny! What high-minded sensitive woman, what woman with any heart could possibly respect a man who . . ."

"Nick. Wait just a second. Don't say another word. I've

got to think." She leaned forward to think; eyes shut, frowning, her hand against her lips. Then open flew her tilted laughing eyes.

"Alice Morell!" she said and Nick sat frozen in his place.

She put a quick kind hand closely over his. "You described her to me once. You said she was a sensitive, high-minded woman. Oh, Nick, you told me she would be a perfect doctor's wife. Don't be unhappy. Because," here Jenny began to laugh and to cry at once, "I really don't want to marry you at all. You see, it's me that's throwing *you* over. And no sensitive or high-minded man would think well of a girl that would do a dirty trick like that ... Please forgive me! I don't know what I'm saying exactly. But I do adore you. I sound so rude and brutal. But I do know it's going to be better for both of us in the end to be rude and brutal now. Nick, I was going to marry you out of gratitude ... for your unselfish loyalty. I dare say we'd make a fine, high-minded, rather happy pair. In fact, I'm sure we would and maybe some day in the future we'll look back to this little stuffy car as the scene of our worst mistake. But ... Look! Let's don't talk any more tonight. It's just too darn embarrassing. Take me back to the hotel. We're near it now, aren't we? And you go think it over. Yes, that's what I really want. Honestly, darling. I'm telling you the truth, the whole truth and nothing but the truth. I feel ... I will feel ... if I'm right. Oh, Nick, please tell me ... am I right?"

Hoarse was his answer addressed with a crimson face bent over his linked hands. "You're right."

When he left her, as she insisted, at the entrance to the hotel Jenny stood, having started through the revolving door and come right out again, to watch him go. He was walking slowly along the pavement, head bent down, his shoulders stooped. He didn't look a captain.

But "There goes a happy man!" thought Jenny in tears.

Very dreary seemed the small hotel room when she had reached it. "I'm glad, at least, it isn't in a tower," she said to her hard single pillow. That night she did not sleep at all, a white long night of noise and close city heat and breathless miserable uncertainty.

Next day she sent a special delivery letter to Mrs. Philip Grise, Castania, Barent, New York State.

"Dear Mrs. Grise, I've a question to ask you. May I come to Castania just once more and say good-bye to you? I'm so part of your tragedy that I can't believe you will feel that I'm an intruder even at this awful time. I want to feel that you have forgiven me as I most truly have forgiven you. I have broken my engagement to Nick Landis. I don't love him and he loves another girl. If you think it wise to do so, tell Adam this. I must still sign myself Jenny Thorne."

She waited there in the grim little hotel until Felicia's message came. A telegram.

"Come as soon as possible. Wire train. Adam will meet you at the station."

But she did not wire the train. She didn't want Adam to meet her at the station.

They met at the gate of Castania, where she dropped her cab at sight of him walking slowly under the sad larch trees.

They met: Adam very grave and shy, she shaking like a dryad halfway transformed into a quaking asp. But before they reached the end of the driveway they knew again that they were lovers and without words they stopped, looked, smiled and deeply kissed.

Afterwards, brave of heart, high-headed, they went together down the steep way towards that haunted house above the river.

Love, Jenny thought, will cast out all its fear.